Jaded 2: The Hunt

Lana Black

Editing by Shayna Turpin

Cover Design by Pretty In Ink Creations

Contents

Content Notes & Trigger Warnings

Thank you for reading Jaded 2: The Hunt!

This is a dark, contemporary reverse harem romance. While the harem is adoring, there are villains who are definitely not. There are dark themes and potential triggers throughout the book, including:

- Captive FMC
- Off-page sexual assault
- Descriptions and discussion of sexual assault
- On-page assault and abuse
- Graphic violence
- Death, grief, loss
- Weapon use
- Verbal and emotionally abusive language and situations.

That's not my name, bitch. –Jade Tanner

CHAPTER ONE

Jade

I DID MY BEST not to move, not to wake the pain. I willed my body not to shiver against the cold. Willed it to be still as I cringed at the sound of the approaching footsteps.

It was better when they thought I was unconscious. They would walk by and if I didn't move or open my eyes, they were more likely to move on to someone else.

Not this time. This was wake-up time for everyone. I heard the hose and shrieks and realized that playing possum wouldn't save me from an ice-cold blast of water to the face.

Tough it out, Jade. Make your body move. Quick!

The last time I got hosed, I spent the night in freezing, soaking wet clothes and an icy puddle of water on the concrete floor of my cage.

No thanks. I'm good without that.

If you weren't ready, if you were crying or trying to avoid the water, they would only hit you harder and longer.

Maybe after the latest torture session, they would feel satisfied with my level of suffering. I'd been dragged out of my cage by those bitches and beaten, then dragged into Berto's "office" to entertain him while he berated me and violated me. That was what, last night? The night before? I'd hit my head pretty hard on the concrete and had to get stitched up, so maybe they'd leave me alone today.

Maybe.

I pressed my face against the bars of my prison, straining to see who was manning the hose. Was it Lydia? Darlene? Missy?

Sometimes that prick Pierce would come by with it, but he was usually too busy. Berto wouldn't lower himself to that kind of activity. It was the job of the staff to provide the daily cleaning, feeding, medical care, and standard issue harassment to "the girls." Or, as Berto and Pierce liked to say, "the stock".

Fun fact: my "keepers" and handlers were just other women that Pierce and Berto had accumulated and chosen to promote. They had names and slept in beds and ate good food. They wore high heels and skirts and giggled a lot when talking to Pierce or Berto. But with us? Oh, there was definitely no sugar. No. There was just rage. It was like they took all their trauma and laser-focused it on us. On their fellow captives.

But that's how it works in life. Shit rolls downhill, right? You don't fight your captors. Nope. You just lash out at your own kind. The ones that your betters have dictated are beneath you. They are the safe way to let loose the rage you feel for being where you are and who you are. Because people in power know full well that those under their heel need an outlet. They wouldn't want them turning on their masters.

My thoughts drifted to the guys. Were they still alive? Were they all in jail? If they weren't, were they looking for me?

Tears welled in my eyes and I willed them back. Crying at the wrong time was an invitation to get fucked with.

Don't cry, Jade. Don't cry. They'll come for you if they can. If they can't, well, you'll survive.

Or I won't. Either way, I pray it's over soon.

There was groaning in the cage to the left of me. Saysha was waking up, too.

The cage to the right was empty. They had dragged the girl out a few days ago and I hadn't seen her since. I didn't know her name, but I knew she'd come from one of Berto's "houses," and she'd worked for him.

"Fuck. Back with the hose again. Fucking cunts," she hissed.

I liked Saysha, but I feared for her. She was a fighter, which was good. But it was going to get her killed. I'd been watching, and it seemed like the best way to survive here was to find a middle ground. Don't be too weak - they'll eat you alive. Don't be too strong, or they'll put you down like a rabid dog.

Don't kiss ass - it's weak. Don't mouth off, it's stupid.

Saysha had a mouth on her, and it got her hurt.

"Shut the fuck up, Saysh. Please."

"Ugh, I'm not afraid of a little water. Or those dumb bitches. Let me at them."

I wasn't afraid of Darlene. Or Missy. They were compliant and sadistic, two qualities Berto appreciated. But they were nothing more than mean girls. And mean girls were just scared girls.

Lydia? Now that one was different. She was a stone-cold sociopath. No fear in her. I got the feeling she wasn't even afraid of Berto and Pierce. Not the way the rest of us were. That was probably her only real weakness. She was too cool for school. One day she would slip and they would slice her throat from ear to ear.

"Ugh. I am so not down for a shower. Fuck this." I swallowed the lump in my throat and glanced around my cage. It was tiny. I was short so I could almost stretch out fully when lying down. I couldn't stand up all the way, but I could sit up just fine. Saysha was tall and couldn't do much but curl up and deal with it.

The only time they let us out was to be raped or otherwise fucked with.

"Clothes off, whores. No exceptions except number eight. Eight? Can you hear me?" Lydia laughed as I held my breath to listen for a response. There was nothing. This meant that "eight" was too hurt to be showered. Probably either unconscious or too traumatized to speak.

"Get your soap ready. Get your buckets near the door."

One girl would be pulled out of her cage and tasked with pulling our waste buckets out. She would empty the buckets in the bathroom and clean them while we were hosed down.

"No. Goddammit," I whispered. "I'm so not in the mood."

Saysha laughed. It was a dark, bitter sound.

"My hair is covered in dried blood and I have to wash the stench of Berto's five closest friends off of me."

I heard the spray of the hose and the sobbing of the girl as the ice-cold water pummeled her.

"Soap up. Hurry, whore. You have less than two minutes to soap up and rinse off."

I rolled my eyes and then winced. When I say everything on my body hurt, that's exactly what I meant.

Next was Saysha.

"Jesus, Five. You are a disgusting mess. Is that cum in your hair still? Nice." Missy laughed while she set the hose on her.

"Yeah, me and your dad had a good time last night."

I groaned quietly as Missy growled and threatened to haul her out of the cage and stomp on her hands.

"That mouth is going to be the death of you, whore," Lydia drawled.

"Literally." Missy howled with laughter and Lydia chuckled in a way that made my skin crawl.

Missy was the one who had it out for Saysha. She tortured her relentlessly and was always "reporting" her behavior to Pierce and Berto, insisting that she needed to be reprimanded and "taken out".

I squeezed my eyes shut and willed myself to undress. I tried to shove my clothes as far into the corner as possible so they would stay dry.

Bracing myself, I watched my keepers come into view.

"This bitch. Grab your soap, shorty."

Every muscle, bone, tendon, and ligament in my body was on fire. They laughed at me as I fought back the tears and struggled to get my oversized shirt over my head. Just as I had it nearly off Missy let loose with the water, spraying me down.

I tried to get my hair wet, and I grabbed the soap, trying to get my armpits at the very least. Tried to rinse off so I wasn't left itching for the next couple of days covered in dry soap.

"That's it. That's a good little whore. Get cleaned up for your master. You've got a big day coming up. You want to be fresh for it."

My teeth chattered so hard I thought they would shatter and the violent shaking triggered a fresh wave of excruciating pain.

The pain sucked, but it paled in comparison to the fear I felt. Fear of what they would do to Saysha.

And for what they would do to me.

"Please. Please come save me," I whispered as they moved on to the next girl, leaving me soaked, shivering, and terrified.

Once in a while, I found myself looking forward to the death I knew was coming. Since I'd been here three women had been killed right in the middle of the room. Executed right in front of us. Others were taken out of their cages and not brought back.

There was no getting out. They would not let us go for good behavior.

"You ever wonder if things could get worse?"

I laughed at Saysha's question because I was just thinking the same thing. Thinking of all the times back home with my parents, with Eddie. All the times I thought it couldn't get worse. I thought about that day they tossed me into the back of the van after the guys robbed the bank. Those were times when I thought it couldn't get worse for me.

Boy, was I wrong.

Chapter Two

Ace

I couldn't function if I thought about what Jade was going through so I pushed those thoughts down and focused on finding her.

We'd torn through the city. Went straight to Berto's home and gunned down six of his men. He was nowhere to be found and no one was talking.

I'd slit two throats and Xander had put holes in what was left. We were ruthless, silent, and scared. Not scared of Berto or Pierce or any of the thugs who were loyal to them. But terrified of what we would find once we finally arrived at where they were holding her.

If they were still holding her.

Xander fell right into killing like it was breathing. The one thing Mick had been trying so hard to prevent. Xander wasn't a killer, he'd said. He shouldn't have to be.

But here he was, and you'd never know he was once the trembling boy with tears and snot running down his face, shaking his head as Berto demanded he put down some poor sap that pissed him off.

When Xander wouldn't do it, he got the shit beat out of him and then had to watch Ian finish the job.

We boosted one of Berto's Mercedes Sedans and rolled through town searching every nook and cranny for Berto but turned up a whole lot of nothing.

One helpful chap said Berto had been losing his touch and ignored the business in favor of other pursuits.

What those pursuits were I didn't know but once we hit the brothels I started getting a picture of what it could be.

Moni was a beautiful woman in her early forties that I'd known since I was a kid. She was quiet and sweet, and tough when she needed to be, and she cared for her girls like a mother. A dysfunctional mother, yeah, but still.

She and Mick were close, or as close as he could be to a woman.

Until Jade, that is.

"I've not seen hide nor hair of Berto or Pierce, that fucker. Not for a month or so."

Xander scratched his chin. "Not unusual, really."

Moni nodded. "True, don't think Berto has been through here in over a year or more, not since he came in and did what he did..."

She started shaking a little, but quickly composed herself.

"But Pierce comes through once or twice a month. Last time he was here..."

Her face darkened, and I felt a chill run through me.

"What? What happened last time?"

She shook her head. "He was weird. Agitated more than usual. He checked out all the girls. Kinda freaked them out the way he was talking to them, the way he was going over them. And when he left, he took Katy's sister, Charla, with him and we haven't seen her since."

She looked down at her feet and swallowed.

"I tried to get him to tell me what he was doing and where he was taking her. He said she was being transferred."

"Transferred?" Xander narrowed his eyes. "What, like taken to a different house?"

She shrugged. "It happens. Sometimes the girls get shuffled around to different areas depending on supply and demand."

"Okay. So it's not unusual then?"

"Yeah, it's not unusual, but I still believe there was something else going on. I didn't buy his story, and there's no way she wouldn't contact her sister."

"Yeah, well Pierce is a lying sack of shit. So there's that." I shook my head and found something niggling in the back of my head. Something just on the edge of my brain or the tip of my tongue, just out of reach. Couldn't quite put my finger on it but there was something. And I didn't like it.

"Fuck. Fuck. Fuck." Xander was wearing a hole in the motel room carpet. Not a hard task considering it was damn near threadbare.

"We gotta get to Mick and Ian."

I shook my head. "Yeah, but we gotta get Jade. Gotta kill Pierce."

"We need them. Two of us versus four of us. What gives us the better chance?"

"You really want to spring them and we don't have Jade? You want to explain to Mick why we didn't get her first?"

Xander paused, considering my words.

"Yeah, but where the fuck is she? How do we find her? She could be anywhere."

I lit a cigarette, ignoring the large 'No Smoking' sign above the switch plate.

"Someone knows. Someone knows where she is."

"You think someone is going to talk?"

I grabbed my blade and ran my finger over it, squinting against the smoke, drawing a thin ribbon of blood across the pad of my thumb.

"Someone will talk if I have anything to do about it."

"Ace. You've cut up half a dozen guys in the last thirty-six hours. You've burned holes in them and threatened to cut off their nuts. Reality is that Berto has been real secretive about something. I bet, the only people who know where he is are with him. His inner circle. Dillon, Joey, Al, and Scotty. We haven't seen them because they are with him. Just like Pierce."

I jerked my head up. Damn, Xander was getting some edge to him. This last catastrophe had changed him for sure. Part of me was sad. The other part, relieved. We lived in a world that punished you for being soft. We had protected him as best we could, but that time was past. He needed that edge now, more than ever.

He continued, still trying to talk me into going his route, but I wasn't convinced, and besides, there was no way we were going to spring the two of them. I didn't know what Xander was thinking.

"I get it. Jade needs us. We need to get to her. But I'm telling you, we can spring Mick and Ian, and the four of us will find her, save her, and make those fuckers pay. But we need them to do it."

"I disagree, Xander. Every minute she is with them..." I trailed off because I wasn't about to say it out loud. And I didn't need to.

Xander visibly shuddered.

"Look, I have an idea. I can do it without you. I can have them out in less than twenty-four hours."

I practically choked.

"Bro. Not to be a dick but there is no way in hell you are getting those guys out. I don't know what you are thinking. We don't even know where they are, right? I'm sorry but you gotta come to terms with reality here. The best thing we can do for Mick and Ian is find Jade and bring her home."

Xander blew out a frustrated breath.

"Home? Where is that? We don't have a home anymore. That safe house is a trap. Our apartment is not our apartment anymore. We are officially homeless."

He was wrong about that.

"Xander, our home is wherever Jade is. Our home is wherever we are together. With her. We get Jade safe and happy, and we are home."

He slumped back down, sitting on the edge of the bed, looking defeated and clearly stewing.

I softened a bit.

"Okay, you tell me your plan. I'll tell you if I think it will work. If it's going to work, if it has a decent chance, we'll try it."

He turned to me, his eyes brightening with the slightest sly little smile playing across his lips.

"Prepare to be amazed, Ace. Your boy is a lot fucking smarter than you think he is."

Chapter Three

Jade

MISSY SNEERED IN CONTEMPT as she shoved the tray at me. "Enjoy it, bitch. I made it special for you."

My stomach roiled at that. "Special" probably meant she spit in it, or worse.

Her face morphed as she pasted on a sweet smile. "You'll notice you have more food than usual. I suggest you eat it all."

I frowned but said nothing.

They didn't exactly starve us, but they made sure we were at least a little hungry at all times. Hungry and sleep deprived. Some girls got starved, but it was usually a punishment for not doing something right. Although "something right" was entirely arbitrary.

"What did you get?" Saysha's voice shook.

"Looks like oatmeal, a banana, a bar. Orange juice."

"Huh."

The portions were bigger than usual. This was a more carefully prepared meal. With a healthy dollop of oatmeal. Full banana. A protein bar and a carton of orange juice.

"What did you get?" I asked as I set the bar aside and grabbed the spoon.

"Nothing."

I swallowed, choking down my bite, suddenly consumed with guilt. This was the kind of shit Missy did to fuck with us because she knew Saysha was my friend, knew we talked even though we weren't supposed to.

"Wait till Missy leaves. I'll share mine with you, no problem. I should be able to scoot my banana over to you, at least."

She sucked in her breath. "No fucking way, Jade. You saw what happened to the last girl who did that."

The last girl who shared her food got pulled out of the cage and three guys came in out of nowhere and beat and raped her right in the middle of the room so we could all see what happened to "trash who think they can be defiant".

"I can't stand the idea of you going hungry, Saysha. Fuck them."

"I can't stand the idea of you getting a rapey beat-down over me while I watch, either," she retorted.

"You need food, Saysh."

"Whatever, I'll be fine."

"Haha, hear that? She says she'll be fine."

My head snapped up. *Ugh, those bitches, always eavesdropping, always sneaking up on us.*

"Hate to break it to you, sis. You are far from fine. You are used up and about to get thrown away."

Lydia crouched into view and shot me a smug glare before returning her attention to Saysha.

"Berto gave the word. You're about to be snuff bait."

My stomach cramped up and the color drained from my face. Snuff bait was what Lydia called it when Berto decided one of the girls needed to die. Sometimes they just quietly disappeared. Other times, he threw "snuff parties" and picked a girl to be taken out and brutally murdered by some of his "boys". And some of those boys weren't just other men from the gang. They were men he invited to participate. Rich men, important men.

It crossed my mind more than once that they paid for the privilege.

His sickness knew no bounds, and Pierce was even worse. We were all caged animals, just waiting to be slaughtered. Tortured, raped, toyed with, and eventually killed.

And now Saysha, my only friend in here, was next.

"Fuck this," I muttered.

Lydia slammed her hand against my cage and I involuntarily jumped, much to my dismay. It pissed me off how afraid I was of these bitches. I'd love the chance to tear them apart or die trying. My hatred for them was growing stronger each day.

"Don't worry, whore, you'll get your turn. Daddy Berto and Pierce have something real special planned for you."

I fixed my eyes on her and something inside me snapped. I was done hoping and praying Mick or Ace was going to come through the door, guns blazing. I was done hoping this would be the day the cops figured out what was going on and would raid the place, saving us.

No one was coming to save me, and I had to get right with it. I was going to die here, and there wasn't anything I could do about it.

So fuck it.

"Yeah? I have something special planned for *you*, cunt. Why don't you let me out of here so I can deliver it?"

For a split second, she broke character. Her jaw dropped slightly and I heard Saysha snort.

"Yeah, cunt. Let us out so we can play. It'll be fun." Saysha cackled and I sadly wondered if she was losing her mind. I sure was.

Missy snarled and called Darlene over.

"Little bitch suddenly thinks she's gonna grow a pair. Pull her out, Missy. Let's make an example so the rest of the cows can see what happens when you run your whore mouth."

Instead of scrambling back and trying to evade them, I readied myself. I positioned myself in a low crouch, my fingertips on the ground, my left foot poised to help launch me out the minute the door swung open.

Darlene was the biggest of the three and easily outweighed me by fifty or more pounds. The other two were more petite, but wiry, cagey, and probably just a little methed out.

If they wanted to kill me, let them.

Missy yanked open the door to my cage and moved aside so Darlene could pull me out. Lydia waited, fists clenched and a look of dark anticipation on her face. She was practically frothing at the mouth.

"Pull the bitch out and let's do this before Smellson comes out and ruins our fun."

"Smellson" was the pervert Berto had supervising the day-to-day operations. Lydia, Missy, and Darlene answered to him when Pierce wasn't around. He was in charge of our medical care if it wasn't something that our twat zookeepers could patch up.

His real name was Nelson, and he had some kind of medical experience. Doctor or nurse, I wasn't sure. But whatever he'd been, the powers that be had yanked his license to practice medicine on account of some inappropriate behavior, which didn't surprise me one bit.

The last time these bitches pulled me out of my cage to beat my ass, I'd cringed away from them, crying and blowing snot bubbles out of my nose, begging them to leave me alone.

Embarrassing.

Not this fucking time.

In the brief window between Missy pulling open the gate and stepping aside to let Darlene at me, I launched myself out of the cage like a rabid spider monkey and made straight for the nearest target, Darlene.

I had the element of surprise, thank God, and she cartwheeled backward, stumbling over her fat feet and I was on her, punching her in the nose. I got a good five quick shots, pummeling the cartilage of her nose into mush, covering my fist and her face in fresh, rosy blood. It was exhilarating.

"What the—"

Lydia let loose a feral growl and lifted me off of Darlene with ease. I'd expected that, though, and used her momentum against her, throwing myself backward and slamming her into the cage.

Darlene scrambled to her feet, howling in pain, and I immediately put the bitch down with a hard kick right to her stupid crotch.

Then, I whipped around to start in on Lydia and was met with a swift, merciless punch right in the mouth, followed by another one to the nose, and a third quick jab to the eye. I saw stars and crumpled to the floor.

From far away, I could hear Saysha screaming every creative obscenity known to man as the three of them started kicking me.

"Hey!"

Smellson, my knight in shining armor, I thought through the haze. He was disgusting and aptly nicknamed. He didn't believe in showers or deodorant and he loved sticking his cock through the cage bars and ordering the girls to suck him off when no one was around.

"Knock it off, or Berto will hear about it. I told you to leave six be. She's slated for the hunt, you dumb whores. Now bring her over here so I can look at her."

"Fuck off, Nelson, this little bitch came at me." Lydia fumed.

"The fuck did you just say, Lydia?" He came closer and Missy and Darlene beat feet, leaving number one bitch to deal with his stinking, pervy ass.

"You didn't see what she did. This fucking piece of trash broke Darlene's nose. She has to be punished, or these other bitches are going to think they can get away with this shit," she hissed.

"Not my problem you can't keep the stock under control. But what is my problem is Pierce left strict orders this one wasn't to be touched. He wanted her in good shape for the hunt. No bruises, well-fed, kept clean. That's your job."

"But—"

"No buts, you hear? If you can't do your job, we'll find someone who can. I'm sure there are plenty of women here who would gladly take your place."

Lydia let loose a shocked laugh, shaking her head in disbelief.

"Are you fucking kidding me?"

Nelson stepped forward, getting in her face and poking his finger at her chest.

"No, bitch. I'm not. You are on thin fucking ice, and Berto is going to hear all about how you are standing here being disrespectful."

"I'm—"

"Enough."

With that, he reached down and grabbed my arm, hauling me up without a word and pulling me into his office. He sat me down in a cushy office chair roughly, then took a seat opposite me. Blood dripped off the tip of my nose and spattered onto the tile floor. He frowned and grabbed a roll of paper towels.

"Clean that up, then we'll look at those cuts and make sure they didn't break anything. Stupid bitches. Can't follow simple directions."

I said nothing and bent down to wipe up the blood, giving an involuntary groan as I leaned over.

Nelson grinned and leaned back in his chair.

"Well, well, well. I thought you were just a quiet little mouse. But I was wrong. You *are* feisty. No wonder Berto wants you for the hunt."

Chapter Four

Ian

SOLITARY CONFINEMENT MIGHT BREAK some guys, but for me, it's a vacation. Unlike most people, I can sit with myself. I can sit and stew in my own juices, unbothered by my demons. Yeah, they poke at me, try to get a rise out of me, but I swat them away like flies and focus on other things.

Like death.

Mine was imminent. I knew that much. Putting me in prison was a guaranteed death sentence once they took me out of confinement and stuck me in general population. Moreno had plenty of men in there who would be happy to take me out.

I was in solitary because he wasn't ready to kill me yet, but I had a sneaking suspicion he'd reconsider once he saw how things were going down. Last time I showered a guard let a little information slip.

Ace and Xander were alive and out there, poking around. Berto had already given the order to ice both of them on account of them mowing down some of his best men and stealing a bunch of his shit.

Stealing his shit was a bold move, and I hoped it paid off for them. I hoped they'd gotten to Jade, and I hoped they would get the fuck out of dodge and live happily ever after.

Something told me they wouldn't be that lucky, and the clock was definitely ticking on what was a pretty pathetic life for me. A life of causing harm, of squandering what should be the best years of my life on stealing, killing, and causing pain.

I had no idea how many people I'd butchered in my life. No dollar number on what I'd taken.

Whatever the figures were, I knew I'd bought myself a first-class ticket to hell.

The sound of my hand cracking across Jade's beautiful face haunted me. The things I'd said to her, the way I treated her like she was beneath me when she was so far above me it wasn't even funny.

She deserved the best of everything in life, and instead, she was probably dead in a ditch somewhere, or worse, held captive by two of the sickest, most violent bastards to walk the earth.

The thought made me sick.

I missed her laugh, smile, and sweetness. She'd changed me and changed the men I considered brothers. A life without her didn't seem worth living.

"Good thing, because I'm not making it out of this place alive."

I'd dozed off after my meal and the sound of my cell door being opened startled me.

The greasy face of Alan the guard met me, his eyes all kinds of shifty. He looked smug as fuck, so I was not at all surprised when he delivered the news.

"It's your lucky day, buddy. You're out of solitary. Ain't that some good news?"

I swallowed and shook off my nerves. This was fine. No doubt they'd take me out quickly. I wouldn't go out alone, though. I'd take as many of those fuckers out as I could.

"Let's go. I'm guessing you are going to be a real popular guy."

"The bitches love me," I said, giving him my best fuck you smile as he cuffed me.

"Oh, so you didn't get the memo?" He laughed. "You're the bitch here."

I curled my lip and smirked but said nothing. I wasn't afraid of dying, but I wasn't exactly looking forward to what was in store for me.

Actually, I *was* afraid of dying. Now that Jade had gotten under my skin, it felt like there had been something to live for. If she was still alive, of course.

Even that kid, that baby who was unlucky enough to have been born into that fucked up family.

I hadn't been able to shake the image of him, sitting on that loser's lap, grinning and drooling. He looked pale, unhealthy.

A kid needed to be loved. Needed to be chubby and rosy-cheeked and healthy. Needed to be at the park, needed to be rocked and held. I seriously doubted anyone but Jade had shown him the love he deserved.

"What was his name? Benny?"

She didn't talk much about him, but I saw it in her eyes the day she saw him on that news program. Saw the pain in her eyes when I asked her about him. Caught her scrolling through the pictures of him on her camera.

Her love and attachment to him were clear, and I bet if she had the chance she would snatch that kid up in a heartbeat and take care of him.

I'd do it for her if I could. But that ship had sailed for all of us. She was probably already dead. Mick had probably died from his wounds and Ace and Xander had already been hunted down.

Or, maybe just maybe they'd gotten her and gotten out. I would hold on to that mental image until I took my last breath.

My cellmate was alright. A rare guy who actually didn't belong here. His name was Dean, and he was funny as hell and had me laughing despite myself. He was someone I could see myself working with.

But I couldn't stay in my cell all day, and I wasn't about to skulk around, trying to avoid anyone I thought might be out to get me.

I sat with Dean at lunch and watched some locals giving me the side eye. My policy was to stay aware and ready, but no way would I cower and rush through my meal. I would eat my food, talk to Dean, and be ready for the moment when it came.

"Look, it's a rat traitor." A voice came from behind me and Dean cocked an eyebrow at me. I shook my head slightly, letting him know I wasn't biting. He returned to his food.

"I'm talking to you, boy."

I'd hoped to get through a meal but clearly, it wasn't happening.

Without turning around I said, "I'm eating my lunch."

Curious eyes fell upon me and I chewed my food and swallowed before slowly turning to see what I was dealing with.

"That's it. Turn around and face me."

I raised my eyebrows and held my hands out.

"Okay, I'm facing you, what now?"

He cleared his throat. A small crowd had gathered and I saw some familiar faces among my fellow inmates. I saw Leonard and Frankie, Niko and Shane. All guys I'd had some kind of history with. Leonard was a guy after Pierce's own heart, a fucked-up douchebag. Shane was alright.

But this guy in front of me was no one I recognized. Didn't matter, he knew who I was, and I realized they had tasked him with taking me out.

"Enjoy your lunch, Ian. It's your last meal. I'm putting you on notice."

"Fuck off, Jimmy," Dean said.

The guy sneered and pointed at Dean. "Hey, I don't have beef with you, but if you don't shut the fuck up, you're as good as dead."

He shrugged and went back to his sandwich.

I had a few seconds to decide how to handle things and I decided at that moment that heading off the problem was my best course of action. I sprang from the bench and barreled into him, knocking the wind out of him and taking him by surprise. He gasped but had no time to do anything and hit the ground.

I grabbed his head and smacked it into the floor, the sound of his skull cracking on the floor had my hairs standing on end. Blood pooled around his head quickly as I punched him in the face, busting his nose and knocking out at least two of his teeth.

Guards finally pulled me off him and had me on the ground just a few feet away from him. I was pretty sure he wasn't dead, but he was definitely fucked-up and hopefully wouldn't be showing up while I was in the shower.

Of course, someone else would be. Or maybe they'd think twice. I could only hope.

The true test was whether they put me in solitary. An attack like that definitely warranted a few days or more in the tank, right?

Instead, they led me back to my cell with nothing more than a warning to "behave myself".

"That's that. I'm a dead man," I grumbled to Dean as we prepared for lights out.

"They aren't coming in here tonight," he said.

"Maybe not. But they are coming."

Sleep didn't come for me. I closed my eyes and saw the faces of those I'd killed over the years. The faces of family long gone but not forgotten. Of those who had abandoned me, hurt me, and loved me. Saw Ace's grin as he joked around and Xander's sweet smile as he put his arms around me. Saw Mick, arms crossed, shades on.

Finally, I saw Jade, eyes wide and terrified, kicking furiously and bravely in the back of that van.

Even then, I knew my life would never be the same.

Morning came and I was still alive. I knew my time was coming, though. It was inevitable, just like birth.

I remembered a girl that lived in our old apartment building. She was cute, smart and ambitious. And she was ready to pop. We all kept an eye on her because she was on her own. The last few weeks she would waddle to the elevator, flushed and breathless.

"Feels like I'm going to be pregnant forever," she'd say.

I laughed and said, "It's going to be any day now, right?"

She shrugged. "Could be a week, could be in two hours. That's the thing. You logically know it can't last forever, but you can't predict when it's going to happen. It's the weirdest kind of limbo."

Birth and death have that in common, right?

"You okay, Ian?" Dean asked, swinging his legs off the bunk.

"Yeah."

The door opened and I sighed.

"Be careful, buddy," he said.

"You know it."

I had two options: Shower as quickly as possible, like lightning speed, or procrastinate. Either way, I didn't want my death to come while I was trying to rinse shampoo out of my hair.

Just didn't sound like fun.

So I took my sweet time undressing and sure enough, I waited just long enough.

One, two, three, four. They filtered in.

Just like the movies.

I'd had more than my fair share of dramatic moments, but getting cornered in the prison shower was definitely upping my game.

Witty banter was Ace's department. Not mine. Part of me wanted to come up with some kind of snarky remark or the perfect insult, but all I had was a dry mouth and a sinking feeling in the pit of my gut.

I didn't want to die.

Kind of a shocker, really. I'd always assumed one day, probably before my 30th birthday, it would happen. I'd be at the wrong place at the wrong time. Maybe it would be revenge. Or perhaps a heist gone wrong. Either way, it was going to happen and I never cared.

But everything was different now. I hated the idea of dying without knowing for sure if Jade was safe. If Mick had pulled through. If I could just know those things I would be okay. I could die with some peace.

"You can fight or not. Doesn't matter, end result is going to be the same," the guy with the sharp object said.

"Shane. Wow. Didn't think you'd be here."

He cocked his head and shrugged, looking at that moment like the kid he was.

"Yeah, well I got orders, you know how it is."

I nodded. "Sure. I get it."

Another guy I didn't recognize gave a hoarse laugh.

"Before you check out I have a message for you. Comes straight from Berto, your boss. You know, the guy who raised you and took care of you. The guy who sacrificed for you and gave you everything."

I shook my head and thought about launching into a tirade about what a toxic, evil bastard he was but I just didn't have the energy. Suddenly, it didn't seem all that important to plead my case or try to win the hearts and minds of Berto groupies.

"What's the message?"

"Berto wants you to know that Mick is dead. He wants you to know that Ace and Xander are going to die slow and they are going to suffer. Finally, he wants you to know that your little whore Jade has been face-fucked by every Moreno boy in a ten-mile radius, and what's left of her is going to end up in the river by the end of the week."

I roared with rage and went straight for the guy, shattering his face in one motion. A searing pain hit me out of nowhere, more of a burn than anything. I didn't care. I was focused on killing this motherfucker. The messenger was going down.

Then, a sharp yelp and a whistle. The guards were breaking it up, but why?

"Brown. Get over here. Get the fuck away from him." The guard seemed annoyed to be coming to my aid, but the men fell back.

"Fuck, look at his face. Gonna have to stitch his ass up before we turn him loose."

"Loose?" Shane's face fell and he paled.

"Yeah, loose. Orders. Don't ask me, I don't fucking know." The guard, a grizzly of a man nicknamed Hoss, shook his head and threw a towel at me. "Put some fucking pressure on that gash before you bleed out. Now let's go."

Three hours later I was dressed and walking through the gates, a free man. The only thing that made a lick of sense to me was that Berto had changed his mind and wanted to kill me himself. No other explanation. Or, he had a change of heart and was going to put me back to work. But that seemed unlikely.

Either way, I was a dead man. That's all I knew.

"You got some kind of fairy godmother or something looking out for you, loser." A guard muttered as I made my way toward the parking lot. I kept my eyes moving, anticipating an attack that could come from anywhere.

That's when I saw him. A figure standing next to a nondescript black luxury sedan.

"Can't be," I breathed, quickening my pace, squinting my eyes, and waiting for him to disappear like a mirage.

Then I got closer and sure as shit, there he was. Mick. Wearing his shades and his too-tight tee shirt that showed off his giant arms. And standing right there next to him was my buddy Ace.

"Holy shit! Holy shit, you guys. What the fuck? Did you... am I fucking hallucinating? Am I dead?"

Then, the crash. I looked around and there was no one else.

"Xander?" My heart sank. Of course it was too good to be true. And Jade? No way in hell we could get that lucky.

The car door opened, and I sucked in my breath as Xander, all tan and lean, emerged with a sad smile playing across his lips and just the faintest hopeful spark in his eyes.

I flung myself at him, engulfing him in a near-violent bear hug as he gasped. When I released him, I attacked Mick and then Ace. Ace let loose a maniacal laugh and Mick winced.

"Easy there, killer. I'm still busted up from the bullet that splintered my ribcage and missed my heart by that much," he winced and held up his hand, his thumb and forefinger about two inches apart.

"Oh, shit. Sorry."

"No problem."

Ace's eyes shifted around the parking lot, and I sensed tension from Mick.

"Let's get the fuck out of here," Xander said. "We'll talk in the car."

I nodded and slid into the back seat with Ace. Mick rode shotgun and Xander drove.

"Where we headed?"

"Motel."

"Really? Is there any place safe at this point?" I found it hard to believe there was any place in Los Angeles where we could lie low.

I dreaded asking about Jade, but I had to.

"Did you find her? Do you know if she's..."

Ace exhaled. Xander visibly flinched and Mick's jaw could cut a diamond.

"Okay, we'll talk about it later. Where are we going and what is our next move? And how the fuck did you get me out of there? You know I was literally about to get stabbed?"

"Ask boy wonder here," Mick joked, ruffling Xander's hair.

Ace nodded. "Yeah, it was all him. Dude has been pulling more surprises out of his ass than... well I don't know what."

He sounded exhausted.

"I went through all Berto's shit. He's got stuff on everyone. And I mean everyone. Sheriff. District attorney. Half the cops on the force. Councilmen and women, you name it. All in nice, neat files. So I went to the people I needed to go to and worked out a deal. The rest is history."

"Holy shit," I said, grinning despite the somber mood. I was so fucking happy to see them, but I knew there was no good news on the Jade front.

"So? Next question, guys. I need to know."

"Short answer: We don't know where she is. We're heading to the Inland Empire where I know we won't run into any Moreno boys. Then, we're going to talk to Jesse."

I scrubbed my hand down my face and took a deep breath.

"Well, the guys who worked me over told me she was... that she was going to end up in a ditch. But they also told me Mick was dead, so there's that."

I decided to leave out a few details.

"Fuck me," muttered Mick.

Ace snapped his head to face me. "We're going to kill every single one of his guys if that's what it takes. Flush out every fucking hidey-hole he has until we find where he's stashed her."

"Yeah, well there is no doubt he still has Jade. Outside of that, I have no idea."

"That's not good enough," Xander growled. "We need answers and no one we've run across has them. We can't waste a bunch of time trying to root out every guy he's got in this town."

"I disagree, Xan. There aren't that many guys. His operation is big, but not that big."

"I know, but he's got other locations. Further out locations. I'm willing to bet money they've taken her out of LA."

He was probably right.

It was a big world out there, and Berto had spots all over it.

She could be anywhere.

Chapter Five

Ian

I SHOWERED WHILE MICK and Ace went out to grab some chow. I was beat all to hell, exhausted mentally and physically, and now that the four of us were finally back together, I felt like I might get a little rest.

But not before we hashed things out.

I dried off and walked into the room, toweling off my hair and trying my damndest to push thoughts of Jade out of my mind.

Xander sat at the table drinking a beer and staring off into space.

"We're going to find her," I said. "Seriously. Don't you worry."

He nodded without enthusiasm.

"Yeah, I knew we'd get to you before something happened. I knew we'd spring you and Mick out of there and you'd both be fine. Ace didn't believe it, but I knew it in my gut."

"See, like I said, she's gonna be okay."

"I don't know, Ian."

I dropped into the chair like I weighed a million pounds and pressed my palms against my eyes.

"You listen to me. You just said you knew in your gut we were going to be okay, and look, here I sit. Mick's bringing back pizza and more beer. See?"

He shook his head. "You don't understand. I had absolute faith you guys were going to be okay, but with Jade... well, I don't have that same feeling."

His eyes darkened and he took a swig of his beer.

"Now that kind of attitude is not what I'm looking for, Xander. We have to think positive. We have to bring every ounce of faith and hope and courage to this if we are going to succeed. You hear me?"

"Yeah, I hear you."

He slouched a little in his chair and started peeling the label off his beer. He eyed me for a minute and I saw the need in his expression.

It wasn't a need for sex, really. But the need for release and comfort.

Sometimes, it was just about that. Especially after anything ugly. To have that release and to feel that feeling of... home. That's what it was about.

I looked him over, licking my lips as I took in his frame, his lips, and then looked into his eyes.

"Come here."

Doubt flashed across his face, but he rose from the chair and approached me.

"They're going to be back—"

"Not for a while. We have time."

He dropped to his knees and started unbuttoning my pants. I couldn't help but laugh.

"I see you were very concerned. Thought I was going to have to talk you into it, guess I was wrong."

He shot me a sly smile and pulled my pants down roughly, exposing my cock, already hard and ready for him.

Without another word he dipped his head down and took it in his mouth, immediately groaning at the way I felt. He loved my cock in his mouth. Always had.

"Fuck," I said, my jaw tensing and my hips pulsing up as my hand grabbed the back of his head.

I leaned my head back against the chair and enjoyed the feel of his mouth on my cock, but when he picked up the pace and started increasing the pressure on me I stopped him.

"I don't want to come now. I want you to get on the bed. Lie down."

He didn't want to stop sucking my cock, I could tell. But I wanted him to get off, and I wanted a different kind of release.

"Thank god for convenience store lube," I said. "Now take off your pants and get on the bed."

He did as he was told and I climbed on top of him as he positioned himself face-down on the bed.

I placed my hand on the back of his neck while I tore the packet of lube open with my teeth and applied it liberally, slicking up my hard cock and dribbling the rest over Xander's tight asshole. I used my thumb to work it in, to gently massage and coax his relaxation as he moaned and raised his ass to meet me.

"Fuck me," he groaned, squirming as I teased his opening with the tip of my cock.

I slid my hand from the back of his neck around to the front, squeezing it just the way he liked while I slid inside him, moaning at the feel of his tight hole around my cock.

"You feel so fucking good."

I felt him swallow and his strained inhale as I slid in and out, increasing the pressure and urgency, because I knew we didn't have long.

Soon I was fucking him mercilessly, fucking away weeks of tension and anger, and uncertainty, fucking away grief and disappointment, worry and fear. Fucking it all away until there was nothing but him and me, and finally, I came hard as sweat ran down my face and dripped onto his back.

I was spent in all ways, and when I collapsed on top of him I truly wished we could just pass out cold for days, just the two of us, the bed, the air conditioner, and more booze so we could keep forgetting.

But we had a mission: find Jade. Find her and save her, if it wasn't too late.

I would never, ever forgive myself if she was lost to us forever. None of us would.

We argued back and forth about the best way to proceed. Ace and Xander wanted to go to Jesse Moreno, and Mick and I wanted to search the city for clues.

Ace was frustrated with that plan and was trying to talk us out of it.

"I told you guys, we've combed the city, searched every nook and cranny. I don't think she's in the city, especially after what Moni told us."

"You said that she had a bad feeling. Explain."

"I guess Pierce took a girl from her place, Katy's sister to be exact, and got weird about it. She left with him and no one's heard from her since. Moni said something felt off about it."

"So you think they stashed her away with some girls?"

Ace shook his head. "Nope. I wish it was that easy."

"You sure?" Mick cocked an eyebrow and glanced at me.

"We've been to every fucking cathouse Berto runs. Talked to a dozen girls and every friend we have that likes to partake in his stock. She's not working for him."

Mick stood up and stretched, and Ace started clearing out wrappers and beer bottles.

"He wouldn't put her out there like that. His beef is more with us than her. I'm betting he's just using her as bait to lure us out."

"If he wanted to use Jade to lure us out, we would have found her by now."

"So what the hell then? Why her? Why is Berto so interested in her?"

Xander smacked his hand on the table to get our attention. His face darkened and the way he looked at us all gave me chills.

"You guys just don't fucking get it, do you?"

"What, Xander? What don't we get?"

"She's their type. And what Berto wants, Berto gets. Trust me, I know."

Chapter Six

Xander

It was a restless night, and I had mixed feelings about seeing my uncle Jesse. He lived in the desert, a good two and a half hours outside of Los Angeles, over three hours with traffic.

We didn't call ahead. Mick decided we should leave early and take our chances at Kiki's Coffee Shack.

You could say that our last coffee run sparked a streak of epically bad luck, but the way I saw it, this was where we first met Jade, and it was her that finally gave our pathetic, jaded, and burned-out crew something to live for.

I'd been stuck inside my shell, relying on the guys to pick up my slack, to be my voice, and to guide me.

They were still my brothers, but for the first time in my life, I felt like I was my own man. I'd already proven to myself that I could fight and win, that I could make decisions, and that my ideas had merit.

If we'd never met Jade, if we'd just done the job and cut out of town I would still be nice guy Xander, shy, quiet, indecisive, forever wondering what I could have been had I not been raised under Berto's thumb.

I guess I'd never know what it would have been like to not have Berto terrorizing me. Or what it would have been like to have my mother around to raise me. Or my father.

I never really hated him for taking my father from me. From what I'd gathered, my dad wasn't any better than Berto. A gangster doing gangster shit. Not caring who he hurt in the process, including me and my mom.

But I knew in my soul she would still be alive. My old man may have been a heartless bastard, but he would have never tortured my mother the way Berto did. She would have stuck around to raise me all the way up. Maybe I'd have ended up more like my family. Maybe I would have grown to be ruthless, heartless, and cold.

But here I was now. Not heartless. But ruthless? Yeah.

Cold? No. Frosty as fuck, though.

We rolled up to Jesse's compound at about 10:00 AM. It was already hot as hell and most likely no one was up at this hour.

The dogs were, though, and the ruckus they created had curious and steely-eyed men wearing faded jeans and full sleeves making their way to the front gate.

One guy, probably in his thirties but looking and walking like he was in his forties, produced a pistol from the waistband of his jeans and pulled off his shades, squinting at me from under the bill of his cap.

"I highly suggest you and your friends turn around and get the fuck on down the road. This is private property."

I laughed and pulled up the sleeve of my shirt. Why Jesse had this loser manning the gate was beyond me.

When his eyes fell to the scar on my arm his eyes widened a little and he motioned for one of his boys to open the gate.

Once upon a time, Uncle Berto thought branding his own was a fun way to build teamwork.

"Think of it like a tattoo," he'd said.

That "tattoo" was my pass through the gates.

"Who are your friends? And who are you, exactly?" he asked, still trying to play tough suspicious guy.

"I'm Jesse's nephew," I said. "Don't worry about anything else. Just take me to my uncle."

I was tired and not in the mood for any bullshit.

He jerked his head to a dusty white ranch-style house down the drive. The property was littered with trailers in various stages of disrepair, along with some brand-new state-of-the-art models. Four-wheel trucks, motorcycles, and a couple of small, run down homes rounded things out. It was dusty and gave definite outlaw vibes.

The screen door swung open and there he was, looking like Sam Fucking Elliot with his gray hair and lopsided grin. He wore jeans, a white tee shirt, and a cowboy hat. In his arms he held a baby wearing nothing but a diaper and an impressively unruly shock of white hair on its head.

"Well, I'll be damned. My nephew come all the way from the big city to see his uncle. Come on over here and meet your newest cousin."

"Cousin?" Mick muttered behind me.

"This your crew, Xander? Come on in. Take off your shoes before coming inside or your auntie will have a cow."

I remained watchful and tense as I walked through the door, shaking my head and laughing to myself. How many aunts could a guy have? I wondered who the latest Ms. Moreno would be. Jesse went through wives like nobody's business.

He wasn't a monster like Berto. At least, not that I knew of. He didn't seem to delight in bringing misery to everyone he touched. But he was a womanizing sonofabitch with a taste for young blondes. He loved working on cars and bikes, loved a good fistfight, loved booze and playing cards, and loved a good barbecue.

He thought of himself as a red-blooded American man's man. Apple pie and whiskey, cigarettes, and red meat. Underage pussy and loud pipes. These were a few of his favorite things.

As I crossed the threshold, he slapped a hand down on my shoulder and cocked his head.

"Your uncle know you're here?"

From the outside, you would swear the inside would be a cluttered mess filled with non-matching furniture, cobwebs, and a sink full of dirty dishes.

Instead, I found myself in a tastefully decorated home that was sparkling clean and clutter-free, unless you counted the baby toys scattered across the living room floor.

"Have a sit, boys. What's going on?"

Jesse had an amiable smile and a twinkle in his eye, but underneath it, I could see his watchful assessment of me, Mick, Ace, and definitely Ian.

A curvy young woman with bleach-blonde hair and enough black eyeliner for five of her friends emerged from the hallway and didn't so much as register the tiniest bit of surprise to see us sitting in her living room. She did glance down at our feet first thing.

"Laurie, come get the baby. I've not seen my nephew in years. I'm sure we have a lot of catching up to do."

She said nothing and he gave no introduction. She simply walked over, Jesse passed her the baby, and she disappeared.

He watched her walk away, eyes fixed on her ass as she made her way across the room. Once she was gone, he turned to me.

"She's a good girl. Been two years and I still ain't sick of her. Must be getting old." He laughed at that, and I did my best to offer a polite grin. Ace chuckled and Mick gave a soft snort. We really didn't feel like small talk, but we couldn't go in after all this time pushing anything.

"So I'm guessing you have some kind of business you want to discuss?"

Well, lucky day. He wants to get right to it.

Jesse was a talker, and he loved telling stories. He was also a staller and a procrastinator. Berto bitched about these things any time Jesse's name came up.

"You boys want some coffee? You're lucky, you know. I'm not usually up this early, but the baby is my alarm clock now."

"Cute kid," Ace remarked. "Congrats."

Jesse sucked in a breath. "Yeah, thought my baby-making days were over after I divorced Genie, but guess the big man had other plans." He shrugged and raised his hands in surrender.

"How many does that make now, Jesse?" Mick asked.

"Six? No, seven. More, if you count the stepkids."

"Huh." Ace raised his eyebrows and I couldn't tell if he was horrified or impressed.

Just as I opened my mouth to spill the story, Jesse held up his hand.

"My sixth sense is telling me you need a favor, nephew. And I suspect that the favor involves pissing off my brother."

Mick cleared his throat.

"You seen your brother lately?" he asked.

Jesse pursed his lips, then answered.

"Haven't seen him. Saw his bitch boy Pierce. Ran through here a couple of weeks ago and grabbed a couple of my boys for an easy job of some sort."

"You know where he's staying?" I asked.

Jesse narrowed his eyes at me and looked me up and down.

"You're a grown man now, Xander. Too old to be playing bullshit games. But from what I hear, that's exactly what you've been up to. And it really baffles me you'd bring your bullshit to my house."

My stomach churned at his words. He wasn't going to help us.

Chapter Seven

Ian

Jesse looked thoughtful as he downed his third cup of coffee while Xander relayed the story we'd agreed to tell him.

It was important to leave some stuff out. It was also important to appeal to his sensibilities, and most importantly, his ego.

"So you mean to tell me you want me to help you guys burn my brother?"

Xander was panicking, I could tell.

"Burn is a strong word, Uncle. What we need to do is find Jade. That's all we're asking."

He set his cup down on the table and gave us a good, long, look-over.

"I'm trying to wrap my head around this. You are going against the Moreno family over a *girl*. That's what I'm hearing. You are risking your lives and the lives of anyone and everyone you care about for a girl. You could be out of the country in the time it took you to come out here and tell me your sad story."

Xander shot me a pleading look and Mick and Ace appeared to be barely holding it together. My gut told me that Jesse knew exactly where we could find Berto, but we had to proceed with caution. He was seconds from telling us to get the fuck off his property, and if we pissed him off, he'd sell us out to Berto in a heartbeat, nephew or not.

"Look, Jesse..." I started, but he shot me a sharp look.

"Nobody 'looks' me in my own house. Watch yourself."

I clamped my mouth shut as Xander gave me the side-eye of death.

But we had to convince him. We'd come all this way and I wasn't leaving without the information we came for. Period.

I altered my approach.

"Sorry, Jesse. I hear what you are saying. But this isn't about going after Berto. I mean, the reality is he's lost his grip lately. Men are talking. And this girl, well, she's no ordinary girl. Berto's real wrapped up in something and I'm thinking his organization is vulnerable."

Xander frowned at me and Mick looked at me like I was crazy.

"I mean, any gang could probably come in and take over. He's not present. He's holed up in his little hideout, distracted. I just talked to some of his best men and they were talking about going elsewhere. Or worse."

Of course, I left out the part where we gunned down half a dozen of those "best men" but he didn't need to hear about all that.

Jesse's ears perked up, just like I knew they would.

When he left Los Angeles for the desert nearly twenty years ago, it was because Berto gave him a choice: Run or die.

Nino was dead, Berto had taken over the family, and Jesse was outgunned and outnumbered.

A few guys went with him and they found a spot in the desert and started running guns and formed a motorcycle gang. They had their hands in a few things, but it was mostly weapons and drugs.

After a few years, Berto and Jesse appeared to bury the hatchet and even worked together sometimes.

But I knew that deep down, Jesse had never forgiven his brother for what he'd done. He never got over what had been taken from him. His spot as top dog in the Moreno family.

"Uncle, I'm not asking for a lot. I just want a little information. We think he's taken her outside the city. Maybe even somewhere out here."

Jesse nodded. "Yeah. He has a place about an hour and a half from where we're at now. I was there when they were building it. A compound where he could go when he wanted to get out of Los Angeles. I've heard from a few boys that he's been there lately."

"Where is it, Uncle? Please tell me. I won't say I heard it from you."

I rolled my eyes. Xander was appealing to Jesse the uncle, not Jesse the businessman or criminal. Xander still didn't comprehend that you couldn't rely on someone's better nature. Or their compassion. Jesse might not be the monster his brother was, but he was not a nice guy, either. There had to be something in it for him, and right now we had nothing. No money, no property, nothing he could use.

"I get it, Jesse. No one wants to step on Berto's toes. Especially not you. We totally understand if you can't give us the location. I'd be worried, too. You have a family and —"

His eyes widened, and he puffed out his chest.

"What the fuck are you saying, kid? You think I'm afraid of that shithead brother of mine? You think I'm out here cowering in the desert?"

I held up my hands in mock surrender. I could sense Mick getting tense, but Ace knew exactly what I was up to.

"Of course not. But the reality is if he wanted he could shut you down in a heartbeat. So, of course you won't cough up his location."

He stood up and motioned for us to stand, too.

"You kids think this is about me being scared? Hell no. This is me doing you a favor. You think you can just roll up to this place, the four of you? You think you can show up and ask him for your girl back? Are you fucking insane? Or just that stupid?"

I opened my mouth to say something, but Xander cut me off.

"Then come with us, Uncle Jesse. Fuck Berto and everything he has put our family through. Fuck him for what he did to my parents, what he did to you. He had no right."

My jaw dropped a little but Ace was grinning from ear to ear. He loved this kind of drama and chaos. Mick didn't like it one bit. I wasn't sure Xander was playing with a full deck at this point.

The unwritten, unspoken agreement in the family was this: No one mentioned what happened. No one mentioned Berto killed his brother and ran the other one out of town. No one mentioned Xander's mother and what he did to her. It was wiped from the records as far as Berto was concerned. He'd even gone as far as to kill anyone who was there when it happened, including men who were loyal to him. He'd done his best to rewrite history, giving entirely false versions of how he came to control the gang.

Mentioning anything different was a fast way to get a bullet in your head.

Jesse regarded his nephew for a moment, then sighed.

"Look, kid. I care for you. I do. But what you are asking is for me to risk the one thing I'm afraid I've gotten real used to."

"What's that?" Xander asked.

"Peace."

My shoulders slumped. Xander's attempt to trigger his uncle's sense of justice and my attempts to tempt him with an easy win and an ego boost weren't exactly having an impact.

It was time to break out the big guns, which is something I hadn't wanted to do. Because once I took this out of the box, there was no putting it back in.

"Can I ask you a question, Jesse?"

"Ask away. Answer is probably no."

I nodded.

"How many daughters do you have?"

He narrowed his eyes at me. A sore point for him. He was a misogynistic son of a bitch, but I also knew he loved his kids, male or female.

"Five."

"Yeah, any of them teenagers?"

His face reddened. "What the fuck is it to you?"

"Land your plane, Ian," Mick warned. I brushed him off and continued.

"It's a dangerous world out there for little girls, you know?"

"I take care of mine, don't you worry. Just what the fuck are you getting at, anyway?"

I stepped in a little closer.

"I'm saying that your brother murdered a fourteen-year-old girl last week. Your brother brutally raped her, then dismembered her body. I'm saying your brother is a fucking monster who thinks that no girl or woman is off-limits. He took his own brother's wife. What makes you think he won't take yours?"

I ventured a look at Xander, Mick, and Ace. Realization dawned on their faces, one by one.

Of course, I couldn't be sure it wasn't just Pierce, but I doubted it. They both had their hand in it. I knew they did. Like a fucking sixth sense. Every time I saw another report about a missing woman or a girl found dead, I knew it was him. I knew it in my soul.

Uncle Berto: Serial rapist and murderer.

And he had Jade.

"What do you want me to do?"

He looked tired. Jesse was just a couple years older than Berto but looked a good deal older. Berto always said the desert aged you. The wind and sand, and sun, dried you out like a prune.

Hell, even his barely legal wife looked older than she should.

"What do you say, Jesse? Come with us. Bring some men. We'll take him down. He won't be expecting it. Take him down and make him pay for what he's been doing. It's not right. As a father, you know it. He needs to get put down. Then, you get it all. His money, houses, businesses. You can take your place. Your rightful place."

His wife crept in and silently listened to everything that we'd said.

Jesse said nothing to her, but she grabbed his hand and he squeezed it. He looked at her and she gave the tiniest nod.

Then he looked at Xander.

"Fine. We go get that girl of yours, although if what you're saying is true, she's probably dead and gone."

Xander winced, and Ace clenched his fists. He looked like he was about to bust a neck vein any second. Mick was cool as a cucumber, but he was Mount Vesuvius, ready to go off any minute.

He heaved a sigh and scrubbed a palm across his stubbly face.

"Let's do it. We go in today. Two hours. We do it my way. But you understand this means a full-on war and if we don't win today, we are in a long-haul battle and there will be consequences."

I nodded.

"We'll win."

Chapter Eight

Jade

NELSON CLEANED MY WOUNDS, bandaged me up, had me sit there with an ice pack, down a bottle of Pedialyte, and a couple of anti-inflammatories. Then, he walked me back to the cages.

We were in what seemed a lot like an airplane hangar divided in half. Half the building housed Smellson's office and some other rooms I knew nothing about - except one. It was like a fucking psycho man-cave and it's where I'd been taken a couple of times to "perform" with the other girls. It was almost like a club, and from some of the screams I'd heard come out of it, I knew lots of bad things happened there.

The other half of the building was the cages. They were situated along the wall. Every wall. I counted about forty-five cages in all. At present, there were probably twenty girls in total. The numbers varied. A few days ago, they'd brought in two more girls.

Yesterday they took one out. She hadn't come back yet.

It was like that. Usually one to three girls came in at a time. And one or two was always leaving.

But there were plenty of vacancies.

Two girls died in the cages. One happened a few days ago. They had dragged her out, kicking and screaming, then brought her back several hours later. Nelson had looked at her and they put her back in her cage.

The next day when Missy and Darlene made their feeding rounds, she was dead.

She was unceremoniously dragged out again. No one said anything about anything.

I cried for hours. So sad not just for her, but for the family that would likely never know what happened to their daughter, sister, girlfriend or wife.

Most girls appeared to be about my age. Late teens, early twenties, I figured. But I'd seen younger girls brought in. There was one a few cages down that didn't look much older than fourteen or fifteen.

Every time she got taken out of the cage, I felt like I was going to throw up.

I'd heard Lydia call her the "main attraction".

Fucking pieces of shit. I wanted to watch them all die. Berto. Pierce. Nelson. Lydia. Missy. Darlene. All the guys who guarded the place. There were plenty of guards. They were supposed to steer clear of the "stockroom" but sometimes they peeked in.

My guess was these guys were the cream of the crop when it came to guys Berto trusted. What Berto was doing here was beyond illegal. This wasn't money laundering or shootouts with other criminals. This wasn't prostitution or drug dealing.

This was mass murder.

I woke up feeling different. Something was going to happen. I felt it in my gut. I didn't know what, but it would either result in my death or my freedom.

Shit, at this point, death is freedom.

Footsteps had my stomach churning. They were coming toward me. It was all three of them and they were looking very smug.

"Wakey-wakey, five."

Missy landed a kick to the cage, and I heard Saysha sputtering in fear and outrage.

"Open it up," Lydia ordered.

Then, she crouched down and peered in at me. She smiled brightly and tapped on the metal bars.

"Oh good. You're bright-eyed and bushy-tailed. That's real good, six. You don't want to miss the show."

"What show? What are you talking about?"

Panic rose in me as I heard more footsteps and two men walked in. They were looking over their shoulder and Darlene snorted and put her hands on her hips.

"You guys are real pussies, you know that?" She pointed at the guy on the left. "I told you, it's fine. Big Daddy B ain't coming back till tonight."

"You sure? Cause Eddie said he's got a hunt today."

She shook her head. "No, silly. It's tomorrow. It's on the board in the office."

He sucked in his breath as Darlene pulled Saysha out of her cage. My blood ran cold as I saw both men grinning, eyeing my friend like she was a piece of meat, which was exactly how they saw us.

"Oh, but first, we get to have a little fun."

"You watching, six?"

I slammed my hand on the cage and the sound reverberated, echoing in the giant space.

"No, what the fuck are you doing?"

Missy giggled and landed a kick right to Saysha's stomach.

"Making you pay for your bullshit, bitch. We can't touch you, but we sure can touch little miss snuff bait right here. She's a dead whore anyway, right, Lydia?"

She laughed her usual maniacal laugh and nodded. "Oh, yeah. Dead as a fucking doornail."

"No. No, you can't," I cried out as Missy and Darlene laughed and clapped while Lydia smirked at me.

The men had forgotten all about the threat of Berto or Pierce. They had Saysha pinned and were pulling off her clothes while she struggled and screamed.

Some of the other girls started crying, and I screamed obscenities at the top of my lungs, beating my fists against the cage.

"Stop it." Lydia smacked the cage back. "I mean it."

"You mean what? You can't do shit to me. You said it yourself."

"Oh really? Your friend is paying for your sins right now. Watch!"

My rage blinded me, I was rabid and there was no fear in me as I slammed my bruised and bloody hands against the cage.

"Fuck you, fuck you and your other two stooges. Can't wait to tell Berto all about it. All about these two clowns. Baldy and fat ass. Nice gold ring. Nice fucking scar on your upper lip, dead man. I'll rat your rapey asses out so fucking fast."

Lydia's eyes widened just a little and she turned back to the men. One of them, the scar guy, jumped up, adjusted himself and started toward me. He pulled out his gun and pointed it right at me.

"Shoot the bitch."

The other guy wiped the sweat from his face, and Saysha curled herself into a ball. All the fight had left her. Blood gushed from her nose and mouth and she was openly sobbing. I squeezed my eyes shut, sure he'd fire off a couple of rounds right into my head. Today was my death day.

"No." Lydia snarled and pushed his hand away. "Are you fucking high? She's Berto's pathetic little prize. He'd fucking kill us all for touching her. Do what you want with the other one. I'll just make something up. Tell him she got sick and died or something. Maybe she had some internal injuries. Whatever. But this one, as much as I'd love to see her get what she deserves, this one is for Berto only."

A clapping sound came from another side of the room, but I couldn't see the source of the sound.

"Wow. Idiots in action, I see."

It was Nelson. Twice this loser had come to my rescue. He was as bad as the others, but he knew how to follow directions and did so diligently. But they outnumbered him and I could see psycho Lydia icing this motherfucker to save her own ass.

"Berto's not gonna like any of this." He tsked and shook his head. I watched him rake his eyes over Saysha and then look at the two men who were now sweating bullets and looking a little lost.

"Now, Nelson. You don't need to say one word about this." Lydia's voice was laced with saccharin and she smiled a sick and knowing smile.

"The fuck I don't, girlie."

"Oh, really? You might want to rethink, or I'll tell the boss about all the times you pulled girls out of the cages for a little after-hours entertainment without permission."

"What the—"

"Oh, you thought I didn't notice you drugging those little ones up and deleting the camera footage? Oh, sweetie. You think you're slick, but you absolutely aren't."

Then came the footsteps.

"None of you are."

There was dead silence for a few heartbeats as everyone froze.

I watched the color drain from Lydia's face and Missy immediately started sobbing.

The two men both stepped forward, splaying their hands and taking that "Oh, sorry boss, didn't know what came over me, surely you understand" demeanor.

But they were fucked. If it wasn't for how messed up Saysha was and how worried I was about this "hunt" I kept hearing about, I'd be thrilled. As it was, I still found myself grinning.

Please, if there is a god, let me see at least one of these motherfuckers go down.

Because at this point it was the most I could hope for. I was fast running out of that tiny glimmer of hope that the guys or the cops would show up. It just would not happen.

Me escaping? Even less likely.

I was definitely going to die. But please, God. Please let me watch Lydia or one of these other bitches die. Please.

Berto was followed in by Pierce and a couple of his bouncers. He gave Saysha a quick glance, then motioned to Nelson. "Put it back in its cage, would you?"

He fixed his eyes on Lydia, her sidekicks, and the two men who were in the middle of raping my friend.

There was a tense and watchful hush all across the room. I knew I wasn't the only one wishing, hoping, and praying for some kind of hollow satisfaction. Lydia was cruel and the way she went about every injustice, every humiliating and horrifically painful punishment, with such unbridled glee, with such utter disregard for our humanity, it was mind-blowing.

She needed to pay, and I was practically drooling in anticipation of her punishment. And seeing those two pigs go down would be the icing on the cake.

Berto put his hand to his chin and tapped his forefinger to his lips, making a grand show of taking his time, thoughtfully considering the situation, and carefully creating the appropriate punishment.

"Lydia, Lydia, Lydia." He shook his head, his eyebrows knit in concern, tinged with sadness.

"Berto—"

He put his finger up and Pierce stood there chuckling to himself, delighted with what was unfolding.

Looking at him made the hairs on the back of my neck stand up, but really, Berto was just as bad as him, if not worse.

"I am beyond disappointed in you. But what did I expect? Women aren't to be trusted, are they, Pierce? Not to be trusted at all."

"What are you going to do?" Missy choked out, sniveling and dripping tears and snot all over the floor.

"What am I going to do? Well, that's a real good question."

He looked to Pierce, then to Nelson. Then turned his gaze to the cages.

"I like to think I am quite careful with selecting my staff. There is a great deal of trust I place in those who I allow into this space."

He paused for effect. Lydia inhaled, gearing up to run her mouth again, but Berto held up a finger.

"Pierce, Lydia doesn't seem to understand the concept of not speaking until she has been spoken to. Seems she has forgotten the lessons we taught her so many years ago, when she was young and bright."

Pierce huffed a mocking laugh.

"She's used up, now. I told you these bitches were useless."

Berto nodded.

"You did. You did indeed."

Darlene looked as though she could pass out at any minute and I continued watching with bated breath.

Nelson had just shoved Saysha back into the cage and I could hear her stifling her sobs.

Then Nelson walked slowly back to the middle of the room.

Berto turned to him and frowned.

"I understand you've been helping yourself to my prized stock. My own personal collection. A collection that I have carefully obtained at substantial risk, with the help of Pierce, my trusted and apparently only loyal associate. This curated collection of females is mine, to do with as I please."

"I only—"

"Once again, I remind you that you work for me. Are paid by me. Were pulled out of the fire by me."

"Yes, boss."

Berto gave the tiniest jerk of his head and slightest gesture and the man flanking Berto pulled out his gun and shot Nelson in the head.

Lydia gasped and Missy dissolved into more tears.

Berto nodded and gestured again, and the same man shot the other two men.

"Good start, Berto. But please don't stop."

I muttered this under my breath, thinking no one would hear me over Missy's sobbing, but she had just stopped to take a breath. Berto and Pierce whipped their heads toward me sharply and Lydia flashed a 'you're dead' glare that delighted me to no end because I knew full well she was as good as dead, even if she didn't realize it.

Berto flashed a grin that was almost friendly, and Pierce offered his own toothy, predatory grin.

"She is the one who started this shit," Lydia hissed.

Berto shook his head.

"You have proven that you have officially lost your grip on these girls. You can't be trusted, and you've just reached the end of your shelf life."

Her lip started trembling and I pressed myself against the cage, feeling a level of bloodthirsty that I'd never known was possible.

It occurred to me then that the trauma I'd endured had changed me.

It occurred to me for the first time that I *could* be Lydia.

I could easily lose my compassion, my empathy. My conscience.

"What do you say, six?"

Berto looked around at the cages.

"How about you, five? Over there in eleven? What would you like to see happen here?"

I watched Pierce's face. He didn't like what Berto was doing. That was the difference between the two of them. Berto was a monster. A horrible, horrible monster. But he sometimes indulged us in odd ways. I'd seen him show small mercies.

But not Pierce. Oh, no. Not him.

The difference between Pierce and Berto was that with Berto it wasn't personal. He had no heart. It was true. But for him, this was fun. We were his playthings. He didn't care about us at all.

But he didn't hate us, either.

Pierce did.

"Why are you asking them? They don't get to decide," he snapped.

Berto cocked an eyebrow at him. Pierce shrugged.

"Or they do."

Berto walked over to me and squatted down so he was at eye level to me.

"Maybe this one wants a last wish to go with her last meal."

My heart sank. It was true. This was the end for me.

I stared into his eyes. They twinkled with amusement and curiosity.

"What do you say, six? You are hereby promoted to judge, jury, and executioner."

He unlatched my cage, and the door swung open. He held out a hand and I took it.

"Come, my little gazelle. Let's let you stretch your legs a little."

I stood up and wiggled my toes against the concrete floor, still not trusting any of this.

But if he was telling the truth...

"Come," he snapped his fingers and pointed in the direction he wanted me to walk, and I complied.

He stopped me directly in front of Lydia. Missy and Darlene stood on either side of her, visibly trembling.

"This is silly, Berto. We have shit to do," Pierce said as he eyed me with a level of contempt that I could physically feel.

"We have time."

I paid Pierce no mind. I imagined he was here to take part in whatever horrible plans they had for me. Whatever. I guess I would find out about that soon enough.

For now, I kept my focus on Lydia.

She was starting to crack.

"Please. Please, I promise I won't let you down again." Her voice trembled and her eyes were leaking big, pitiful tears.

Her breaking only caused more panic between the other two, and I couldn't help but smile.

"See that, Pierce. There's the fire I was talking about."

Pierce scoffed. "There's no fire in this whore. I don't know why you think so highly of her. At least Lydia was of some use. Just shoot the bitch and take your favorite little fox to her pen to wait for the horn to sound."

His words went through one ear and out the other. I didn't care what Pierce was going on about.

"Here, love. Take this." Berto pressed a gun into my hand.

Pierce literally jumped.

"What in God's name are you doing? Have you gone mad?"

"Shh. Don't get your trousers in a bunch."

The men with Berto pointed their guns at my head.

He leaned into me.

"You have one chance, dear. And believe me, if you so much as move or breathe the wrong way, your brains will be all over the floor, do you understand?"

I nodded.

"So, what will it be? Mercy? Or will you dole out punishment? The choice is yours."

"You mean I can let her live?" I said.

Lydia's eyes lit up. Her eyes pleaded with me.

"Of course. You are the judge and jury, that's what I said."

"So if I do, she can just go back to work? No consequences?" I stepped toward her, keeping the gun low.

"Yes. Your choice."

I turned my head and looked at Saysha. She was pressed up against the bars, her eyes lit with unholy rage, and when I gave her a wink and a smile, she responded with a bloody, giddy, crazed grin.

"Hey, Lydia," I said.

"Y-yes. Please. Please, six—"

"That's not my name, bitch."

She started crying.

I raised the gun and pulled back the hammer.

"What's my name, Lydia?"

Her eyes widened and she shook her head slightly.

"What is it?"

"I don't know. I don't know." She was really crying now. I could see the fear and panic in her eyes.

"Okay, I'll give you three guesses."

She shook her head harder.

"No. No, please."

"Definitely not my name. Try again."

I heard Berto chuckle.

"What? That wasn't a guess." She choked a little and started looking around wildly.

"Oh, are you looking around to see if someone is coming to save you?"

She was breathing hard, her chest heaving.

I nodded. "I did that for a couple of days, too. Every time the door opened I thought maybe it was someone coming to save me. But it was just you bitches."

Pierce cleared his throat.

"This is crazy, Berto. Take that fucking gun away from her."

"Shut up, Pierce. This is fun."

Lydia latched on to Pierce's dissent.

"Pierce. C'mon. You know me. You know I am loyal."

Pierce rolled his eyes.

"You mistake my protest for concern. You are nothing to me. No more than any of this other trash. Shut the fuck up."

"Wow, great benefits this job has, yeah?" I snarked at her.

"You have one more guess. What do you think my name is?"

She dropped to her knees and started slapping the concrete with her hands.

"You can't fucking do this. You won't get away with this."

I laughed. "Are you fucking kidding me? Won't get away with this? Are you new?"

There was a smattering of laughter from the guards and from within the cages.

"Last chance, bitch. Guess my name and I'll give you mercy."

She stared at me, a mix of raw fear and unbridled hatred. Her eyes were wide and I could see the wheels turning. What did I look like? I'd been told that I looked like a Jessica. Or a Vanessa.

Finally, she spat out her best guess.

"Tiffany?"

That guess took me aback, I have to admit. I couldn't imagine myself as a Tiffany at all.

"Nope. That's not me."

She opened her mouth to say something.

I'll never know what she was going to say because at that moment I pulled the trigger.

Her head snapped back and for a split second, she just kind of wobbled around a bit on her knees, then collapsed onto the ground while Darlene and Missy shrieked and sobbed.

Berto clapped loudly, and I heard Saysha's hoarse laugh from the cage.

I was quickly relieved of my gun and it was only then that I realized in that moment I could have blown Pierce away.

Why wouldn't I just do that? I was dead anyway.

In that moment I could have taken him out.

But no, I was more focused on making that bitch pay.

"What about the other two? Hm?"

Berto looked at me, full of anticipation. He was genuinely having fun.

I shrugged.

"I think they would look good in a cage."

He nodded.

"It's done then."

He motioned for his men and they sprang into action, dragging Missy and Darlene to the empty cages.

"Now, you."

I swallowed and retreated into myself. I was going to die. Painfully.

He snapped his fingers and more of his men materialized.

"Get her ready."

"Ready for what?" I couldn't help but ask, even though a part of me didn't want to know.

Hands were on me now, guiding me, pulling me along. I didn't struggle. There was no point. There was no fight in me.

The last bit of fight in me died on the floor with that bitch Lydia. I was done now.

And, selfish as it was, I found myself grateful that it was me being led away, not Saysha. Because I couldn't stand that pain. The pain of my friend dragged away to her death while I watched, helpless to do anything. Waiting for hours after she was taken away, hoping she might be back.

Hearing her screams.

Days going by and no Saysha.

Then, finally, a new girl shoved in what had once been her home.

No, instead it would be Saysha who would lie awake tonight crying for me and wondering how long before her inevitable end.

They took me to a room with a comfortable bed. There was a small fridge stocked with bottled water, a small plate of fruit, yogurt, and juice.

There was a bathroom stocked with toiletries and fluffy towels. I wandered around the room, shaking my head in confusion because this absolutely made no sense.

About an hour later a voice came in over some hidden speaker.

"Normally I would have you examined by a medical professional to ensure you were in good health, but he's dead and I have yet to find a replacement. You'll enjoy a delicious meal tonight. In the morning, you'll be fed a healthy breakfast. You'll shower and change into the clothing provided. Then you will await further instructions."

"This is weird," I muttered as I examined the clothing he spoke of. There was a pair of sturdy yet lightweight pants, underwear in my size - sensible underwear no less, a sports bra, tee shirt, and a lightweight jacket that looked expensive.

"Very weird."

An odd knot formed in my gut as I tried to imagine what was going to happen, and although I couldn't exactly articulate it, I knew.

Chapter Nine

Mick

How long had it been since that meeting with Berto in the warehouse? It felt like weeks, months, even. I really didn't know.

Maybe a month? At least two weeks. I'd been in the hospital recovering from a gunshot wound for several days. Then, tossed in a cell.

It had been two days since getting sprung, and now we were waiting on Jesse's men to get their shit together so we could find Jade.

Until today I'd been filled with a manic hope. She was alive. She was okay. Maybe not okay okay, but she would live. And she would heal, and we would love and care for her through the process.

Hell, we all needed to heal.

But today was different. That hope was dimming. The feeling of dread in my gut was growing.

Something was wrong. And this shit was taking too long.

Ace materialized beside me. He crossed his arms and stared into space, mirroring me. He didn't speak because he knew I was a fucking mess and when I'm a fucking mess, it's best not to talk to me.

"How fucking long does it take to get a few men together and hit the road? We need to get out of here." I clenched and unclenched my fists and Ace sighed in agreement.

"This isn't just getting a few men together. Berto's compound is a small nation unto itself with a high level of security and highly trained men who are ready to die to protect what's behind the walls."

I turned around to see Jesse's oldest son, Griff, standing in front of me with a shotgun draped over his shoulder and a smirk on his face.

"I get it, but..."

"You don't get shit. Do you know what my dad is risking going on this fucking suicide mission? I can't believe he let you talk him into this." He shook his head and walked off.

"I didn't talk your dad into anything. Trust me. If he didn't want to do this, he wouldn't."

Griff looked back and tilted his head, seeming to consider my words.

"We've gotten along fine with them for years. They leave us alone. We leave them alone."

"Yeah, well, he's doing shit that's way beyond fine. Shit that isn't okay."

Griff shrugged.

"Yeah? How does that affect me?"

Ace turned to face him.

"Because inevitably, he is going to get caught and when he gets caught, everyone associated with him is going to go down."

Griff shook his head.

"I doubt that."

Jesse walked over to us, followed by a couple more men who looked about Ace's age. And two women. One of them looked about my age, the other barely out of her teens.

"You guys can take my truck," the older woman said. "We'll ride."

The woman looked familiar. As though he could read my mind Jesse smiled.

"Nattie is my second wife. She's a good one. Gave me two kids. She's my ride or die." He smiled at her and winked. And I'll be damned if that grown-ass woman didn't blush like a schoolgirl.

"They going with?" Ace jerked his thumb toward the women. Jesse rolled his eyes, and the women scrunched their faces, looking at each other like they couldn't believe Ace would say such a thing.

In Berto's world women worked, alright. They worked on the streets or in brothels or clubs. Sometimes they did a little spying or a little digging for information.

But they weren't doing this kind of work. Ace wasn't familiar with organizations that had women packing iron and working alongside the men. Berto was a sexist prick and believed a woman's place was on her knees, as he'd said a million and one times.

I was really, really looking forward to taking the sick fuck out. He needed to be put down a long time ago, and I was angry with myself for not doing it sooner.

I think we all were at this point.

Thirty minutes later, we were on our way. Jesse said little about where Berto was. Just that it was heavily guarded and that they would know we were on our way long before we arrived at the gate.

"Be ready for the welcome wagon to show up around ten minutes before we arrive at the compound. They'll see us coming and send people out. That's fine. That gives us an opportunity to take some guys out before we even get there."

Jesse was sitting in the back of a pickup truck loaded with what looked like some pretty heavy artillery. Stuff we never messed with. It really looked like we were going to war.

"We've got a half dozen trucks and twice that many bikes. We are hitting them with everything we have. If we don't get them taken out, the next place that gets hit is ours."

Griffen shouldered past me and muttered, "Our place gets hit and I will make sure you die a painful death. All four of you."

"Don't pay him any mind, boys. He's just grumpy because I pulled him out of bed before noon. Now let's get this shitshow on the road. I'd like to be home in time for dinner."

The compound was a couple hundred miles away, and as we made our way down the dusty highway, I couldn't help but think of Jade and what she must be going through right now.

If she was even still alive.

CHAPTER TEN

Jade

SAYSHA AND I WANDERED the vast desert, running from an unseen foe. She slipped off the side of a narrow path and hung off the edge by her fingertips. I tried so hard to get to her before she let go, but it was too late. I didn't make it and she fell screaming to her death on the rocks below.

The sound of the door opening woke me. The guard sneered at me and set a tray on the nightstand.

Groggy and still half stuck in my nightmare, I sat up, shaking my head to clear the cobwebs.

I found scrambled eggs, sliced fruit, whole grain toast, juice, coffee, and water.

I had been downing all the water I could drink throughout the night. Lydia and the girls were pretty stingy with the water and during the day the hangar was boiling hot.

That's why they always hosed us down in the evenings. Because the desert gets damn cold at night.

I inhaled the food, nearly choking to death when I inhaled a bit of scrambled egg.

The hot water ran over my body, a luxury I swore I would never take for granted again if I lived through this and somehow escaped. To just stand up and feel warm...

Tears mingled with the water as I soaped up and stood there, determined to enjoy the hot water till it ran out.

I dressed in the clothes that were provided and sat back down on the bed, resisting the urge to pace.

I have to conserve my energy. I'm going to need it for something.

But would I? Really? Did anything matter?

After what seemed like hours, the door opened and an older woman motioned for me to follow her.

"Let's go, six. No talking. I do the talking."

I nodded and followed her. She was new, or someone I'd never seen. I noted the hollows of her cheeks and her ruddy, pockmarked complexion. But it was her eyes that really got me, so clearly haunted by the things she'd seen and taken part in. Her movements were jerky and her eyes were constantly moving.

She was either on drugs or beaten into hypervigilance. Probably both. My guess was she'd been a working girl who got old and Berto kept her around as a babysitter for the young ones.

"Here are some supplies. This is all you get. Don't waste it. Conserve it. Not that it matters, but whatever." She shrugged and handed me an aluminum bottle filled with water. She showed me how it hooked onto the belt provided with my pants.

"These, too," she said as she handed me two protein bars.

I shoved them into a zippered pocket and then glanced at her hair, which was pulled back and secured with an elastic.

"Can I have your hair tie? Please," I asked, smiling as much as I could muster, which wasn't much.

She frowned and her eyes kept roving, looking off to one side, then the other. She seemed very concerned with my question, but finally nodded and took her hair down, fluffing it up a little before handing me the elastic. I piled my hair up on top of my head and secured it as firmly as possible. Couldn't have it getting into my eyes.

"Come with me," she said after looking me up and down. If I wasn't mistaken, she looked sad.

Because she knows you're going to die.

How women could do this shit to each other was beyond me.

Really? Because you sure didn't have a problem putting a bullet in Lydia and having Missy and Darlene shoved into cages.

They were bitches; they deserved it.

Yeah, how much longer before you'd be just like them? What if they put you in charge? What if you were holding the keys and your life depended on torturing those girls?

I'd rather die.

You sure?

While I continued my one-sided philosophical discussion, they loaded me into a small box truck. It was torture sitting in the stifling vehicle for what seemed like ages, but we finally got moving.

I couldn't say how long. Maybe thirty minutes? I had no grasp of time anymore. Could have been ten minutes, could have been an hour. At this point I felt like I was losing it.

"Stay cool, Jade. Stay cool. If you don't panic, you might be able to get away," I whispered to myself.

Are you fucking crazy? You think they would let that happen? The game will be rigged so far in their favor there is no possibility of winning.

"Way to stay positive. Fuck, now I'm talking to myself."

The doors flew open, blasting me with sunlight and dust. They hauled me out of the truck and I fought to keep my balance and my composure.

It took me a minute to adjust to the brightness, but my eyes finally cooperated. I saw I was standing in the middle of the desert amid scrubby brushes, Joshua trees, and rocks. That was it. Not far in the distance were some rocky hills. More rock than hill.

I tried to ignore the chilling resemblance. Those rocky hills were straight out of last night's bad dream.

And before me stood three people. Berto. Pierce.

And Saysha.

My beautiful friend was bruised from head to toe. Her clothing was shredded to ribbons, and her right eye nearly swollen shut.

She sobbed quietly while Pierce stood there, gripping her by her arm, smiling his signature toothy, predatory, slimy grin.

"Six. At long last." Berto beamed at me, then looked at Saysha. He cocked an eyebrow.

"Welcome to the hunt. You are privileged. Most of my stock won't see the light of day once they go to the cages. But you two get one last opportunity to feel the sun on your skin and the ground under your feet."

I noted that while I was clean and dressed in protective clothing, Saysha was wearing our standard "uniform" of baggy, elastic waist shorts and an oversized tee shirt.

She wasn't wearing shoes.

"What is this? Why is she here?" I swallowed hard and tried my damndest to keep the panic out of my voice.

"This one? She's here for the kickoff."

What the fuck is this?

"There are rules, six. You get a head start. A generous head start. Ten minutes. Choose your direction carefully. One direction might lead you to the main road. And that main road might have a car or two on it."

Doubtful.

"Nearest town is over twenty miles away. That's a long way, but theoretically, you could make it. If you were going the right way, and if you didn't get too dehydrated."

"And if you don't get caught first."

"Ah, yes. Rather big catch. Don't get caught, six. You are prey. We are hunters. If we catch up to you, it's over. You are our prize. Like any other deer or antelope or boar or moose. You are game."

Once again, I looked at Saysha. She tried to give me a brave smile, and I felt sick because there was something very wrong with her being with us.

"Why did you bring her here?" I repeated.

Saysha looked at me and gave me a weak smile. "Give them hell, Jade."

"Saysha..."

"Enough." Pierce snapped.

Berto sighed and turned to me.

"Pierce and I have a lot of history. And he is my partner and friend. One of the few I can count on."

"Pierce is a cocksucker," I blurted out before I could stop myself.

Pierce's face reddened and he raised his hand but Berto shook his head.

"Pierce has no patience. But I do."

I watched Pierce shrug and drop his hand. Berto continued.

"But he's right, it's only getting warmer out. We have plenty of water and supplies here. You, on the other hand, are quite limited. It behooves you to get the party started, don't you think?"

I swallowed nervously and once again looked at Saysha. She looked down and a tear dripped off the tip of her nose.

"Say goodbye to your friend, six. She is here to see you off."

Pierce pushed her toward me and I wrapped my arms around her as I let loose the sobs I'd been holding back.

Pierce snorted, rolling his eyes at me.

"Okay Berto, now show me a woman who doesn't get emotional. I have yet to see it."

He smirked and then gestured toward the other truck. Not the one I was in, that one was right behind us. There was another one, maybe twenty yards away.

Bert turned to Saysha, his eyes cold.

"Okay ladies, it's the big game. And there is no big game without a kickoff. Five, I'm going to count to three. When I say 'three' you head for the truck you arrived in. If I were you, I'd run."

"No," I whispered. "No, just leave her out of this."

Berto turned toward me.

"You have problems of your own, six. Because I don't have to tell you what happens when we catch our prey, now do I?"

"You kill me. Yeah, I get it."

"How cute. She thinks she gets it."

Pierce laughed a hearty laugh at that then shook his head.

"I don't think you do, pretty. See, hunters don't just shoot a deer and walk away from it. They don't just hunt down and kill a prize like you and leave it to rot in the dirt. That's... just a waste."

I felt like I was going to puke or shit my pants, but that didn't slow down my mouth any.

"You gonna eat me?"

Now it was Berto's turn to laugh.

"No, but we are going to taste you. And we are going to savor every single scream. Every tear, every beg for mercy. Every cry of exquisite pain and suffering as we carve that pretty little body of yours up like a Thanksgiving turkey."

My breath caught in my throat and I felt the color drain from my face as I realized the truth.

These guys were the killers. The ones who had been kidnapping girls all over Southern California and mutilating them. Torturing them. Raping them. Cutting off limbs. Dumping them in creeks and shallow graves.

And I was next.

"Okay, remember, six, you get a ten-minute head start. Hell, Pierce, I think I'm gonna give our petite little princess fifteen."

"You serious? Why? Fuck her. I don't understand why you give her special treatment."

Special treatment. Jesus.

"Listen up, pretty. This is important. The hunt starts when I fire this gun, do you understand? If you're smart, you'll run. Run far and fast and put as much distance between you and us. Don't waste time."

I looked at my feet. I was already feeling like I could pass out. Was already wanting to curl up into the fetal position and cry and scream. Already my mouth was dry and I desperately needed a toilet.

"Okay, Pierce, you ready?"

"Born ready."

"You, five, you remember what I said. I count to three and you haul your sorry ass to that truck."

I shook my head, "No, stop! This is crazy, leave her alone."

He ignored me.

"One... two..."

"Please, just let her—"

"Three."

My chest heaved as I watched her run, her bare feet moving as fast as she could go. She knew what was coming. She didn't just run straight. She cut left, then right, but it didn't matter.

Pierce raised his gun and fired.

Saysha went down and I crumbled.

My knees hit the ground as I screamed. The scream caught in my throat as I saw her raise her head up and try to roll over. She was alive.

Stupidly, I felt hope. Maybe they would haul her into the truck and patch her up?

Instead, Pierce walked over to her and put a bullet in her head while I was frozen and unable to stop him.

"I told you, six. Run. The clock is ticking."

I couldn't move. I couldn't speak.

The only thing I felt like I could do was kill them. What I would have given in that moment to have that gun back in my hand.

I would sell my soul to the devil if I could just have that gun.

"Run along little gazelle," Berto said in a singsong voice.

"No. Fuck you and your stupid hunt."

"Really?" He tsked.

"Really," I replied.

He drew his leg back and landed a kick to my ribs. I grunted and winced and clutched at my side, then glared up at him through my tears.

"Fuck you."

Pierce laughed and came to a stop next to Berto.

"See? Ungrateful cunt. This is what I'm talking about. You can't show any kindness. No favors. They deserve nothing."

Incredible. I should cease to be amazed by this guy's thought process but I still found my jaw dropping.

"You fucking killed my friend. Sorry if I'm a little 'ungratef ul.'"

"Yeah, and that friend is costing you a generous head start. Because you are an idiot and you deserve to die. Now fucking run, you dumb bitch."

Berto smiled at me.

"If you do not provide the sport we are counting on, I promise you that whatever horrors we had in store for you once caught will be delivered to you tenfold. As bad as you think it could be, I promise it will be beyond what you could imagine. I will skin you alive. I will cut off your limbs slowly while you squirm and shriek. When you pass out, I will patch you up enough to make sure you don't die, and when you come to, I will cut you up some more."

I was numb at this point. Probably in shock. But deep inside, that self-preservation instinct finally kicked in. With some effort, I rose to my feet and faced my soon-to-be killers.

"Good girl." Berto smirked. Then the smirk faded, leaving nothing but cold, murderous intent in his eyes.

"Now run."

Chapter Eleven

Ace

I FELT LIKE MICK and Ian were losing hope. I could see it in Ian's eyes. Mick had his stupid sunglasses on so you couldn't see his eyes but I could tell by how quiet he was. His silence said everything: He thought she was already dead.

Me and Xander though, we knew she was alive. She was alive and we were going to fucking roll up like knights in goddamn shining armor and save our beautiful princess.

Then, we'd kill every fucking piece of shit that had anything to do with hurting her. Anyone left loyal to Berto was fair game. Word would get out fast once we started taking heads. The Moreno family was done. Only ones left would be Jesse's crew and Xander.

And then we were going to get the fuck out of this shithole and find a nice island to set up house in.

That's how it was going to be. Period.

I rode with Ian. Mick and Xander were ahead of us. We made our way down a mostly deserted highway, occasionally passing an RV or van, sometimes a few bikes. The desert sun was blistering and even in the truck with the windows up and the air conditioning, you couldn't escape the heat and the dry air.

They loaded the truck up with weapons, including - and I'm not kidding here - a rocket launcher that Jesse packed "to get us through the door" if need be.

Jesse emphasized to me that Berto's desert compound made his Los Angeles industrial hideaway look like the straw house from the Three Little Pigs.

We were the wolves, and we needed to blow the brick house down.

Jade would be safe. And I would find that rat fuck Pierce and the two of us would spend a little one-on-one time together.

Then, fuck the place. Burn it down. Burn down the entire Moreno family organization. Jesse could take it over, or fucking put an end to it. I really didn't give a fuck. I just wanted Jade, and I wanted to get the fuck away from anything and everything that reminded me of this fucked up life.

Except, of course, my brothers. And Jade.

I had a feeling Ian wasn't ready to leave the lifestyle. For a long time, I didn't think I was, either. I enjoy getting blood on my hands. Been told many times I'm a psychotic son of a bitch, and maybe I am.

Hell, if I couldn't stay away from it, I'd just do some freelance work on the side. But I'd keep it the fuck out of my house.

Then there was Xander.

Something had changed and I wasn't sure how I felt about it. He wasn't the same kid he'd been before. Not since Jade, not since that night Berto put a knife to his throat and he watched Jade get hauled away. Some kind of switch had flipped and he'd gone from the guy who wouldn't hurt a fly unless he had to, and then he'd beat the shit out of himself for it, to a guy who didn't think twice about icing a motherfucker, and more and more I got the feeling he liked it.

"I brought snacks," I said after a good thirty minutes of silence.

Xander smiled and replied, "Of course you did."

"Hey, we still gotta eat."

"That's like, your motto, Ace. You know that? No matter what is happening, no matter what we have going on, you always say the same thing."

"It's true. You can't live life on an empty stomach. You have to fuel up so you can keep going."

I handed him a bag that contained some fresh fruit, a couple of sandwiches, some water, and a container of cookies that Jesse's wife had made "for the road".

He grabbed an apple and took a bite, munching thoughtfully as I drove.

"What happens after this?"

His question caught me off guard.

"Don't you think we should keep our focus on the here and now? On just getting Jade and getting the fuck out of here?"

He nodded. "I guess. I just wonder what happens after we have her. We're gonna have to kill Berto and Pierce."

That drew a laugh out of me.

"Oh, Xander. We don't have to. We *get* to."

He grinned.

"Excellent point, Ace."

I took a swig of water and scarfed down a cookie. I thought about the life Jesse was leading. He was a pig for sure, but he was also clearly a family guy who kept his people close. He had a wife baking cookies and raising babies. His home was a home, despite whatever it was he was doing behind the scenes.

"Everything is going to be okay, Xander."

He nodded. "I know."

"It's going to work out. We'll find our way. I know we will."

"Yeah, we will." He looked out at the dusty road ahead and I glanced at him, marveling at how old he looked in the moment.

"We have no choice. We have to make it right."

Someone had sounded the alarm, just like Jesse said they would. Xander had pointed to some trucks off in the distance about a half an hour earlier, but we hadn't seen a vehicle on the road in over an hour.

Minutes later, three jeeps and a van hustled toward us with guns blazing.

Right out of the gate a couple of Jesse's guys went down. But that's as far as it went. We parted like a stream and within minutes were surrounding his guys. We pummeled the shit out of those pricks, leaving over a dozen men dead and riddled with bullets. It was easy. Too easy, I suppose.

The good news was our two guys that were down were just hurt. Bullets had grazed one, the other guy had a slug in his arm. Painful but not fatal. We had first aid supplies in one of our vans and got him dug out and patched up.

"Good as new." A young woman who introduced herself as Maria said.

There were a few women in our crew and I hated that they were there. Even Jesse's ex, who looked like she could probably kick my ass. She was a mother. If she and Jesse both bought the farm, then two or three of Jesse's kids would have no parents left. Sure, they were adults, but still.

"Okay, the hard part is coming. There will be more. They will be tougher. This was to feel us out. We've spent ammo and we are down a couple of guys. But we've prepared for this, so stick to the plan."

The "plan" was simple: Blow our way in there. I was nervous about using the rocket launcher. What if Jade got hurt?

But Jesse insisted it would be fine.

When we arrived at the compound, we fought past two more packs of Berto's men. They were well-armed and trained, but it wasn't hard to pick them off. As one of Berto's guys, I knew how these guys operated. I knew the playbook they were operating from.

One guy came at me, rammed my truck and for a split second, I thought I was a goner as he pulled up alongside me, pointed his gun, and took aim.

I flipped him off and gave him a winning smile but it all turned out okay, Jesse's ex motored right up alongside him and blew his head off. He went off the road, down a slope, and flipped over.

Done deal.

And then we were there.

"This is it." Xander and I parked the truck, crawled in the back, and brought out the big guns. We were armed to the hilt, but my two favorite companions were the star of my show: My nine-inch blade and a small hammer I'd had for years.

We were pals.

One of the bigger trucks pulled ahead of the crowd and gunned it right for the gate. He or she, I couldn't really tell, broke it wide open, revealing a fenced compound that contained two hangars and a few newer-looking trailers. Nice, high-end models.

We were here, and honestly, I was underwhelmed. This wasn't the fortress I thought it would be.

Of course, there were about a dozen men waiting there for us, and immediately we took fire, our first actual loss, and plenty of injuries.

But we kept coming, and at the end of it, they were just outnumbered.

"C'mon," Jesse yelled.

"We'll split here. You guys go check that hangar. Billy, take some guys and go through the trailers."

"Mick, you and Xander come with me. Ian and Ace, you guys go hit the other hangar."

I didn't like splitting up, but Mick and Xander took off before I could say anything, and Ian was pulling me along with Maria and a handful of men to check the hangar.

My optimism was fading fast. Something shifted once we found ourselves in Berto's territory. I could feel his fucking evil in this place. I could smell the hopelessness and the pain. It was fucking tangible, and it scared the hell out of me.

Once inside, my heart dropped into my gut. We'd gone in through a side door and found ourselves in an open space. It was stifling in there, and I could smell the fear.

Then I saw the cages.

"Jesus," Maria muttered.

"What the—" Ian said. His jaw dropped, and I stopped dead in my tracks.

There were girls huddled in the cages. Over a dozen of them. They pressed their faces against the metal bars and some were crying out, begging to be let free.

This wasn't what I expected. This was something far worse than what I was expecting.

But the worst part was that Jade wasn't there.

Maria and two of the men rushed to let the girls out. There were sobs, hysterical sobs. Laughter, even.

One girl looked like she was just a kid. Maybe thirteen or fourteen. She clung to Maria, sobbing for her mother.

Some girls were clearly in shock, and a few looked so out of it, either they were drugged or half dead.

"We need to get them some water. Hell, they need fucking medical care," Ian shouted.

"We've got medical care."

Two of the men motioned for us to head into the other part of the building, where we found a room stocked with supplies. There were water bottles, painkillers, gauze, and antibiotics. The girls huddled together, begging us to call the police, begging us to get them out of there before "he came back".

I assumed they meant Berto or Pierce.

"This is fucking insane," Ian raged.

"Yeah, but where the fuck is Jade?"

He shook his head.

"Maybe she's in the other building."

But I knew she wasn't. She wasn't here.

Jesse and the others filtered in and confirmed what I knew. There were no other women in the compound.

"What the fuck was he doing?" Jesse was trying to wrap his head around what we'd found, but I was far less interested in what he was doing. I just wanted to know where the fuck Jade was.

"Okay, okay. Ladies, please. I know you're scared, I know you need help and care and we are going to take care of you. Protect you."

Mick had come in and immediately went into protective dad mode. No one else had calmed these girls down, they were terrified, and I had the distinct impression that they had all lost hope, and refused to let themselves believe that this was it, that they were really safe.

But Mick was the kind of guy who inspired confidence, and once he started talking, they calmed down.

"Now, I'm looking for a girl. Her name is Jade. Have any of you met a Jade?"

His voice was nearly hoarse, and I could tell by his strained tone that he was terrified.

"Jade? Anyone?"

Some of the girls just looked at us and each other in stunned silence, but one girl stood on shaking legs and raised her hand.

"We don't know each other's names. We just have numbers. They beat us if we talk or use names."

My jaw dropped.

"Yeah," another girl piped in, "unless she was next to one of us, we wouldn't know anything but numbers."

I looked at the cages and sure enough; they were all numbered.

"Okay, who is missing? What number should be here but isn't?"

Xander was pacing and Ian was losing it, I could tell.

Another girl spoke up.

"There are always girls coming in, and going out. Sometimes they come back, sometimes they don't." She sounded broken when she said it and something inside me broke a little just hearing the sadness in her voice.

"Okay, she's got long blonde hair. Light blonde. She's short, real short. Twenty-one years old. Blue eyes."

There was a ripple of whispers, shrugs, and shaking heads.

"He just described half of us." One girl muttered.

The same girl who spoke up first snapped her fingers.

"Maybe you're looking for six."

"Six?" I felt my insides churn.

There were some nods and murmurs.

"Okay, where is six? What do you know about her?"

This excited the girls a little, and at that moment I noticed that two of the women were edging their way apart from the rest.

"Ask this bitch." Another girl said, motioning toward the curly-haired girl who was dressed differently than the rest.

The young girl blurted out, "Six blew away Lydia. They gave her a gun and she fucking shot the bitch dead in the face."

There were some claps and hoots and the curly-haired girl made a break for it.

"So this six is a pretty little blonde girl who shot someone?"

There were enthusiastic nods.

Billy grabbed the curly girl and pointed a gun at the brunette who was also trying to make a run for it.

"Don't fucking think so, ladies."

I turned to the girl who was eyeing us warily. Something about her and her friend was different from the rest of the girls.

"Where is she? Where is six?"

Curly tried to twist away from Billy, but it wasn't happening.

"Tell us where the fuck she is," Mick warned.

"They took her out. Took her out for a hunt."

This was the answer I was dreading. And that's when Ian snapped.

"Fuck," he shouted.

I ignored him.

"What the fuck does that mean? Tell me now or I will blow out your fucking kneecaps."

The brunette started sobbing.

"They take the girls out into the desert and hunt them down and kill them. Do fucked up stuff to them. Six was their prized prey, they said. They left over an hour ago."

Jesse shook his head in disbelief. "My brother is a stone-cold psycho. Worse than I ever could have thought. Fuck me."

"Where?" Ian bellowed at her as he reached for her arm and pulled her up and off her feet, shaking her till her teeth chattered.

"Where the fuck did they take her?"

She was hysterical now, and Mick and Xander had to grab him and pull him off of her.

"Settle down, Ian."

The curly-haired girl screamed.

"I don't know, they don't tell us. They just put them in trucks and drive out into the desert."

I snapped my fingers.

"I saw two trucks off in the distance on our way in, they were quite a ways off the road and I thought nothing of it. About ten miles from here."

Chapter Twelve

Jade

I STUMBLED OVER A rock and nearly lost my balance. I winced as my ankle turned, sending shooting pain up the side of my calf.

"Fuck, Jade. Don't be that chick. Don't fucking sprain your fucking ankle and start sniveling and crawling. My god."

Talking to myself was the only thing keeping me sane. I'd gone high, there was a bit of a rise and some larger rock formations and denser brush. They probably expected me to go in this direction but what did it matter?

I was not as far from a road as I thought.

In the distance a truck rumbled along, kicking up clouds of dust. My heart felt like it could explode but there was no way the truck would see me, even if I jumped and flailed. All that would do is draw Pierce and Berto.

They'd geared up with knives, guns, water, flashlights, the whole shebang.

I had a dwindling bottle of water, two protein bars, and my "survival tools" which did not include a gun or a machete, or a big ass flashlight.

Instead, they'd been kind enough to provide me with a tiny pocket knife and an LCD flashlight that I couldn't knock anyone upside the head with.

"And here they are, geared up like they are hunting something dangerous."

Maybe you could be dangerous?

The thought intrigued me.

After all, I'd taken down that bitch Lydia. Didn't even give it a second thought. In fact, I had to admit I kind of enjoyed it.

"What the fuck does that say about you, Jade??"

Says you have potential.

I wondered if Ace would be proud of me.

If Xander would be horrified.

If Mick would think I was too far gone.

If Ian would decide I was untrustworthy, after all.

Had life prepared me for this?

No.

As fucked up as my upbringing had been, it didn't prepare me for survival. It prepared me for dependence. To cower, freeze, and fawn.

I was only prepared to fail.

"Fuck that."

I shook my head as I started down the slope, scooting myself down so I didn't lose my balance and fall into the cacti that were scattered about. I slid a bit, and some rocks fell off of a larger rock, skittering down the slope.

Humans are apex predators.

Stupid Eddie had said that to me many times. When he said humans, he meant men, but the wheels started turning. I mean, yeah, I was at a distinct disadvantage, but I was a human. That made me a predator, right?

"I need weapons."

They had eyes on me now. They most likely had binoculars. I took my head start, jogging away from them, waiting till I couldn't see them anymore, then switching directions and keeping parallel to the road.

They expected me to head straight for it but I wasn't stupid.

I wondered if they had night vision goggles. The thought of being out here long enough for it to get dark made me sick to my stomach.

Fact: I'm not an "outdoor girl".

Not like this, anyway.

I'd already seen one snake and a couple of lizards. The vultures circling overhead didn't inspire confidence.

I stopped walking for a few minutes and sat down so I could listen. There weren't any proper trees, just huge, bushy plants big enough to provide a little shade and cover. Still, the foliage was sturdy and the ground was littered with sticks and branches.

I looked around and found a couple of decent sized sticks and felt around in my pocket for the sharp rock I'd grabbed earlier. I also found a heavy stone that felt nice and comfy in my fist. It gave my punch some weight and if I smacked someone upside the head with it, I felt confident I could do a little damage to the skull.

Definitely the nose.

The desert was silent. There was only the slightest breeze. Insects buzzed in the air, but it was just a little white noise.

No voices. No footsteps. No vehicles in the distance.

Just me and the big, empty sky.

I took a few sips of water and considered my protein bar, but just wasn't feeling it.

While I was sitting there I took in my immediate surroundings.

It was after noon and from what I could tell I was headed north. That didn't help me much since I did not know where I was.

Everything was so fuzzy. It could be Nevada, Arizona, or even Mexico. My gut told me I was still in California and I knew there were parts of the Mojave desert that saw little traffic. I didn't want to lose sight of the road, but there was no cover in that direction. It would be so easy to see me and pick me off.

There were rocks and shrubs to the west. The rocks provided shade, cover, and some nooks and crannies I could hide in.

I continued north for the time being, knowing that they were right behind me, and I most likely didn't have long.

The "head start" was a joke. It gave me just enough time to get out of their sight, but not enough of one to really put much distance between me and them. And, it was clear enough which direction I'd started going in. All they did was stand there and watch me run off.

They would catch me. If they didn't catch me, then I would die from dehydration and heat stroke. Or a snake bite, or a hungry coyote. Something.

Unless I got super lucky and someone came along. Maybe somebody out on a camping trip. Out riding dirt bikes or something. Maybe if I got closer to the road someone would drive by and see me.

But I knew better. Once again, there was nobody coming.

I had to save myself.

Closing my eyes I took a few deep breaths. I felt the stick in my hand and envisioned myself as a warrior, a survivor.

Something *had* shifted in me.

They wanted to hunt and chase their quivering prey. They wanted the smell of fear and the sounds of my terrified screams.

They wanted me exhausted, bleeding, and desperate so they could laugh while I crawled away on bloody hands and knees, begging for my life.

"Fuck all that."

There was no way to outrun them.

All I had was the ability to do the opposite of what they expected.

Because they wouldn't expect me to lie in wait for them. They wouldn't expect me to stalk them back. To fight back. To hunt them.

The sharp rock could slit a throat wide open. Better than the puny two-inch blade they'd given me.

A sharp stick was perfect for plunging into a vulnerable eye socket.

Flying rocks could distract or injure.

What did I have to lose?

If I ran, I was dead.

If I didn't fight back, I was dead.
So why not go out fighting back?

Chapter Thirteen

Xander

Some of us left on foot, others on bikes, still others on trucks. We had to find her. When the girl told me what Berto and Pierce intended to do to Jade, how they were going to run her down like an animal, torture, and kill her…

It was hard not to puke. I examined all the men we'd fought and won against, hoping one or two of them would still be alive so I could kill them again.

"Kid, you are stressing me out."

Fifteen women were on their way to Jesse's ranch. Some hurt pretty badly. They were all malnourished and dehydrated. One said she thought she might be pregnant.

A young woman sobbed uncontrollably because they'd taken her sister, too. Unfortunately, we didn't show up in time to save her.

Some of them were girls from Berto's prostitution ring. No one was going to miss them. They'd come from foster homes and the streets. They were runaways, throwaways, and outcasts.

The others were young women and girls who had been taken away from normal lives and families. One of them I recognized from news stories.

Now they were safe and on their way to get help.

"Sorry, Uncle. I'm just worried we won't get there in time."

I scanned the desert landscape, looking for any sign of her. Of them.

Please, let us find her before they do. Please, please, if there is a god out there, let us find her first.

"We'll find her." He lit a cigarette and offered me one. I declined and kept scanning.

"You think they know? That we are after them?"

My phone rang and I held up a finger before he could answer me.

It was Ian.

"Hey, we found tracks."

My heart thumped so hard in my chest that I was sure I would drop dead of a cardiac event any minute.

"What kind of tracks?"

He blew out a breath.

"Hers, theirs, and wheels."

I pinched the bridge of my nose.

"What does that mean?"

"Means I found some smaller footprints followed by larger footprints, and tire tracks because they are riding ATVs to catch up to her."

"Fucking losers. They got her on foot, but they are riding ATVs."

"Yeah."

I thought for a second. "Okay, we'll come over to where you guys are. But do you think they've caught up to her yet?"

He was quiet for a minute.

"I don't know."

"Fuck."

"Well, do you think they know we are after them?"

"Depends on where they are now. We are following the tracks on foot and sending out trucks in the direction they looked to be going."

We'd taken a couple of dirt bikes from Berto's men when we offed them. One of them was in the back.

"Uncle, stop the truck. I need to ride over there. I'll get there quicker."

He nodded and stopped the truck.

"Careful, nephew. Remember who you are dealing with," he said.

"Yeah, I know. A killer. A psychopath. A total douchebag."

He grinned.

"You get him cornered, hold him there. Wait for me. I'll handle him, okay?"

"Yeah."

I was already out of the truck and pulling down the ramp.

A couple of minutes later I was going hard on that throttle, headed in the direction that Ian had given me.

"He's going to die. If she's hurt, he's going to die slow."

Soon I was catching up with the rest of my crew. Ian was also on two wheels. Mick and Ace were in a truck. Jesse was bringing up the rear, and some of the other guys were back at the compound in case they cut and run or grabbed her and took her back.

The trail had gone cold because we were no longer in the dirt. We were in a hilly area and no longer had good, clear visibility.

Ian had pulled over and hiked up into the rocks since there was no taking even the dirt bike up the rocky path.

"Check it out, Xan. There's some broken branches, and over here it looks disturbed, like someone has been through here."

He was right. I wouldn't have noticed but there were some scrubby bushes and on one side there were a bunch of broken twigs. Some of the dirt and rocks were disturbed and out of place.

"Look, here."

Ian nodded. "Good eye. Someone has for sure been up here."

Mick and Ace stayed in the truck to drive around while we explored the area on foot. We didn't know just how long they'd been in this direction and just because they'd been through here didn't mean they were still in this area.

As we made our way through the brush and rocks and the way became more demanding, I doubted Jade would have continued on this path. It was getting treacherous, and down below there was still plenty of cover and flatter, safer ground.

"Should we go down and get back on the bikes? No way she'd be up here, and we didn't see their ATVs. They must have moved on. Maybe checked it out and left? She wouldn't be up here."

Ian chewed his lip and looked ahead, shielding his eyes. It was closing in on four p.m. and the heat was suffocating. There was no breeze and the day was still, the only sound was the sound of truck engines in the distance.

He shrugged and nodded. "Yeah, let's poke around a little more, though. Look for more tracks."

"Okay." I shook my head and found myself irritated. I was sure she wouldn't be anywhere near this hazard. We were wasting our time.

I was just about to say fuck it and head down the path when Ian stilled.

"Shh. Shut up."

"I'm just breathing, bro."

"Well, stop."

I stilled and tried to quiet my breath.

"Do you hear that?" he asked.

I strained my ears but heard nothing.

"Look, another footprint."

We kept going. This time we kept chitchat to a minimum and stopped every few minutes to listen. There was a straightaway with boulders on either side. Up ahead the trail rose and from where we were it looked like there were hiding places, nooks you could crawl into or under and hope you weren't seen.

Perhaps Jade had tucked herself away here, waiting for them to pass her by. Perhaps they had moved on, unsatisfied and thinking she'd gone another direction. Maybe she would see us and bolt out of some little crevice or cave, wrap her arms around me, sobbing with relief that her nightmare was over.

"Fuck." Ian hissed.

"What? What is it?" I picked up my pace, feeling tightness in my chest as I watched Ian's face go from intense concentration to utter horror.

He said nothing but kept staring at something just ahead.

"What is it? Tell me." I demanded.

He sighed and wiped the sweat from his brow.

"Blood."

Chapter Fourteen

Jade

From my vantage point I could see the rapey twins were on their way, riding comfortably on ATVs, wearing wide-brimmed hats to guard them against the sun. When they stopped, they drank deeply from large jugs of water.

"I should fucking steal that shit."

I wet my lips and reached for my bottle, but willed myself to conserve it.

"Not yet."

In the unlikely event that this went into overtime, I would need what I had. My focus in the last hour had been to conserve my energy. Avoid sweating. Stay in the shade. Don't get worked up.

I found a nice little nook with a view and spent time whittling my sticks into sharp points. Next, I collected some large rocks and found some assorted hiding spots to tuck myself into.

High ground was safe ground. I could see them coming and strike when ready.

Or I could launch myself off the tallest rock and crack my skull about fifty feet below.

A smile played across my lips as I envisioned myself jumping to my death, robbing them of their catch just as they thought they had reached their prize.

Or, I could just slit my own fucking throat right after I told them to go fuck themselves.

But mostly, I wanted to live.

And I wanted them to suffer.

They were still standing around, leisurely taking in the view. Eating, I think.

"Not a bad idea."

It was almost battle time. I should probably get a snack in and maybe a few sips of water.

Besides, it was best to open my bar now, while there was still a good bit of distance and they couldn't hear me.

While I munched I studied the shiny aluminum water bottle.

"Fucking dicks. Giving me this goddamn disco ball of a water bottle. Here, look at me! Here I am!"

My clothes were brightly colored so I would be more visible.

Fuckers. They were cheating on so many levels. This was not equal. This was so not fair.

"Fuck 'em."

The jacket had a white mesh lining. I turned it inside out and rubbed dirt all over it, and did the same with my pants. My tee was white. I poured a tiny bit of my precious water into my hands and used it to make a paste that I rubbed all over my shirt.

It wasn't perfect, but it was less "hey, look at me!" than before.

"Uh-oh." I buried the wrapper of my protein bar in the dirt and stashed my water bottle. Couldn't have it clanging around as I moved. It seemed like everything they did was intentionally planned to make me louder, more visible, and more emotionally fucked up.

I blinked back tears thinking of Saysha, running on bare feet away, knowing instinctively that this was it. She was going to die, but still tried to get away, dodging, trying not to be an easy target.

And Pierce's laughter. Berto's. She was the kickoff. She was the flag.

"Pieces of shit."

I crouched and peered between the bushes. Sure enough, they had fucking binoculars.

"Fucking assholes," I muttered.

I crouched lower, keeping still and studying their movements. They were going to hoof it right up here. That was fine.

I replayed my plan for the hundredth time. There was an incline between two giant boulders that was the best way to get where I was. Unless they came from a completely different direction, but from my tucked away spot it would be really hard to sneak up on me.

I would stay still, really still, waiting for the first one to arrive at the opening, and I would strike. My sharpened stick was at the ready, and I would plunge it right into him, then push him back and hopefully into the other guy.

I had several piles of hefty stones to launch at them, and a small stash of sticks for stabbing.

My goal was to put up a fight. To kill, wound, or maim. Then I would make a break for the ATVs and get the fuck out of dodge.

Go for help. Make my way to the nearest town and get the police over to the compound to set the girls free.

"Unless they own the police here, too."

That was a sobering thought, but I couldn't worry about that shit now. I just needed to focus on staying alive.

"Fuck," I whispered as I watched them ascend the hill I was preparing to die on.

They were relaxed. This wasn't a big deal. It was only a matter of time before they found me, and I was no threat to them.

Good.

Pierce led Berto up the winding, natural pathway. You could diverge from it, but it was the way that made the most sense.

As they made their way up, there was a good stretch where they couldn't possibly see me, but I could hear them. I stood for a moment, checking out the distance between myself and their ATVs.

Earlier I had courted the idea of finding my way back down. Luring them up high as they followed my footprints but already halfway down so all I would have to do was make a run for it. By the time they realized that I'd already made my way down the hill, they wouldn't be able to catch me.

Unfortunately, their bullets would. It was a chance I wasn't willing to take.

This was just as crazy, though. What were the chances I could pull it off?

I thought about every other time in my life I'd tried to fight back against people who wanted to hurt me. Eddie. My parents. That slime ball who sexually abused me all those years. Bullies from school.

As I nestled into my nook to wait for Pierce's slimy ass to get in reach, I reflected on that time I got "the talk" from my dad.

"Thing with bullies, they don't want to be confronted. Once you call them out, once you stand up to them, it's over. They'll leave you alone."

Fucking shit advice. All that happened when I stood up for myself was I got my ass kicked harder.

"Good times."

They were getting closer. My throat was dry and I had to pee, but I dared not move at this point. That time had passed.

Fuck, fuck, fuck. You should have just run. You should have just kept going. Put as much distance between you and them as possible. Idiot.

But no. I wasn't an idiot. It would be idiotic to run when I'm on foot with no supplies and they are on ATVs fully stocked.

No, this was best.

I could hear them now.

"You see those little tracks?" Berto said as he pointed at the ground.

"Yep, dumb bitch didn't even try to cover her tracks. Didn't even try to put us on the wrong path. I'm telling you, Berto, bitches are dumb. Maybe we should hunt a man sometime."

I couldn't help but smile.

Because I did, in fact, cover my tracks. While this cute little path had been the most obvious way up, it's not actually how I came up. I scrambled up the rocks so I wouldn't leave tracks.

When I decided that this was the best spot for an ambush, I took the rocks down a little ways and then walked in the nice, soft dirt right where I wanted them to go.

And if by chance, they made it past this point, they not only wouldn't see me, they would go up further and see my footprints all over the fucking place. In circles. Back and forth. Going to dead ends. *Yeah, but I'm a dumb bitch.*

Hunt a fucking man, please.

The sound of engines distracted me from my rumination. I listened and then shook my head. Must be my imagination.

Then, they got louder.

Not my imagination.

Must just be some more of their guys. Right?

But what if it isn't?

The thought that someone else was around that wasn't a murdering, raping, douchebag was enticing. If I could just signal them...

But that would mean moving. Yelling. Running. Blowing my cover and putting myself in danger.

Besides, Berto and Pierce were close enough now that I could hear their conversations, and they weren't saying anything about the vehicles I was hearing. So they must not be worried. And if they weren't worried, it was probably just their guys.

Chickenshits called for backup?

I could hear the crunching of their boots on the dirt and rocks.

My heart was pounding so loud I was worried it would give me away. Wouldn't be the first time my heart betrayed me.

Once again my thoughts flitted to Ace, Mick, Ian, and Xander.

What were they doing? Where were they? Were they still alive?

Had Berto killed them? Were they sent to rot in prison?

Or, had they skipped town, never to return? Forgetting all about me?

Pierce was still leading the way, and that meant he was my target.

I was low and he was tall. I needed to hurt him badly. Which meant I needed to get close.

Earlier I'd thought about launching some rocks at them. The idea of pitching a softball-sized stone and smashing Pierce's fucked up face in was enough to give me chills. But I'd sucked at softball, and couldn't take the chance of missing and giving away my position.

One of them muttered something under their breath but it was unintelligible. Closer. Then a little closer.

Almost.

When Pierce stepped on the dried twigs I'd buried just under the sand, that was my cue. They both looked down in surprise. I tossed the golf ball sized rock I'd been holding high, so it would arc over their heads and land to the left of them.

That was taking a chance, too, of course. What if they saw where it came from? I was taking for granted the noise would perplex them and I was right.

The rock landed and they snapped their heads to the side. I quickly and silently pounced, driving my sharpened stick into the soft part of Pierce's side, then attempting to angle up and shove it in further.

Thing is, I'd never stabbed anyone. It's harder than it looks. And an inch-diameter sharpened stick isn't quite the weapon you'd think it was.

It was brittle and no sooner did it penetrate through his clothes and into his skin, it broke.

But the effect was still what I'd planned. Between the sticks, the rock, and the sharp object I'd just embedded in his side, he windmilled his arms, then went backward, yelping in pain and rage.

It caught Berto off guard and sure enough, Pierce took him right to the ground.

I resisted the urge to jump and clap and instead went for my ammo. I grabbed two good-sized rocks and hefted them toward the not-so-happy hunters and was pleased to hear a satisfying thunk as one rock made contact.

"Fucking bitch." Pierce roared, but Berto the psycho laughed good-naturedly.

"See? Fire. I knew it."

"Who does she think she is?" Pierce was struggling to his feet when I launched another rock at him, hitting him on the elbow.

That's when Berto raised his gun and fired off two shots.

A white-hot pain seared my shoulder, and I was sure he had shot me. I scrambled back up the hill as Berto fired off another round, laughing and yelling at Pierce to either keep up or get out of the way.

"This is a hunt!" he exclaimed. "This is why I picked her."

"She's a cunt. She needs to die now. Before they get closer."

Before they get closer? What the fuck? Who? Before who gets closer?

I went straight for my little nook, breathing heavily and wincing in pain.

There wasn't much time to check my wound, but I needed to know how bad it was.

I pulled up the short sleeve of my tee shirt and saw blood. But upon examination, it didn't look like anything but a deep cut. The bullet had grazed a rock and maybe I got hit with some shrapnel.

Close one. Too close.

Now what?

"Where are you, my gazelle? Licking your wound? You find a nice, cozy little hole to burrow in?"

From where I was I could see Berto climbing up. He had blood trickling down the side of his face. Haha, good. Fucker.

I had more rocks here. I could launch another one when he got closer, but it needed to count because they'd backed me into a corner.

Blood was pouring out of the wound on my shoulder and it burned and throbbed. I still wondered if it wasn't a bullet lodged in there, but I didn't think so.

"Here kitty, kitty..."

His tone suggested that he already knew exactly where I was. It was so smug and satisfied.

Perhaps I wasn't the first girl to have this bright idea. The idea of lying low, conserving energy, and fighting back. I suppose I thought every other girl had just run and run until she couldn't run anymore.

But maybe I was predictable.

"Come on out, bitch," Pierce said. His voice was so nasally and outraged, I had to clamp my hand over my mouth to keep from laughing. I was terrified of the man but even in my fear, there was a part of me that instinctively knew he was pathetic shit.

"She's close. I can smell her," Berto said. He positively gushed sadistic glee and chills ran up and down my spine. I'd fucked right up. I should have climbed right up over the rocks and been making my way down by now. Should have gone to the left and down the side, and made a run for the ATVs. At least I would stand a chance.

They would find me here. It was a good spot but eventually, they'd find me. Knowing these guys, they had most likely mapped out every hiding spot long ago.

Fuck. Fuck. Fuck.

All I could do was make a stand as best I could.

I focused my intention on smashing Pierce's skull with the stone I held in my hand. Felt his warm blood dripping down my wrist, envisioned his eyes, wide open in shock as he fell backward, cracking the rest of his skull open on the rocks below.

Food for the vultures. Circle of life.

Once again I heard them speaking in low, hushed tones. They had to figure I was close by and didn't want me to hear their plans.

Don't freak out. Don't freak out. Don't freak out.

What was I going to do?

Just fight. Fuck it.

They were close, now. I heard the ominous crunch of boots on the ground. The low chuckles, the clearing of a throat, and the sound of spittle hitting the dirt.

I'm fucked. I'm gonna die. It's going to hurt.

I thought about the knife. How long would it take for me to bleed out if I sliced my wrists now? What, I had maybe five minutes. Maybe.

They had turned the corner. I could hear Berto breathing with the effort of the climb. His breathing was always slightly labored. This is a fact that only lent to his creepy, disgusting, frightening presence. He was a perverted Darth Vader, a greasy, disgusting, sadistic version, dressed in gold chains and too much hair product.

"This way," Pierce said.

"No, over here." Berto was getting too close.

"I think she's this way," Pierce insisted.

"Go that way, then. I say she's this way."

"Fine. I'll be back in a minute."

"You hear something?" Pierce muttered.

"Probably our little gazelle."

"Maybe."

"Be ready for anything, Pierce."

I could hear Pierce muttering as he separated from Berto and I wondered what they were talking about. Was someone else nearby? Who?

I scrunched myself against the rock, ignoring the bugs that were seeking refuge from the heat.

Please don't let there be snakes here.

"Come out and play, little one. I've been waiting so long for this moment."

Okay, yeah, sure. Let me reveal myself. Sounds like a solid idea.

"You've been very brave, dear."

I rolled my eyes.

I've been very stupid. I should be miles from here by now. This was dumb.

"But I'm afraid your time is up."

I held my breath.

He walked right past me.

"Do you know how many girls have made it past one night? How many have actually made it until morning?"

I had to bite my tongue to keep myself from asking how many.

"Just one. One. Of all the prey I've set loose in this desert exactly one of them managed to elude us until morning."

I squeezed my eyes shut. He walked past me and I missed my opportunity to launch a rock at his head. To stab him in the neck with my little blade. To knock him off balance and send him stumbling back onto the rocks below.

I fucked up again.

And then the unthinkable happened. After what seemed like an eternity of remaining still and hoping for enough distance between us to make a run down the hill for it, Berto's greasy face popped into view.

"Ah, there you are my little piggy. Right where I thought you would be."

I swallowed and felt just the slightest trickle of urine run down my thigh.

He reached his fat arm out and grabbed me by the hair. I fought the urge to knife him right there.

I allowed myself to be dragged out of the hole without a struggle and waited until he had pulled my face close to his.

Just before I swung my arm toward him he frowned as though he was wondering what I had planned. After all, I didn't put up the fight he was looking for.

He was fast, I was faster. I plunged my stick into him, into the soft flesh just below the jaw.

Success!

He grunted and his eyes went wide with shock. Briefly, he let go of me and for a sweet moment, I felt the rush of triumph.

I fucking nailed him.

Too soon to celebrate, though.

His fist made contact with my face.

One short jab to stun me, and a second, full-force slug of the fist to knock my ass out.

Chapter Fifteen

Ian

There was fresh blood on the ground and smeared on the neighboring rocks. The sun seemed especially bright and the air thin as I steadied myself, aware of my dry mouth and the color leaving my face.

Too much blood.

"Stay behind me," I said to Xander.

"Fuck you."

I was still trying to protect him, and truth be told, he'd always allowed me to.

It wasn't because I thought him weak, it's just that to me, he was worth protecting. Not just protecting him from harm, but protecting him from becoming like me. Like Ace.

Too fucking late. That ship has officially sailed.

As evidenced by the fact that Xander had scrambled over boulders and taken the lead.

I heard voices.

Berto.

I heard muffled sobs.

Jade.

She was alive.

Xander was out of sight, and I panicked. I couldn't lose them.

And where was Pierce?

The space between the rocks on either side of me narrowed, and I squeezed through, feeling claustrophobic and frantic.

Once I navigated the tight spot, things opened up. There was brush growing out of rock crevices, cacti, more rocks, and a flat pathway to the right of me.

I jogged in that direction and stopped cold at the sight before me.

Berto had Jade on a ledge. She was on her knees, face bloodied, eyes closed.

He looked like he'd taken a little beating himself. I noted the dried blood on his face.

I couldn't see Pierce anywhere, but I saw Xander, slowly approaching.

Berto had a gun pointed at him.

"Let her go!" Xander roared. "Kill me if you want, but fucking let her go."

Berto chuckled.

"I fully intend to kill you, and anyone else you have with you."

"Yeah?" I said, catching up to Xander, but still creeping.

"That's right, Ian."

"Pierce!" Berto called out. "I've got our prey here, ready and waiting. And some bonus prizes, too."

I laughed. "You've got your hands full, Berto, and you won't win this time."

"Oh, that's where you are wrong."

I had already drawn my gun, but all Xander had was a knife in his hand.

"Put down the gun, Ian."

"Nope."

"Fine," he stepped closer to the edge, dragging a limp, bloody Jade dangerously close.

"You fucking hurt her and you're dead."

"Oh, Ian. I've already hurt her. And this is just the beginning."

I swallowed and tried to calculate my odds. If I shot Berto and he let go of Jade she could fall down. It wasn't a super high drop, but the rocks were jagged and she could die from that kind of fall.

If I wasn't fast enough, he could easily shoot Xander and drop Jade.

"Think about it, son. You can't win, I'm telling you."

I put the gun down.

"Good boy."

He smirked and looked at Jade, then at Xander.

"My backup should be here any time."

Now it was my turn to smirk.

"You radioed for backup?"

"Yeah. That's right."

"That's interesting because when I left your compound, every single man there was bleeding out on the ground. Every one. You must have talked to one of our guys."

His face darkened, and for a second I saw the fear. He knew I was telling the truth.

"Where's Pierce?" I asked.

"I'm going to kill this bitch. I'm going to slit her throat and dump her off this cliff."

"I don't think so," I said.

"Really? You want to test me?"

I saw movement from Jade. Just the slightest. She had something in her hand.

Before I could compute what I was seeing, Jade, who had obviously been playing possum, swung her arm and plunged what looked like a small pocket knife into the meat of his upper thigh.

He didn't see it coming at all and immediately cried out in pain, letting loose his grip on her hair. She rolled herself backward, scrambling away from the edge and crab-walking to the side.

I went to grab my gun, but Xander lunged at him before I could say a word to stop him.

"You piece of shit. I only wish Mick and Ace were here."

Xander moved with confidence, graceful like a dancer, but deadly. Berto tried to fight him off, but Xander couldn't be fought off. He was a man on a mission, and that mission was to kill his uncle.

"Look around, Uncle. This is your graveyard. This is your last resting place. You are the one who is going to rot in the fucking desert. You'll rot while the buzzards feast on your entrails and not a fucking soul in the world will miss your fucking sorry ass."

"Please..."

Berto tried to plead and fight but in the end, Xander's knife found his throat and the blood spattered onto the sand while his body jerked and squirmed. Just as the light was leaving his eyes, Xander tossed him onto the rocks below.

Everything happened so fast, it made my head spin. One minute we were stumbling upon a nightmare scene where Jade looked nearly lifeless, beaten to a pulp, and Berto was brandishing a gun, with Pierce no doubt just around the corner.

But that's not how it ended.

It ended with Jade alive - albeit totally fucked up, and Xander standing atop the rocks, victorious, while Berto's smashed up body was bleeding out below.

Ace, Jesse, and Mick came rushing up toward us, guns drawn, and I saw Mick's face when he saw Jade, swollen and bloody, yet very much alive. Xander had already gathered her up in his arms and was making his way toward us.

"What about Pierce? Did you guys get him?"

Ace turned toward me, his face contorted into an incredulous mix of confusion and anger.

"What? I thought maybe you guys had him up here."

"He's long gone. That slippery little rat bastard probably ran at the first sign there was trouble."

"Fucking coward," Mick said.

Ace was seething, and I knew he'd be pissed later that he didn't get his chance to bludgeon the fucker. But now we had more important matters, like getting Jade out of this godforsaken desert and fixed up, pronto.

I approached as she started talking.

"Thirsty," she croaked.

I pressed the bottle to her lips. She was trying to look at us, but her eyes were so swollen she could barely open them.

"You came." She finally gasped as she went limp and her eyes rolled back in her head.

Chapter Sixteen

Jade

THEY WERE GOING TO take me to the compound and get me patched up there, but I freaked out.

"No fucking way. No. I don't want to go back there," I moaned as Ace gingerly wiped the blood from my face.

"There's some kind of infirmary there and—"

"Yeah, I fucking know. I've spent time there," I snapped.

"Look..." Mick began.

"Let me stop you right there. I'm not fucking going near that place again, so I suggest you turn around and take me someplace else. Someplace far away. I don't want to ever, ever, ever, see, smell, or hear that place again. Do you understand?"

Mick swallowed and Xander rubbed my back. We were in the back of Jesse's truck. He was Xander's other uncle, and that meant he was fucking suspicious.

"You trust him?" I whispered to Xander.

He gave a half-hearted nod and I closed my eyes.

Great, another monster to deal with.

"Okay, okay. We skip the compound."

Jesse adjusted the rearview mirror and eyed me, smiling.

"I see why my nephew was so insistent. You are an angel."

My eyes were swollen nearly shut and my face was puffy and bruised. But sure, I looked like an angel.

"I can't believe Pierce got away," I muttered.

"Don't worry, baby. We'll find him."

Mick turned to face me, slinging an arm over the seat and reaching for my hand. I raised it to grasp him and winced. Every bone and muscle in my body hurt.

"We won't let him or anyone hurt you ever again," Mick said. Even with his shades on, I could see the sincerity on his face. But as long as Pierce was on the loose and we were hanging out with the elder Moreno, I wouldn't feel safe.

"What about the others?" I blurted. Visions of Saysha flashed before my eyes. I struggled out of my slouching position and tapped Jesse on the shoulder.

"Wait, we have to get my friend."

"All the girls that were at the compound are already on their way to my place," Jesse said.

"No, she wasn't in the cage." I swallowed, then continued. "She's dead. They shot her in front of me before they started hunting me. She was lying in the dirt near those box trucks they put us in."

"We'll be coming up on those in a few minutes if they are still there," Mick said.

"We can't leave her body there. We have to bury her. Or something."

"We can't bury her. Someone will look for her. We have to let the police find her."

"Fuck that," Jesse said. "No police involvement. None. We patch up the girls and drop 'em off where they need to go. We find Jade's friend and load her up. I know a spot we can bury her. Real nice."

I nodded. "No one is looking for her." My eyes teared up, and I brushed them away, causing fresh pain to my sensitive skin.

Xander looked at me and his eyes were a mix of pain, anger, and sorrow. I could feel him, feel how much he'd missed me, how hard he fought for me.

Ace, too. All of them. I didn't know how they did it. Didn't know how they got out of the spots they were in, how they didn't get themselves killed. How they found me, just in the nick of time.

My only sadness was that they didn't come in time to save Saysha.

Pierce would pay for that. If it was the last thing I did.

The rest of the ride out to Jesse's place was a blur. I faded in and out of sleep a few times. Cried fresh tears of pain, grief, and rage when we finally came upon Saysha's body, unceremoniously shoved into the back of the box truck along with some of their supplies.

We decided to clean her up a little on the spot, wrap her up, and transport her in that truck.

From what I understood, Jesse's people grabbed most of what was in the hangars and trailers. They loaded up the dirt bikes and ATVs. They took photos and pilfered the weapons and supplies.

Eventually, we rolled through an open gate into a dusty collection of houses and trailers. There was a large house in the center, with outbuildings and a barn.

"Welcome to my ranch." Jesse beamed.

There were barking dogs and playing children. Looked like there could easily be a hundred people here. And they were very interested in me.

Ace helped me out of the truck and I felt dozens of eyes on me.

"Bring her into my house," Jesse instructed. "We'll get her all patched up."

I wanted to see the others. The women who I'd seen suffer along with me.

And, I needed to know about Missy and Darlene. What happened to them? Were they brought here, too?

But everything was happening so fast, I didn't have time to ask questions, didn't have time to orient myself. It was all a blur. Jesse's wife, Laurie, handed me a pile of clothes to wear.

"Here, you can wear these. I have a ton of clothes I can't fit into since the baby. But we are basically the same size."

I smiled and thanked her. She wasn't any older than me, married with a baby to a weathered criminal over twice her age. I was full of judgment, but when Mick poked his head into the bedroom to check on me, I had to shove that judgment right out the window.

"You okay?"

I nodded. One by one, they'd come in to check on me. Laurie had helped me get cleaned up, and showed a surprising level of skill in cleaning and bandaging my wounds. I had a couple of deeper cuts and she deftly closed them up with butterfly bandages.

"That should do it. They aren't bleeding anymore, so you should be good."

"Thanks. I really appreciate it."

She eyed me quietly while checking over the stitches Jesse had given me earlier.

"These should heal up fine. He's good. Stitched up plenty of us."

I nodded, wondering why stitches were something you needed a lot of here.

After she left I changed clothes with great effort. She was right, her pre-baby jeans and t-shirt fit me just fine. She gave me some slip-on shoes and an extra brush.

The door opened as I was trying my damndest to brush the knots out of my hair. Every movement sent pain shooting through my body. My left arm was useless since the shrapnel wound had gone from a medium burn to a well-done throbbing, searing pain that punished me every time I tried to move it.

"Here, let me get that for you."

Ace tip-toed into the bedroom and gently perched himself on the edge of the bed, taking the brush out of my hand.

"You don't have to," I said. I felt shy around the guys suddenly, and after what I'd been through, I had a weird thing where I didn't want to be left alone, but I didn't want anyone near me, either.

I really didn't want anyone touching me, not even him.

He gathered my hair in his hands, but when his knuckle brushed against the back of my neck, I flinched.

"Oh my god, baby. I'm so sorry for everything you have been through. I'll be super careful and I won't touch you, okay? Just going to help you get the knots out of your hair. Is that alright?"

I nodded miserably and stared at my feet while he gently combed through my knotted hair.

Two or three times during my captivity, they gave me a brush so I could make myself presentable.

The rest of the time I combed through it with my fingers as best I could, but the last several days I'd given up and just let it do its thing. What was the point?

"My god, Jade. What did they do to you?" he asked as I blew out a violent exhale. I'd been holding my breath as he worked, totally unaware I was doing it until I became lightheaded.

I shrugged away from him.

"We need to find Pierce. Find him and kill him. Before he kills another girl."

I turned to look at Ace, and his eyes darkened. He nodded, saying nothing. But his eyes told me everything I needed to know. He understood it wasn't just about preventing him from killing again. It was personal.

As he nodded, I reached out as though to grasp his hand. Instead, I took the brush from him.

"I — I'm sorry, Ace. I just need time."

Chapter Seventeen

Jade

When I woke up, Ian was sleeping in a chair next to the bed, his arms folded across his chest, his sleeping face grim.

Slowly I sat up, lamenting the empty water glass on the nightstand, and squeezing my eyes shut against the thundering pain in my head.

I'd fallen asleep with my body curled in the fetal position, making myself as small as possible, as though my sleeping body had forgotten I was no longer caged. Twice I'd woken up in a panic, hearing the sounds of screams and the grating noise of the cages opening, and the chuckles and mocking words of Berto's goons and those bitches he had working for him.

Uncurling my body took a steely effort and I clenched my teeth to avoid moaning and whining as my muscles and bones protested my every move. I didn't want to wake Ian. He'd been up all night watching over me.

The sunlight streaming through the window illuminated him, the hard shadows showing off his sculpted cheeks and jaw. Those same shadows also defined the hollows under his eyes from what was probably weeks of sleep deprivation.

Ian was a gorgeous man, but he looked like hell.

He opened one eye and smiled, stretching his long and lean muscled arms.

"Hey, Jade. How are you feeling?"

He'd woken to me staring creepily at him and I blushed and shifted my gaze to my hands, examining the cuts and bruises all over them, some old, some new.

"Like fresh, hot shit."

He nodded. "Understandable. Looks like some of the swelling has gone down, but damn, you've gone full raccoon."

His voice tried to be light but I heard it. The edge, the quiet fury, the sadness, and discomfort. Ian wasn't used to taking care of others. Except Xander, maybe. But not a woman. And yet, here he was, watching over me, and asking me how I was.

The thing about him was that I didn't feel much pressure to be better than I was. Xander and Ace were so stricken by how bad I looked, and the pain it caused them made me want to crawl into a hole and die. And it made me want to avoid them and lie and say I was feeling better than I was. I truly appreciated their concern, but it was hard.

Ian cared, I knew he did. But somehow it was easier to just... be real with him. He could handle my pain without falling apart, and I needed that.

"Hey, what about the girls? The others? And those bitches who were working for them."

"Bitches? Oh, the redhead, and the other mouthy one."

I nodded vigorously. "Yeah, them."

He chuckled. "The skinny brunette with the mouth cut out of here as soon as she could. Don't know anything else about her. The redhead is still here, trying like crazy to attach herself to somebody, anybody. She's gunning for one of Jesse's higher up crew."

"Figures. She's an ass-kissing hoochie, and she caused me and the other girls a lot of fucking pain."

He raised his brows. "Really? Like what? Was she really working for them? She was in a cage, too."

"Yeah, because I put her there. Her and the other one. And..."

I stopped there because the realization that I'd willingly and happily taken a life hit me hard out of nowhere.

"And what?"

I swallowed.

"I killed one of them. Lydia."

He pursed his lips thoughtfully and nodded.

"Shit happens, Jade."

"Yeah."

"You ready to get out of this room? Or do you need more time?"

I shrugged. I didn't know how long I'd been sleeping but it felt like forever. At this point I was just trying to shut out the screams and luxuriate in the novelty of a soft bed I could stretch out in.

"Yeah. Let me take a shower, and I'll come out."

"Okay, I'll leave you to it."

He stood up and for a moment looked down at me, a tenderness in his eyes that looked so foreign to me.

"I'm glad to have you back. I'm so glad we made it in time, and so sorry we didn't make it sooner. I promise you, Jade, I promise we'll find him and make him pay."

My throat tightened and hot tears threatened to roll down my cheeks.

"Yeah, I'm glad to be... back. I mean, back where? It's not like this is home, right? Or, is it?"

He shook his head. "No, this is not home. We're just here until we can figure something else out."

"Okay. But are we really safe here?"

"Yeah, we're safe. Don't worry, Jade. I swear I won't let anyone hurt you. Ever again."

Eventually, I made my way out of the guest bedroom and out into the living room. Laurie was playing with her little baby girl. Ace was cooking, and Jesse and Ian were talking in hushed tones.

I didn't see Xander or Mick.

"There she is." Ace grinned and Ian nodded at me, fixing his gaze on me, seeming to stare into my soul.

Jesse rose from his spot on the couch, extending his hand.

"Jade, I haven't formally introduced myself. I'm Jesse, and I'm real pleased to meet you. My nephew hasn't shut up about you since he got here."

My insides churned with fear because he was Moreno and Xander was the only Moreno I trusted, but the guys seemed comfortable enough with him, and his wife didn't look skittish or display any signs of being mistreated.

Besides, if it wasn't for his help, I wouldn't be standing here. I'd be dead. Or maybe still being tortured and raped.

I took his hand and offered a smile.

"Nice to meet you, Jesse. And thank you so much for all you did."

He shook his head. "Nah, you don't need to thank me."

"I'm sorry, I know some of your guys got hurt..."

"Getting hurt comes with the territory. We've all gotten hurt for a lot less." He chuckled and smacked Laurie on the ass as she walked by. She flashed him a flirty grin.

"Are you hungry? Of course you are. You need to eat." Ace was looking at me with an expression that made my heart feel a little like it was going to explode. There was an intensity in his eyes, but also this kind of... awe. And genuine happiness. Part of me wanted to launch myself at him, wrap my arms around him, tell him how fucking happy and grateful I was to be alive, safe, and with them.

But I couldn't. Part of me was still in that cage.

"Yeah, I'll eat," I answered.

Trying to be normal and casual was proving difficult. Sitting around a table with men and women talking and laughing and enjoying their food seemed like a betrayal to every girl who had gone into that hellhole and not come out.

Saysha. The girl with the tattoos. The beautiful little thing with the flowing black hair. The one who cried for her mother. The one who cried for her baby.

I needed to see the others. Laurie mentioned that there were a few who were still around, healing, and getting stronger. Some had already gone home, but those that were left had no home. There would be no missing person reports for these girls. Any homes they may have had either weren't there anymore or weren't worth going back to.

"Where are the other girls?" I asked as I put down my fork. I'd managed a few bites but just couldn't eat anymore. My stomach had shrunk to nothing, anyway, so there wasn't much room.

"Honey, you need some meat on your bones. You'll blow away in this desert wind," Jesse said, his voice all gravelly and good-natured. He had a fatherly way about him that was welcoming and comforting, but I still couldn't trust him.

It's just you. You don't trust anyone. Hell, you don't even want the guys you supposedly love to touch you, so why would you trust this man? Especially a Moreno.

Xander was a Moreno, and if he wasn't evil, perhaps Jesse wasn't, either. Criminal? Sure. Scumbag? Definitely. But there was honor among thieves, and he wasn't any different from any of the men I grew up around. Pervy, temperamental, and always out for himself. Par for the course. Didn't make him a murdering monster.

"Jade, I think you should just rest so you can get better," Ace said. His eyes were uncharacteristically puppy-like, brilliant and blue, and pleading with me. I couldn't help but smile. Which hurt, by the way. My lips were still cracked and swollen.

"I am getting better, but I'm done with bed rest. I need to see them. We all went through the same thing together."

They will understand me in a way you can't.

I didn't say that part out loud, because I didn't want to hurt their feelings, but it was the truth. Everyone was walking on eggshells around me and treating me like I was some delicate piece of fine china.

And in some ways, I was. My sanity was hanging by a thread and my body was broken in ways they couldn't even imagine. I was still hurting from things that had happened to me weeks ago.

I needed to see their faces. See that they were getting better, see that they had hope. I needed to sit with them and know that they knew what had happened to me because it happened to them, too.

"Can you just take me to them?" I said. My voice sounded flat, and I saw Ace and Jesse exchange glances.

Ian nodded. "Yeah. Let's go."

Chapter Eighteen

Ace

WATCHING JADE WALK OUT of Jesse's house gave me an immediate case of the shakes. It was like a trauma response. She was with Ian, though. I'd considered tagging along, but it seemed like she was more relaxed with Ian, so I let her go.

Besides, hanging out with Jesse and his boys was enlightening. I'd learned a bit about his operation and how his club was organized. His homestead, as he liked to call it, felt comfortable enough for me in those moments when I was stupid enough to let my guard down, and I could see why his guys - and girls - stuck with him.

He was charismatic. A complete womanizer, but one of those womanizers that don't make women *feel* womanized. He was funny and jolly and gave off a vibe that made you feel taken care of. I watched him with his wife, his ex-wife, another girl he was clearly intimate with, and all his kids.

He was a fucking cult leader, really. His charisma made people want to please him, follow him, and do things his way.

Dangerous. He's straight up dangerous.

That's how I felt, anyway, and at this point, I just wanted to get the fuck away from this god awful desert. I needed the ocean, and I needed to leave this life behind. Most importantly, I needed to take Jade away from here. Take her away someplace safe.

But first, I needed to find and kill Pierce.

"You boys are welcome to stay here as long as you like, you know."

It was like he was reading my mind. I had just spent the last ten minutes trying to figure out the best and fastest way to get the fuck out of the country. I scanned my brain files, trying to remember who it was that had passports for us, and if he was still someone we could trust.

"Hey, thanks, Jesse. You know we appreciate that. Like Mick said, we need to get on our way. Just letting Jade heal up a little." I shot him my patented "gee, I think you're swell," smile and he clapped me on the shoulder.

"Of course. Just remember, word is getting around about what happened. People talk, and it's already gotten out that Berto is dead at Xander's hand. Me and my boys, we don't give a fuck, you know that. Hell, his blood is technically on our hands, too. And I don't fear anyone coming out this way to pick a fight. They do, we'll handle it."

"You think there might be some backlash for us?" I pulled at my chin and thought about it.

"Well, you've taken out a powerful gang leader and left a vacuum. There are going to be guys with something to prove, and one way to please the Berto fanboys is to take out the guy who took him out. Then, step up as the shiny new leader."

I didn't think about that. When Berto killed Nino, he took care to slaughter his inner circle immediately. This move sent a message, leaving behind those that would fall into line easily.

"What about you, Jesse? Why don't you step up?"

He heaved a sigh and pinched the bridge of his nose.

"No fucking way, Ace. I hate Los Angeles, for starters. Sure, I could make this headquarters and have a couple of my trusted guys post up there to handle things, but why deal with the headache? I'm a family man in the way my brothers never were. My priority is making sure my people are taken care of with as little bullshit as possible. I'm not a risk taker."

That was a straight lie.

"You took a colossal risk attacking the compound, knowing some of your people could die. Knowing that it could cause a showdown with your brother and maybe kill one of you. That was a hell of a risk for someone who isn't a risk taker."

"So it was. But I'm a romantic at heart, son. And seeing Xander's sad puppy dog eyes when he was talking about that girl just got me. And I'm not one to condone the fuckery he was producing. Too much."

"Yeah, still. You keep to yourself. This put a spotlight on you."

"That it did. I suppose deep down, I never forgave Berto for what he did. I stuffed it down and tried to tell myself it was all in the past, water under the bridge. Then you guys showed up and it triggered something. Doesn't mean I want his job."

I sat on the porch shooting the shit with Jesse for a good hour, gleaning as much information about him, his operation, his inside info on the Moreno family, and what he knew about Pierce.

"Pierce is a piece of shit, of course. You know that. I never understood what my brother saw in him and I avoided dealing with him as much as I could. He's a fucking psycho, that's for damn sure."

"Any idea where he might go? Where I could find him?"

Jesse looked at me as though he was trying to size me up.

"You sure you want to go that route?"

I jerked my head to face him.

"What do you mean?"

"I mean, Pierce is a bottom-feeding lowlife, but he's also dangerous. Far more dangerous than my brother ever was. You got your girl and your freedom. So maybe you call that good enough. Would hate to see shit go downhill when you've made it to the top, you know?"

"You scared of him?" I asked, knowing I was walking a thin line.

He scoffed at me, shaking his head.

"Fuck no. I fear no man. But I think sometimes you should just be grateful you came out ahead. Just take the win and be grateful for it. Just my two cents, son. Take it or leave it."

I nodded. "Good advice, Jesse. Thanks."

He smiled and offered me a beer. I shook my head, wiped the palms of my hands on my jeans, and stood up.

"It's been real nice talking with you, Jesse, and I really appreciate all you've done for us."

"Anytime. You boys are like family. Mick and I go back a long way, and I was one of the first people to see Xander after he was born. He's my nephew, and I know you and Ian are solid guys. Guys I wouldn't mind having around."

I nodded. "That means a lot."

"I guess you're going to go fetch that pretty little thing of yours. Don't blame you. She's something special, alright."

"She is."

I kept the smile pasted on my face, but I did not like him talking about her. Couldn't say why. But where I was at, after all that had happened? I didn't want another man looking at her, talking to her, talking about her. Period.

"Ace, I meant what I said. About having you guys on my team. You could have a good life here. Think about it."

I nodded again and headed across the compound. There was a house just down the end of the dirt road where I was told Jade would be. Mick and Xander were still gone with one of Jesse's men on a supply run. Ian was sitting on the porch, which let me know Jade wanted her privacy.

That was fine. We could wait on that porch all night if that's what she wanted. But that's as far away from her as we would go.

Chapter Nineteen

Jade

I MADE MY WAY up the first two porch steps of the little white house but struggled by the third. Without a word, Ian swept me up in his arms and carried me the rest of the way.

I instinctively flinched at his touch but quickly relaxed. I was already tired, and my body had all but given up. Ace was right. I needed more rest.

But I had to see them. To see with my own eyes that at least some of them had survived.

Ian put me down and opened the door for me.

Through the doors, I found a smallish, wood-paneled living room that looked straight out of the seventies. The only reason that I, a twenty-one-year-old Gen Z girl could know this was out of the seventies was because it looked a lot like my parent's house, which was also straight out of the bell bottom and shag carpet generation.

There was a sagging couch and a coffee table littered with ashtrays and empty liquor bottles.

Completely opposite of the tidy, well-decorated house Jesse lived in, it looked more like what I would expect from this kind of place. A place that was running drugs and guns, that "loaned" money and pulled bullshit jobs that did little other than pay the bills.

Sitting on the couch were two of the girls I knew from the hellscape. The one with the blonde hair was number fourteen. Didn't know her name. The other girl was eleven. She still had ugly brown and yellow bruises all over her face. Fourteen had a bandaged up arm. They both looked red-eyed and puffy from crying, and as I walked in, fourteen lit a cigarette with a shaking hand.

Both these girls were already in the cages when I arrived.

"Hey," I said, motioning Ian to stay back. "Could you give me some time?" I whispered.

He eyed the girls and tried to get a look into the hallway, and I had to put my arm out to block him from searching the house for potential threats.

"Ian, chill. I'll call you if I need you."

Fourteen and eleven eyed him warily and then me. I saw the recognition, but it wasn't until after Ian reluctantly went out the front door that they jumped up and clustered around me.

"Oh my god. It's you. You're alive." Eleven threw her arms around me and I tried not to tense up as the pain shot through my shoulder down my arm.

"Oof, sorry." She pulled back, noting my pained expression. "You're fucked up. Yikes. Here, sit down."

Fourteen said nothing but sat next to me and held out the pack of cigarettes. I declined and as eleven sat on the other side of me, another girl stepped into the room. She had stitches along the side of her cheek and walked with a limp.

"Eight," I whispered.

She carefully lowered herself into a chair and stared at me before bursting into tears.

"Thought you were dead."

"I almost was."

They all nodded.

"I don't know your names," I said.

Fourteen sighed and gave a rueful smile.

"Yeah. It took me about six hours after they pulled me out of my cage to remember my name. And then, I was afraid to tell anyone."

She stuck out her hand. "My name is Allison."

I took her hand. "I'm Jade."

A sad, fleeting smile graced her pale face, and she cleared her throat.

"I'm sorry about your friend."

I swallowed and nodded. "Yeah. Saysha was a good one. I miss her."

Eleven piped in. "I'm Sara."

Finally, eight introduced herself.

"I'm Rose."

We were silent for a moment. The weight of all the ones who didn't make it hovered around us.

"How many were saved?" I asked. I didn't want to push them, but I also needed answers.

Allison answered, she seemed the most "normal" if you could call any of us that.

"There were fifteen of us. Including Missy and Darlene. One girl was already dead in her cage. So that made twelve. Darlene ran off not long after we got here."

"And Missy?" I felt my chest tighten and my pulse quicken. The anger took me by surprise, but it shouldn't have.

Allison gave a shrug and reached for a bottle sitting on the table.

"Missy found herself a man, I guess. One of the guys. Been seeing her come and go on the back of his bike. She's staying with him in one of those trailers."

My jaw tightened and I balled my fists.

"You gonna kill her, too?" Rose asked. She raised her eyebrows and I felt the other girl's eyes on me, too. They didn't look concerned, just genuinely curious.

"Maybe." That was my honest answer. I didn't know what I would do when I came face to face with that sadistic little twat.

"What about the rest?"

"They left. They had families or friends to go to."

Those words landed heavily in my heart.

Nowhere to go.

Even I would have had somewhere to go if push came to shove. My parents were horrible, but I could go to them.

Well, maybe.

Doubt it. God, you are still delusional, aren't you, Jade? You don't have a family.

The baby.

I squeezed my eyes tight, trying to stop the thoughts of him from pouring in. The thought of him being raised by Eddie, my parents. I shuddered.

There wasn't much else to say. We could sit around and talk about how bad it was. How scared we were. Compare horror stories.

But who the hell wants to do that?

"Here." Allison poured a shot and handed it to me.

Sara grabbed her glass and raised it.

"I've been drinking since I got here." She gave a bitter, jagged-sounding little laugh.

"Here, Rose. Take your glass," Allison said, her tone hushed and gentle.

Rose reached for it and I could see how weak she was, how fragile.

Allison waited until we all had our glasses raised, then she smiled. Her eyes sparked and her face practically glowed with defiance.

"Here's to us, the bitches who wouldn't die."

"The bitches who wouldn't die." We said in unison.

I've never been a big drinker, but before I knew it, I'd knocked back three shots of whatever they were pouring and I was getting sloppy. The alcohol was a salve, easing the pain inside me, filling me with warmth, and numbing the physical pain. It also made conversation come easier. I hadn't really been able to talk about the things that had happened, but now, with the women who had lived it with me, and a little bit of truth juice, I could finally start processing.

Was it healthy processing? Probably not. But it was a start.

"Do you feel guilty?"

Allison was the most talkative of the three, and even though she was as traumatized as we were, she seemed to take life in stride, mostly.

I nodded. "Yeah, I do. I feel guilty that I got away. The others didn't."

Rose nodded as well. She didn't say much, just sat in the faded armchair, knees pulled up to her chest, arms wrapped firmly around them.

"Yeah," Sara said. "Me too."

Allison sighed. "Survivor's guilt. I read about it in an article once. People who survive plane crashes and car accidents get it. Also, soldiers."

"Makes sense," I said.

Sara shook her head and poured another shot.

"It's a sick joke. We made it, right? We should celebrate every single second we are free and alive. But I feel like I never can. Like it's spitting in their faces if I laugh or feel good."

Allison laughed darkly, brushing her hair out of her face. "Who feels good? I know I don't. Feels like I've been hit by a truck. I fear my own shadow and I want to kill every man I see."

Now it was my turn to laugh.

"Yeah. I'm with you there. But it's not just men. It's women. I swear there is just something extra about being betrayed by a woman. It's worse, somehow."

"Yeah, well after what I saw you do to Lydia, remind me to never piss you off."

Sara and Allison laughed and even Rose let loose a little giggle.

"What's my name, bitch?" Sara said, pointing a finger gun at Allison.

"Okay, okay. One more shot. We gotta drink to that shit. I never considered myself a bloodthirsty bitch, never had the stomach for violence, but goddamn if I didn't cheer for you when you pulled that trigger."

Allison poured some more shots, spilling alcohol all over the table and floor while she was at it. We were all officially shitfaced.

"What say we go find that ginger bitch, Missy?" she joked.

"Haha, yeah. We could go pay her a visit at her boyfriend's little trailer, shake her up a bit. Dole out a little retribution," said Sara.

I shook my head. "Nah, I don't have the energy for that bitch. I need another week to get my mojo back."

The three of them nodded in agreement, surveying bruises, wincing over sore muscles, gingerly testing body parts that had been put through unimaginable torture.

I smiled and swallowed the lump in my throat. Part of me believed I should feel guilty for what I'd done. Taken a human life. The life of a fellow woman.

But here's the thing: I couldn't feel bad. I couldn't muster up even one iota of regret or remorse.

And I felt certain that if I had the chance to do it again, even knowing the outcome... there was no doubt in my mind that I would.

Chapter Twenty

Mick

While Ace and Ian were shadowing Jade's every move and Xander was having some kind of weird internal crisis, I was strategizing our next moves.

Before everything went to hell, I had a guy hooking us up with passports. With today's technology, it's no simple task. I needed to follow up with him and make sure our deal still stood.

I downed another cup of coffee and rubbed my eyes. I hadn't slept well since we'd arrived back with Jade. Now that I was awake I decided to go look in on her.

"Hey, you okay?"

I handed her a glass of water. She took a sip, then wrinkled her nose.

"Ugh. I don't want to puke again."

"You puked?"

She looked green around the gills. Her face was pale, accentuating the horrible bruising around her eyes, her cheeks, her neck, and on the left corner of her lip.

"Yeah, like ten times. Every time I get up, I have to yak."

I laughed and sat on the edge of the bed. It killed me to see my princess looking like this. A murderous rage surged through me and I couldn't wait to get my hands on Pierce and anyone else still alive who took part.

"Anything I can get you?"

She collapsed back onto her pillow and shook her head back and forth. This brought on a fresh wave of nausea.

"Ohhhh. Ugh. I think I have alcohol poisoning," she said, moaning. "Even shaking my head back and forth makes me dizzy and sick."

I brushed the hair back from her eyes and tried to keep my expression neutral.

"What are you thinking about?" she asked. Her voice was soft and her eyebrows arched in the cutest way. Looking at her broke my heart in ways I didn't think were even possible.

"Nothing, sweetheart. Working on getting us out of here."

"Really? When? Where?"

"Yes, and soon. Not sure where. Where would you go?" I asked.

Everything in me wanted to gather her up in my arms. Even though she pretended not to be, she was fragile. And skittish. I watched her watching everything and everyone. She hadn't let her guard down even once. Constantly flinching and looking over her shoulder.

She thought for a few minutes. "I don't know, but I don't like the desert. I never want to see the desert again. So I guess somewhere in the mountains. Or the tropics."

"Okay, Ace agrees with you wholeheartedly on the 'no desert' thing. We all agree that palm trees and beaches are good shit. We'll figure it out, don't you worry."

For a few minutes, I just sat there, helping her up to sip water, arranging her pillows, and gathering up her laundry so I could do it later. I didn't want her lifting a finger.

Reluctantly, I left her side, wanting so badly to gather her in my arms and hold her close. She'd dozed off and was snoring softly. I dared not even touch her cheek lest I disturb her peace.

"I love you."

I left Jade to sleep off the rest of her hangover. Ian was getting antsy. Ace was edgy and had flatly informed me that he hated this place, wasn't fond of Jesse, and that the dry desert air was fucking with his sinuses.

Xander was imploding. The shift in him gave me a sinking feeling. I didn't like it, and it busted me up knowing that I had failed. I'd wanted to get us out of the life before it hardened him.

Too late.

I nudged him and gestured toward the door.

"Walk with me."

He fell in step next to me and scowled at his feet as we walked. His anger and frustration were palpable. I tried to soothe him.

"Hey, I know you want to find Pierce. Ace wants to find Pierce. Ian wants to find Pierce. I want to find him and end him."

"Yeah, so why are we still here? We could be out there looking for him now. I just know he's back in LA."

I shrugged.

"No, you don't. He could be anywhere. He could be in Vegas or Mexico. We don't know."

"So let's find him. I've talked to a couple of guys who claim he's in the area. They don't know what he's up—"

"Wait, you've been talking to whom? I thought we were laying low, not tipping anyone off where we were?"

Xander rolled his eyes, looking far more like an angsty teen in that moment than a grown man.

"First off, you're high if you think people don't know where to find us. Second, 'talking' to people doesn't mean telling them our business."

"I know, Xander, but I'd just prefer not to put ourselves on anyone's radar right now."

"Mick we are all over everyone's radar right now. There are guys who have worked close to Berto for years..."

"Yeah, and we killed most of them," I said.

"Not all of them. There's plenty more. And then there are the assholes who will want to move in on his territory."

"Fuck 'em, let them have it. It's not like you are stepping up. Jesse doesn't want it. The Moreno family is done. It's dissolved. Some ambitious, enterprising dickhead will pick up the pieces and make something out of what's left. Not our concern."

I watched him take that in, and was surprised to see doubt creep across his face. He didn't seem to like what he was hearing.

"What? You not okay with that?"

He leaned his head back, crossing his arms across his chest and staring out into the empty sky.

"I mean, my dad built it up from nothing. It was nothing when he took over. He made it what it is."

"So? I thought you hated it? Hated the lifestyle. You wanted out, right? Now is your chance, kid. Your chance to put it behind you and make something new, something that's yours."

He stared back at me with his dark eyes.

"That is what you want, right Xander?"

He sighed. "Yeah, that's what I want. It's just that it's all I've ever known. Even when I hated it. Who am I without it?"

I put a hand on his shoulder.

"We all get to figure that out."

He nodded and chewed the corner of his lip like he always did when he was feeling uncertain.

"Why don't you go keep an eye on Jade? I need to figure out some stuff. We're getting out of here soon."

"Go where?"

"I have ideas for a temporary spot until we make our move out of here."

"Out of the country?"

"Yeah, that's what we talked about. Somewhere in the Caribbean, I'm thinking."

"Yeah, I mean, sure. That sounds okay."

"Jade wants out of here. I don't think she feels safe here, you know?"

Xander walked back toward the house, then turned to face me.

"I doubt she's gonna feel safe anywhere, especially knowing that monster Pierce is out there, free to keep killing innocent girls. Maybe come back for her."

That statement made my blood boil.

"We won't let another goddamn thing happen to her, you know that."

He spit out a bitter laugh.

"Yeah? She got put in a cage on our watch. He came right in and took her like it was nothing, and we couldn't fucking stop him."

Chapter Twenty-One

Jade

I WOKE UP TO find Xander in the chair next to my bed and couldn't help but smile. One by one, they all found their way into that chair. I was never alone, which was mostly good. Sometimes, though, I felt like I wanted nothing more than to be alone forever. In some cabin atop a mountain high, far from anyone. Those thoughts were brief, though. I wasn't the alone type. I needed my guys, as much as I loathed the fact.

It felt good to know they worried about me, that they didn't want to let me out of their sight. I felt safe, and with each day that went by, I felt safer, knowing they would never leave me alone again.

"Hey, you." I smiled and gingerly stretched my body, as usual, reveling in the bed's softness and the fact that I could stretch out without brushing up against metal bars.

He returned my smile. "Hey, angel."

"You watching me sleep like a creeper?" I joked.

He blushed a little and smiled shyly, which was quickly replaced with a mischievous twinkle.

"Yeah. I've been sitting here for hours staring at you. You know you sleep with your mouth wide open and snore like a walrus?"

My jaw dropped, and for a second I bought it.

"What? Seriously?"

He laughed. "It's adorable. I love it."

I shook my head. "Are you bullshitting me? Do I seriously sleep with my mouth hanging open?"

He nodded. "And you drool, too."

I was horrified, but the twinkle in his eyes gave him away.

"You are so full of shit."

His smile lit up the room, and it warmed my heart to see it.

"You got me. You weren't snoring, and your mouth wasn't hanging open. Although I think you might have been drooling a little."

I shrugged and smiled. "Whatever."

A few seconds went by and there was no more conversation. Conversation was something I struggled with since my rescue.

I hoped he would carry the conversation, but he remained silent. The weird, old-fashioned analog clock on the night-stand had a second hand that made a clicking sound with each second, bringing attention to the silence between us.

Five seconds. Ten seconds. Half a minute. A full minute.

I sighed. He shifted in his seat.

I started wishing he would leave and then felt guilty for wishing it. I loved Xander and longed to connect with him and the other guys but I just couldn't seem to do it.

Finally, "It's good to see you smile, Jade."

Oddly enough, I'd just been thinking the same thing. Xander and Ace were both like sunshine. Even when shit was less than ideal. Xander kept this gentle, hopeful, positive vibe. Ace was manically positive.

But since this... he was different.

"Yeah, I could say the same. This is like the first time I've seen you smile in days."

He swallowed and gave a slight nod.

"Yeah, well, I'm a little preoccupied."

"Sure, I get it. You want to talk?"

I hoped he would say yes. Spill his guts, give me something to focus on besides me.

"I mean, there's not much to say. And I don't want to upset you by talking about..." He trailed off.

"About Pierce? And how he's still out there? About Berto, and what's going to happen now that he's dead?"

He looked over at me, his eyes wide with concern.

"I'm serious, Jade. I don't want to bring stuff up and make things worse for you. You're still healing."

"I am healing. Every day. But trust me, bringing up Pierce and Berto and talking to me about what is happening next isn't going to trigger me. I'm already triggered. I am still living in a nightmare, Xander. I see their faces twenty-four seven. They invade my dreams. Every sound I hear, every time a door opens or I hear footsteps behind me. I hear screams constantly. I see the faces of the girls who they murdered. There is no avoiding it, and you aren't doing me any favors by keeping me out of the loop. You can talk to me. I can handle it. I know I can handle it because I've been handling it."

His face darkened, and I saw his fists close.

"Those fucking bastards. I swear, I will make Pierce pay..."

"Yeah, me too. Take a number." I laughed bitterly. "I wish we could just keep killing all of them over and over again."

He looked at me and something in his face shifted. There was a little smile playing at the corner of his lips. His eyes shone.

"I swear, Jade. If we can catch him alive, we can just keep him somewhere and torture him. Take turns on him. Draw it out, let him suffer."

Heat prickled all over my body. That wave of tightness hit my chest, but this time it felt good. Felt like a rush.

"Put him in a cage," I said.

He nodded. "Yeah."

After Xander left my room I got up. I took a long shower, letting the water run over my body, easing the ache in my bones. Most of my cuts had healed.

The swelling in my face was almost gone. The bruises had faded, covering most of my face in splotches of brown and yellow.

"So gross."

Laurie had brought me more clothes and her stuff was cute. I slid on a pair of jeans and a cropped tee.

I combed through my hair and eyed the makeup she'd told me I could use.

"Concealer. Lots of concealer."

It took me a few minutes but I covered the bruises. I applied some mascara and some lipstick and surveyed the results.

"Not bad. You nearly look like a normal human being. A human who wasn't tortured in a cage for weeks. Good deal."

After a few minutes of pacing and working up the courage, I opened the door to see Mick, Ian, Xander, and Ace all sitting there with Jesse, Laurie, Jesse's ex, and their son, Griffin.

They all turned to look at me and I couldn't help but notice the way both Jesse and Griff looked at me. I didn't like it, but then again, men had been looking at me like that since I was twelve.

My guys looked at me, too. But the overriding expression I noticed on their faces was relief. And love. It warmed me through and through and I felt the flutters in my stomach, the happy butterflies, for the first time since I'd been here.

"Am I interrupting something?" I asked. Their voices had been hushed and there was tension.

"No Ma'am, you're just in time." Jesse pasted on a wide grin and Laurie leaned into him, mirroring his smile and beaming at me.

"I'm so glad to see you up and feeling better. You look fantastic," she said.

"Yeah, I'm doing better."

It's true. I was. That drinking session with my besties from the torture cages was therapeutic on a level I couldn't have imagined. At first, I thought I'd made a mistake.

After the drinking and commiserating, the retelling of traumatic tales, and the crying on each other's laps, I landed in my bed courtesy of Ian and spent the night sobbing and puking while the room spun. But all that sobbing and puking proved to be a massive catharsis, and I felt a little lighter, a little less fucked up.

Ace patted the spot next to him and I made my way over, still feeling eyes on me and not really liking it much.

"So what's going on? What are we talking about?"

Mick cleared his throat and smiled.

"We're talking about leaving. It's time. We're heading out of here, princess."

Turns out, not everyone was on board with this. Jesse wanted us to stay. And when I went over to see the girls, they were sad, too.

"Nooo. I don't want you to leave." Sara stuck out her lower lip and hugged me. "I was just telling Allison how good it felt to have us together here. It's not bad, you know. I'm getting used to just being here, and they don't seem to have a problem with it, either."

"Yeah? But then what? You're stuck out in the middle of nowhere. What are you going to do? What kind of future do you have here?"

She shrugged. "I haven't had a future for a long time. It's nice to just be. No one is asking anything of us... yet. Maybe I'll find a man. There's enough of them around." She giggled and nudged Allison.

Rose sat in her chair, staring into space. She wasn't okay.

"I guess. Look. We're getting out of here, but I want to stay in touch. Do you have a phone?"

Allison nodded. "Yeah, Laurie brought us some prepaid burner phones the other day." She giggled again. "She's super nice to us. Brought us clothes, snacks. We have this place to ourselves."

I frowned. "Nothing is free, Allie. You know that."

She nodded. "Yeah. But nothing can be worse than what we've been through. What? They want us to have a little fun? Pull some kind of job? Nothing we haven't done before."

She hugged me again, pulled away, and Sara hugged me next. I walked over to Rose and knelt down next to the chair.

"Hey. You take care of yourself, okay? Go slow. It's going to be okay."

She reached out her hand, and I squeezed it.

"Be careful out there, Jade," she said.

Chapter Twenty-Two

Jade

I WOKE FROM A different dream. Up till today, I was dreaming about being crammed into a cage smelling of piss, or Saysha running, and this time it was me pulling the trigger. Or, being inches away from Xander when Berto shoved me off the edge of the cliff and I tumbled head first onto the jagged boulders below. My nights were a smorgasbord of terror and I was quite used to it.

But this time, my dream took me back to a memory. A night when I was back in my old home with my parents and my shithead boyfriend Eddie.

It was one of those nights that Eddie's son Benny stayed with us. Normally, on those nights, Eddie didn't bother coming home. He would spend about an hour halfheartedly playing with him, commenting on how big and strong he was, how smart he was, and anything else he could say that stroked his ego.

Then, the minute the baby fussed or soiled his diaper, he was out.

Of course, those nights were the best. It was best when Eddie just left. When my parents got drunk or took their pills and passed out early. Then, it was just me and Benny. I'd make his bottles and give him his bath. Play with him, sing to him, read to him. I'd do my best to give him the love he deserved, to make up for the neglect he suffered most of the time.

But once in a while, Eddie stuck around. Those nights were the worst. Because if the baby cried and I couldn't soothe him fast enough, he would fly into a rage. Scream at the baby. Scream at me. Hit me if I interfered.

A few times he shook the baby, and once he slapped him. I freaked out and tried to call the police. The one and only time. And I regretted it.

It wasn't Eddie who went after me that night; it was my father. He hit me so hard I saw stars and was on the floor, dazed. My mom kicked me. Eddie laughed while the baby screamed.

I remembered little else about that night, but I dreamed about it. The dream was so real that for a minute I thought that everything since had been the dream. That the bank robbery had never happened. That I'd never been in the cage.

When I opened my eyes, Ian's concerned face hovered over mine.

"Jade, you're having a nightmare. Wake up."

He gently stroked my arm, careful not to move suddenly or invade my space too much.

"Yeah. Shit. It all happened."

He nodded, as though he knew exactly what I was talking about.

"Yeah."

Today was moving day. I didn't have much to pack up. Laurie had given me some clothes, and I had my toiletries. That was it. My grandmother's ring? Gone. My camera with the pictures of the baby? Gone along with my purse, keys, and random stupid shit that shouldn't mean anything, but when you have nothing those little things mean a lot.

"Where are we going? What kind of place? How far away?"

I was brimming with questions and excitement, and also fear.

I knew the guys had concerns about Moreno's remaining men, his loyalists, coming after us, coming to avenge Berto's death.

Ace said that even guys who didn't give a rat's ass about Berto might come after us just for street cred.

Mick shook his head at my questions. "Don't worry about it."

I frowned and curled my lip. "Or, you could just tell me it's a surprise. That sounds a lot better."

He smiled. "It is a surprise."

I stared at my fingernails. I'd spent the last few hours in Jesse's desert compound doing nails with the girls. Even Laurie showed up and hung out with us.

Every time I saw her with her baby I thought about little Benny and wondered how he was doing.

I looked up and Ian and Ace were both staring at me. I shrugged and wiped my eyes.

"Just thinking about... about the baby. I don't know why. Stupid, right?"

Ian shook his head. "Not stupid. You bonded with him and he's stuck with horrible people. Now that you aren't in full survival mode, I'm not surprised you are thinking about him."

Ace nodded in agreement.

Xander was in the front passenger seat. He turned and looked at me.

"He'll be okay. We had fucked up childhoods and look, we all turned out fine."

Ace playfully smacked him on the back of his head for that one.

"Yeah, I don't think that's going to make her feel better."

I shook my head and craned my neck, trying to see any signs on the freeway that would clue me in to where we were going. I was sandwiched between Ace and Ian, and I couldn't see much out of the windows of the double-cab truck.

"How long before we get there?" I asked.

"Why, you need to stop and use the bathroom?" Mick asked.

"No, just curious."

He nodded. "It's going to be awhile. Just relax, take a nap, or something. We'll get there when we get there."

He was unusually gruff this morning, something Jesse had said to him didn't sit well.

I didn't press him, but I was curious. The send off we got was full of smiles and well wishes, and it felt genuine.

And we were gone. Long gone. On our way to a safe place while we waited for passports. Then, we were leaving the country.

At least, that was the plan. For me, I would believe it when I had my feet firmly on the ground in a new place, far, far, far away from the Morenos. Far from Los Angeles. Far from the desert, far from anyone who even knew who Berto or Pierce was.

That's where I wanted to be. A world where they didn't exist and could never hurt me or anyone I loved ever again.

Was that too much to ask?

I woke with a start as the truck rolled to a stop. So I'd drifted off, after all. Irritation flared up as I rubbed the sleep out of my eyes. I'd wanted to stay awake so I could pay attention to where we were and how we got there. Honestly, I was getting tired of being kept in the dark. What city was this place in? How far from Los Angeles? From that dusty murder desert?

"We're here," Mick said, his voice uncharacteristically bright.

I grumbled as I collected myself, reaching in my hand-me-down purse for a stick of gum and my lip balm.

"Here where? What city?"

"Just come on. Come see it." Mick grinned like he was a kid on Christmas, and Ace gave a low whistle of approval.

"Holy shit," Xander murmured.

Ian was silent as he offered his hand to help me out of the truck, but when he turned to face the house, his eyebrows shot up and he nodded his head.

Me? My jaw dropped.

"This is where we are going to stay? Are you serious?" I practically screeched as I started walking down the path that led to the front of the house.

The coastal air teased my nostrils, and the breeze cooled what was probably an upper-eighties day in Southern California.

"I can hear the waves," I whispered.

The front doors opened to reveal a massive living space, filled with modern furnishings.

But what really got me were the floor to ceiling windows with views of the beach. The waves crashed onto the shore and I could see surfers in the water along with boats out further.

It was mid-afternoon, and I was starving, but the sight of the ocean had me wanting to peel off my clothes and jump in the water.

"This is incredible." Ace said. He put an arm around my shoulder and pulled me in. I ignored the urge to shrug him off, and instead leaned in.

"It is."

"So how long we staying here, boss?" Ace asked.

Mick pulled at his goatee and grinned. "Until we are ready to move on. At least a week or two. We'll see how things go. I'm going to meet with my guy about those passports, and start looking into transportation."

"Come on, let's go find your room." Mick held out his hand, and I took it, allowing him to lead me out of the living area down a wide hall.

"It's the third door on the right," he said.

"Cool, right near the bathroom," I observed.

He just laughed and opened the door.

Once again, my jaw dropped.

The bedroom was enormous, nearly as big as the living area. There was a king-size bed to the left, and directly across from the door were more floor to ceiling windows with a view of the ocean.

I gasped. "There's a balcony!"

Mick nodded and opened a sliding door that led out to a large terrace, complete with a table, chairs, and sun loungers.

"Oh my god. This is insane." I went to the railing and breathed in the ocean air, closing my eyes against the warmth of the sun and giggling as the wind ruffled my hair in the most delicious way.

"There's more. Come inside."

I clapped my hands. "No way, I'm living out here."

He laughed. "Come on, you're going to want to see this."

We went back inside and I explored the room some more. There was a sitting area that faced the windows, with the bed to the left. To the right, there was an arched entry. I walked through it and my hand instinctively went to my chest.

"I'm dead. Seriously. Dead. My heart can't handle this shit."

Before me was a bathroom that probably was as big as a studio apartment or master bedroom in a normal house.

There was a huge sunken bathtub, a shower big enough for all five of us, and two doors. One led to the toilet.

There was also a vanity with two sinks and lots of cupboards and drawers. I poked around, then turned to see what was behind door number two.

"Jesus," I blurted.

It was a walk-in closet with a chandelier, dripping in crystals and finery. There were shelves, drawers, space to hang all the clothes I didn't have, and an upholstered bench.

It was a fucking princess suite. It was massive. It was mine.

"Tell me we never have to leave. Tell me."

He shook his head and laughed, his eyes twinkling with affection and something close to happiness.

"Jade, just enjoy it. I promise where we go next you'll love just as much. I want nothing but the best for you. You deserve to live like a princess, and I'm going to make it my life's work to make sure that's what you get."

I grinned while tears sprang to my eyes. I brushed the back of my hand across my eyes and made a run for the bed, leaping onto it and noting it had good bounce but was also supportive.

"It's perfect."

"Good. Now, I know you don't have much as far as clothes or any of your girlie shit, but don't worry. We'll change that. Online shopping is your friend."

"Oh, hell yeah," I said.

"When can I go down there? To the beach?"

He pretended to give it serious consideration, then shook his head.

"Right now. Let's go."

Chapter Twenty-Three

Ian

I CLAIMED THE BEDROOM next to Jade.

The beach house was tri-level, with two master suites, and three smaller bedrooms that all had en-suite bathrooms and were still huge. The place was ridiculous and honestly felt a little over-the-top and not very secure.

"Come with me," Mick said.

He led me to a home theater room with a 75-inch screen, recliners, a huge sectional, and a bar.

"Holy shit, Mick. What is this costing? How did you even find this place?"

"Jesse knows a guy who knows a guy. He set us up."

I nodded.

"Yeah, and what about the money? I know this place isn't free."

"Xander grabbed a small fortune when he raided Berto's warehouse and residence. Information, weapons, money, and more. The kid did good, and that's what is funding us right now."

"Yeah, he told me about some of the stuff he grabbed. I guess I just didn't realize it was enough to afford a place like this."

"Yeah, well I have some connections of my own, too. Now I just have to get us out of the area permanently."

I looked at the luxurious entertainment room, tried to envision myself eating popcorn and drinking beer while watching some action flick or something. It seemed far-fetched.

"Relax, Ian."

"Relax? Are you serious? I feel exposed here. It's too over the top. It's too accessible. There are people all over that beach. They could be anyone. Too easy for someone to sneak up on us. And, we are still in Los Angeles."

Mick shook his head.

"Wrong. Not easy at all."

He walked over to the screen and ran a finger behind it.

The wall to the side of it opened up and I couldn't help but laugh. Yet another safe room.

"Okay, cool. We had one of those at the last house and guess what? It didn't help."

"Fuck's sake, Ian," Mick growled and turned to face me. "I get it. We fucked up. We fucked up big time. But that's the last time. It's the last time anyone touches Jade. It's the last time we walk into a trap. You hear me? The last fucking time."

I put my hands up in surrender.

"Okay, boss. I hear you."

He nodded and motioned for me to follow him.

This safe room was bigger than the last one but set up the same. A living and sleeping area, stock room, plenty of surveillance.

"Look. We've got cameras all over the place. At any potential point of entry. Outside. All over the house, the driveway, the street, and the path to the beach. The system sends alerts anytime anyone comes or goes. Any time someone approaches. There is facial recognition that alerts me if someone other than us shows up or comes anywhere near us. We just have to set it up."

"Wow. Impressive."

He nodded.

"No one comes in here without our knowledge. We stick together. We don't fuck up."

"We stay with Jade, at least two of us, at all times."

"How long before someone knows we are here?" I still didn't trust this situation. We were way too close to Moreno territory. Way too close to people who would recognize one or more of us.

"It's called hiding in plain sight, Ian. As long as we play it cool, we'll be okay. You know none of the guys would be caught dead in the village. We can have groceries delivered, shop online. And that beach? That beach is full of rich yuppies and their little dogs. No one is going to notice us."

I nodded. "Yeah, and the only two people in this house who would fit in on that beach are Jade and Xander. Maybe you. I guess some people might see you and assume you are a rich sugar daddy."

"Cute. Keep a shirt on, Ian. Wear a hat and some shades and you'll be fine. Same with Ace."

I rolled my shoulders back and tried to relax.

Mick lowered his voice.

"Ian, how is Xander? I mean, I'm kind of worried about him. He's talking like he doesn't want to leave the business behind. Like he's more concerned about getting revenge than being safe and getting Jade somewhere safe."

I cocked my head, studying his face for a minute before I responded.

"Mick, we have to find Pierce. Not just to make him pay for what he did to Jade, but to keep him from doing it again. You saw how many girls were in those cages. You've seen the news. He's a cold-blooded killer of innocents. He kills for sport. We have to stop him."

Mick nodded. "Yeah, he needs to be stopped. So we drop a dime, tip off the good cops. But we get the fuck out of here. As soon as those passports are done."

"Yeah? And then what? I get it, we've got some money. We've got a lot of money. But we are criminals, Mick. That's our life. That's what we know. It's not so easy to walk away."

The look Mick gave me when I said that made me feel like I'd just made a mistake.

Probably should have worded it a little differently.

"Are you fucking kidding me? Ian? Are you serious?" He shook his head. "Of course you're serious. I knew you would be the one to want to stay in the lifestyle."

Okay, now he's pissing me off.

"Oh, you knew? Me? Just me? What about Ace? He'll be chomping at the bit to smash a head in before too long. You think he can reign in that impulse? He's a fucking killer. Berto's own reaper. What do you think he's going to do off leash? With no one feeding him a steady diet of jobs?"

Now it was Mick who was pissed.

"Ace is on board with my plan. He doesn't want this anymore. He wants to settle down."

"Keep telling yourself that, Mick."

I walked away, leaving him standing there stewing. His heart was in the right place, but he was too idealistic. Yeah, we probably should get the fuck out of this place. But then again, where would we go to? Who would we be?

I needed to be around Jade. Since we'd arrived at the house she was busy exploring and finding little ways to make the place her own.

"Hey!" she said, her face glowing and her grin wide. Her eyes sparkled for the first time in days. I couldn't help but smile.

"You like it, huh?" I surveyed her space. It was a huge suite fit for a queen, not a princess. She sat cross-legged on the bed, her pale blonde locks tumbling over her shoulders and down her back.

Her face was finally looking normal. The swelling was gone and you had to look to see the bruises. With makeup on, you couldn't see them at all.

"I freaking love it, are you kidding me? Did you go outside? Did you smell the ocean? And you can hear the waves, Ian. Even with the doors and windows closed. I'm going to fall asleep listening to the ocean."

She closed her eyes and smiled, sitting there like some enlightened being, meditating and radiating like the sun.

Her happiness unlocked my own. I mean, I wasn't happy, happy, but I felt a twinge of happiness, of contentment. If Jade was feeling good, I could only feel so bad, right?

"We walked down to the beach earlier, me and Mick and Xander. It's so pretty. The sand is so soft, and I got my feet wet in the ocean."

She was absolutely beaming.

"I'm so glad to see you smiling, Jade."

I swallowed and looked down at my feet. She was so beautiful, so excited about the simple things. Unbelievably stoked about hearing the waves and smelling the ocean.

"I've always loved the beach," I said.

"Really?"

"Yeah, I grew up here. Not that I've had a lot of time to hang out but I have always come here when I needed to clear my head, to find some peace."

"Me too. I mean, no one really let me come to the beach much, but once in a while I got to."

Her face turned all wistful, and I wanted to crush the people in her life who had just snatched away her light with not so much as a thought.

"I used to surf back in the day," I said.

Her eyes widened. "Seriously? You know how to surf?"

I couldn't help but laugh. "Back in the day" wasn't really all that long ago. A few years.

"Yeah. I learned when I went with Ber — I mean I just — I was in Hawaii for a month, and I had some rare downtime. I learned at Waikiki beach and did a little surfing in this area when I could."

She looked a little flustered, and I internally cursed myself for bringing up that piece of shit.

"Ian, don't worry about it. You can say his name. Yeah, I'm still shaken up. Probably will be for a long time, but I can handle it, okay?"

I nodded. "Yeah, I know."

"So you were in Hawaii with Berto, what, do gangsters take vacations?"

"Yeah. I mean, not really. He was buying a house there as an investment, and he was just soaking up the bars and girls and dabbling in a few things. Nothing major. He doesn't have people there or anything."

She cocked an eyebrow. "Really? No Moreno gang in Hawaii?"

I shook my head. "Not that I know of."

"Huh. But he bought a house there?"

A lightbulb went off.

"Yeah. He did."

She tapped her chin with her forefinger.

"So, he's just got a house in Hawaii sitting there?"

I smiled. That's my girl.

"Yeah, he sure does."

Chapter Twenty-Four

Xander

I SAT AT THE desk in my bedroom and continued hacking into every single piece of technology I'd lifted from Berto's warehouse headquarters.

When Ace and I started our journey to getting Mick and Ian sprung from jail and trying to find Jade, I had cleaned out everything in his office that looked even remotely important. Laptops, towers, paper files, recording devices, cameras.

We'd even come back and found more. Weapons. Cash. Jewelry. More paperwork.

But once we started intensifying our search for Jade, I'd just kind of forgotten about things. I mean, we'd cleared several hundred thousand dollars in cash. Crazy, but Berto was a firm believer in having as much cash on hand as possible.

Then we found her, and for days and weeks, everything was just a blur. I got caught up in how we could find Pierce, worrying about Jade, wondering what was going to happen to the empire that my father had built, and the distraction of my uncle Jesse's gang, how he ran things, what kind of lifestyle he was living. There were things I didn't agree with, sure, but there was something to be said for a guy who ran his organization with a firm but loose grip and was adored by his people. And he put family first.

It was alluring, and I wondered if it would be possible to recreate what my father had started and what my uncle Berto had twisted.

"How can I untwist it?" I asked aloud.

"Untwist what?"

Ian had entered the room in his usual stealth fashion. I could always hear Ace coming because his mouth preceded him, and Mick had heavy footsteps for a guy who was supposed to be such a smooth criminal.

But Ian? He was forever sneaking up on me.

"Dude, you could knock," I said, feigning irritation. I mean, technically I was irritated but I was happy he was here. There was a distance between us since we found Jade. She occupied our thoughts most of the time. We were processing the horrors we'd come upon, not to mention what we'd been through individually before finally coming to this point. A point where we could hopefully breathe easy. At least for a little while.

"Just came to see how you were doing, is all."

I could tell from his tone that Mick had gotten to him. Mick was worried about me. He didn't need to be. For the first time probably ever, I was actually doing just fine.

"I'm good. How are you?"

He took a seat on the bed and I swiveled my fancy office chair around to face him.

We locked eyes for a minute and I felt that familiar spark, that desire. It was good. Familiar. Safe.

"Good. I guess. I don't know. This place is cool, but I don't feel like it's safe. I am frustrated that Pierce is still out there. And I don't like not knowing what's going to happen next."

I nodded. "Yeah. I hear you. So what are we going to do about it?"

He looked at me and smiled.

"I'm going to grab us some beers. Let's talk."

When he left I turned my attention back to the screen. Berto had accounts. Property. Information on law enforcement and local politicians. Assets. Offshore bank accounts. He'd amassed a fortune I could barely wrap my head around.

Growing up, I lived in his main house, a large estate in Los Angeles with a view of the Hollywood sign. It's where we lived. He had his "headquarters" which included a large commercial office building and warehouse.

Other than that? I knew he owned some real estate. I knew he had investments in several businesses. But I never knew about the desert compound.

"Fuck, I forgot about the house in Hawaii."

He'd taken me there when he first bought it. It wasn't long after my mom had died, and I spent most of my time holed up in my room. Having fun on the beach, eating shave ice, and going to parties in hotel rooms in Honolulu seemed like a gross betrayal to my mother.

"Fucking bastard. He laughed at me. Laughed at my grief."

My stomach turned as I relived the torment the man had shown me.

"Hey, whatcha looking at?"

Ian walked up behind me and pressed a beer into my waiting hand.

I leaned back in my chair, leaning into him, tilting my head back to look at him.

"Remember that fucking house in Hawaii?"

He nodded. "Yeah, that's when I learned to surf. Was just telling Jade all about it. Great time."

His words, although innocent enough, were like a punch in the gut.

"Yeah. Great time."

"What?"

I shook my head. "Nothing."

"What else does Uncle Dickhead have?" he asked.

"Accounts in the Cayman Islands, Swiss accounts, safe deposit boxes, deeds to property, a fucking box of Rolex watches..."

"Uh, pretty sure that box of Rolex watches is Mick's."

"Oh."

I'd found a bunch of shit and stuck it in storage in the Inland Empire. I'd gone with Mick to grab it so we could go through it once we'd settled in.

"So, you have access to all of it?"

"A lot of it. Some of these accounts, I might not be able to get into them. Some properties, I mean, at some point... I don't know. He's dead, it complicates things."

Ian grabbed my chair and spun it to face him. His eyes looked like they could pop out of his head.

"Did he have a will?"

That gave me pause. He'd mentioned his legacy, and he had mentioned a will.

"I guess guys like him think they'll live forever, right?" Ian looked at me, his eyes searching for confirmation.

He posed a valid question. Berto had to know he could die at any time. If not at the hands of a rival or pissed-off relative, then a heart attack or a stroke. Something.

"I mean, I guess he could have left it to Jesse, or one of his kids."

Except I didn't think so.

Ian jumped up from the bed and instantly started pacing.

"What if he left everything to Pierce?"

"No way. He didn't have any feelings about Pierce. He wasn't a real friend to him. I'm willing to bet he had guys working for him he cared about way more than Pierce. He was just a guy he trusted because they were both the same level of sick."

"True."

Ian sat back down and looked thoughtfully at the monitor screen.

"I say we get what we can. Drain any account you can get access to. We have all his cash. I say we get his cars. Strip his house. Take everything of his that isn't nailed down. And, I say we figure out where his will is."

I rolled the chair to the two file cabinets Mick and Ace had hauled up earlier.

"Yeah, I've been through most of these files, but I'm going back through. I could have missed something."

"I'd be willing to bet the will is in his house."

"Maybe. But what difference does it make?"

"He has that place in Hawaii. And other houses, too. I think a place in Vegas. Unless he sold it. Point is, the more of that shit we get, the better. Anyway, it's your stuff. Yours to do with what you want."

He was wrong about that.

"Technically, Jesse is his next of kin."

Ian looked shocked for a minute and opened his mouth to protest, but realization replaced his shock quickly.

"I didn't think about that. You're right."

"Funny he said nothing about it. I mean, him and his guys picked the compound clean, but they said nothing about his Los Angeles stuff. Doesn't that strike you as weird?"

Ian looked at me, then cocked his head, squinting his eyes and pursing his lips.

"Don't hurt yourself over it, Ian. Just thinking it's a little odd."

He laughed and fake-punched my shoulder. "Funny."

"I mean, Jesse isn't hurting for money. He doesn't seem interested in taking over the family business. Doesn't seem to want to leave his ranch, and like you said, he didn't say anything."

"Yeah. I guess you're right," I said.

A few minutes went by. We polished off our beers and I smiled at the tension between the two of us. It had been too long.

But there was something on my mind. Something I couldn't talk to anyone else about. Not Mick. Not Ace. Not Jade. Ian was the only one.

"What else is going on with you? What's been on your mind?"

I chuckled at that. Ian read my mind. Or maybe this was him finally getting to the point of why he came in here in the first place.

"I don't know. I've been looking through all these receipts, these books, files. Berto had a lot of irons in the fire, had his hands in a lot of things."

"Yeah, but we knew that, right?"

I nodded. "Yeah, but now what happens? There are people who depended on him for their livelihood."

Ian looked confused.

"Okay, well I'm guessing that someone else will swoop in and take over. They'll probably barely notice the difference."

"Maybe. But he owned some legitimate businesses. He funded them and protected them. What are they going to do now?"

"Okay, what are you getting at? You want to stay? You want to run in his place?"

I searched his eyes to see where he was with it. I couldn't read him.

"What if I said yes? What if I said we need to go hunt down Pierce and kill him, anyone who works for him, and anyone left who doesn't fall in line? What if I said we could run things together, the four of us. The right way?"

He sighed and scrubbed his hand across the back of his neck.

"Xander, it's not what I'm going to say. It's what Mick and Ace are going to say."

"Yeah, I know. But I want to know what you say."

He looked me dead in the eye.

"I say you're fucking out of your mind."

I slumped, disappointed. I guess I'd thought he might back me.

Then, his face lit up, and he flashed a sexy as fuck grin.

"Sign me up."

Chapter Twenty-Five

Jade

THREE WEEKS HAD GONE by in our beachside mansion. Over five weeks now since my rescue.

"What's in this bag?" Ace popped his head into the bedroom to deliver more packages to me. I'd developed just a slight shopping addiction since Mick had handed me a credit card and told me to "have fun with it".

"Bathing suits." I smiled.

His eyes lit up and I blushed. I'd already bought a few other suits, several cute outfits, a large haul of makeup, new sheets and bedding, and half a dozen pairs of shoes.

"Well, let me know when you're ready to head down."

"Okay. I'll be ready in a little while."

Xander and Ace were with me, Mick and Ian were out doing something hush-hush. There was a lot of that going on. I knew they'd gone out a few times to follow up on Pierce leads, and other times to go find things that had belonged to Berto.

They didn't talk to me about it much, and I didn't ask. I'd made the decision that I would focus on myself. I was going to heal and enjoy this little slice of luxurious paradise while it lasted.

One thing life had taught me over the years, and especially over the last few months, was that nothing was permanent, and anything could be taken away.

"Ah, there you are."

I ripped open my packages and tossed my new suits on the bed. But what I was really excited about were my new books. I'd ordered two of them and smiled as I put them up on their shelf.

I'd decided that I had a responsibility to better myself and since I wasn't going to go to therapy I would just start reading and learning more about myself.

I'd joined an online social media group for survivors of abuse and sexual assault. I'd purchased a book and a workbook to help me work through my trauma. Just for fun, I'd ordered a couple of astrology and manifestation books.

It seemed a little silly to me, but I was desperate to grow past what I'd been living through.

There was only one thing that really kept dogging me. One thing I didn't think I could get a handle on or move past.

My need to make Pierce suffer. I dreamed about his blood on my hands. I fantasized about slowly torturing him and laughing in his face while I did it.

A part of me longed for violence and excitement, no matter how much I breathed and meditated.

There was no way I was letting this go.

"Nice." I checked myself out in the mirror and smiled. I was finally feeling comfortable in my body. Outside of a few scars, there were no outside signs of the trauma I'd been through. The bruises were finally gone.

"Love it. Absolutely love it. That's definitely my favorite one." Ace had come back, and I waved him in.

"Seriously. That's your suit."

I giggled. He said that about each new suit I ordered, but as I surveyed the sapphire blue high-waisted bikini, I couldn't help but agree. The color looked good against my skin, the halter top was super cute, and the bottoms gave the suit a chic, vintage vibe that I was really digging.

"The beach is that way." Ace pasted on a goofy grin and pointed toward the windows.

"Yeah... got it." I laughed.

"Hold on, let me grab my bag."

Once I'd secured my bag, fully stocked with snacks, water bottles, beach towels, and sunscreen, we headed down the two flights of stairs to the ground floor, and out the back gate to the path that led to the beach.

The sound and smell of the ocean had nurtured me and healed me in a big way.

I was still hurting inside. I still had panic attacks, nightmares, dark thoughts, and persistent fantasies of revenge.

"Come on, let's run," I said to Ace.

He nodded and we started jogging along the sand. I'd read that trauma stays stuck in the body, and that movement could help free it so I could let it go. Sometimes I would sprint along the shore, running until it felt like my heart would burst and I would collapse onto the sand, breathless and laughing till I cried.

Those tears were different than any tears I'd ever cried before because I could literally feel the toxicity leaving me. I let those tears flow freely, and I always felt better, lighter, and freer after.

Dancing was my other obsession. On days when I didn't go to the beach, I would put on my headphones and hit play, then sing and dance my heart out. I told myself that any time I danced or moved my body; I was releasing the pain and trauma and fear from every cell.

It was working. I was feeling better every day. I was smiling and laughing. And for the first time since my rescue, I was looking at my guys and feeling that stirring inside me. That want and desire.

My fear was that if I gave in to it, I would regret it. That I would set myself back. I was a survivor of extreme sexual violence, and while I logically knew my guys weren't a threat, the trauma was still fresh.

Today, though, I gazed frequently at Ace as we jogged along the beach. He had his hat on backward and a long-sleeved tee shirt on to hide his tattoos, but he looked delicious. His stride, his smile, his attitude, everything about him was drawing me in and I found myself flirting despite myself.

"Whew." I slowed to a stop, then leaned over, my hands resting on my knees as I caught my breath.

"You're building your endurance," Ace observed. "You couldn't run that far, that long even a few days ago."

He was right. I was getting stronger. The body that had been so broken just a few weeks ago was getting stronger than it had been before everything happened. I was working out, running, dancing, swimming.

I was proud of myself. Proud that I didn't give in to the darkness and fear.

Proud of myself for surviving.

I flopped down onto my towel and grabbed the sunscreen out of my bag, handing it to Ace with a cheeky grin, batting my eyelashes at him like a dork.

Baby steps, Jade.

"Will you do my back?" I asked, hoping this wasn't too much, that it wasn't a mistake. I wasn't ready for all of it, but some physical contact, some attention, and some flirting sounded good.

"I'd be honored." He smiled warmly at me and motioned for me to turn around.

I was facing the water, watching the sun sparkles dancing on the mellow waves. I could hear people laughing and talking, hear the seagulls crying out overhead, and I could hear the ocean, filling my ears. Filling my soul.

Mick was a genius. It's like he knew what I needed to a T.

Ace was silent as he smoothed the coconut-scented lotion on my back. His touch was gentle, and it felt... almost platonic, but not quite. He was being careful, and it only made me love him more.

"How is that?" he asked.

I closed my eyes. "Wonderful. Thank you."

He said nothing but kept it up, rubbing the lotion into my lower back, gently lifting my hair out of the way, and then rubbing the excess on my shoulders and upper arms.

"Don't forget your nose and the tops of your ears."

I smiled and twisted my hair into a loose bun at the nape of my neck, then grabbed the hat from my bag.

We chilled on the beach for several minutes in perfect silence. It felt good to just be. To just have him at my side.

Then, I saw her.

Instinctively, I grabbed Ace's forearm and squeezed. He sat bolt upright and scanned the beach for signs of a threat.

"What is it?" he said, his voice low and tense.

"It's... my cousin. Tish. Holy shit, what do I do? I haven't seen her since..."

I had sunglasses and a hat on and we hadn't seen each other in nearly three years, but when she turned and looked my way, the recognition on her face was instant.

She clapped her hand over her mouth to keep from squealing, and I just froze.

"Fuck." Ace muttered.

It was too late to get up and casually walk away. She knew it was me.

"Jade?"

I smiled and stood up, awkwardly brushing the sand off my hands as she flung herself at me.

"Oh my God, I knew it was you. Holy shit, I can't believe it. I thought..."

She stopped and as she broke off from our hug, she took my sunglasses off.

"Jade, I thought you were dead. Everyone thinks you are dead."

I couldn't look her in the eyes.

Tish was pretty much my only friend in life. I grew up with her. She was my mom's sister's kid, and they used to live in the same neighborhood as we did. Went to the same schools. Hung out with the same people. Had the same life, basically.

But, she met a guy. A guy who was actually halfway decent. They got married; she moved away, and there went my best friend.

"Jade, look at me. What's going on? Eddie told me flat out that you were dead. He said you'd done some horrible things and betrayed your family, and that you got in some kind of accident or something."

I frowned and shook my head, confused why Eddie would make up my death. Guess he just knew I wasn't coming back, ever. But to say I was dead? Come on.

"Oh, shit, Tish. You're crying."

Tears were streaming down her face, and she hugged me fiercely.

"I'm so happy. I'm so... I don't..."

She pulled away.

"Where have you been? What are you doing here? Is this..." She gestured at Ace.

"He's a friend, yeah."

I chewed my lip and glanced at Ace, who was looking understandably perplexed.

"Hey, can you give us a sec?"

Ace frowned and shook his head slightly. I pleaded with my eyes and he relented.

"I'll be right over there, Jade."

I nodded and smiled and mouthed 'thank you'.

"Look, Tish. I'm kind of laying low right now. I've been through a lot of fucked up shit..."

"Yeah, I mean, I heard about the kidnapping. Then he said you had some kind of Stockholm syndrome and shit. Is that guy... is he....?"

Oh shit, Jade. Clean this up. Fix it now.

I shook my head violently and forced a laugh.

"Him? Oh, no way. No, I just met him a few weeks ago. He's cool. Just a guy."

She looked doubtful, but then relaxed.

"As long as you are okay, Jade. I'm so glad you're okay. You look good."

"Thanks, Tish."

I grabbed her hand and motioned toward the beach blanket.

"Here, sit with me for a minute."

She smiled and then something caught her eye. She smiled and waved at a man holding a squirming, red-faced toddler. He laughed and waved and headed back toward the water.

"Oh my god, is that?" I laughed in disbelief.

"Haha, yep. That's hubby. Dad bod in effect."

"And that's..."

She smiled. "Zoey. Two years old now."

I shook my head and tears sprang to my eyes. I'd missed it all. We'd always promised each other that our children would grow up like siblings like we did.

She looked at me, and her expression shifted, like clouds passing over the sun.

"Hey, you hear about Eddie's mom?"

I frowned. "No, what about her?"

"She died. Had a stroke, it was bad. But she went back home, developed pneumonia, and died."

My jaw dropped.

"Wow, so what's happening with... with..."

I choked a little on my words. I just couldn't say his fucking name.

"Eddie? Oh, Jade. It's bad. He's staying with your parents and the baby. He's using real bad."

I swallowed roughly and felt my stomach turning and my chest tightening. There was no way the baby was being cared for properly. Not even close.

"Hey, Jade?"

"Yeah?"

"I'm going to give you my phone number. Just put it in your phone. I won't ask for yours because I have a feeling you won't give it to me. But I'm here for you, and if you need anything, anything at all, you call me, okay?"

I nodded and hugged her again. This time the tears wouldn't stay back.

"I missed you, Tish. So much. I promise when the time is right, I'll call."

"You better."

She got up, took a last look at me, and walked back to her family.

Seconds later, Ace plopped down and we watched as they gathered their beach chairs and sand toys and made their way toward the parking lot.

"Okay, let's get back to the house. We need to talk about what just happened."

Chapter Twenty-Six

Jade

When we got back to the house Ace was looking frantic. I personally didn't get what the big deal was. It was my cousin and best friend for years and she had my back, always. I was happy to have seen her.

But I was absolutely freaking out about Benny. The urge to hijack the truck and speed down to my parents' house and snatch the baby was strong. He needed to be saved. He deserved to be saved.

"What are we going to do about this," Ace muttered as we walked into the kitchen. I was starving after our vigorous run.

"Ace. Seriously? What do you mean, what are we going to do? There isn't anything to be done. I ran into my cousin, that's all. She's not the enemy."

"Wait, what happened?" Ian strolled in and scowled at Ace. "You guys ran into someone? What the fuck?"

Mick and Xander were right on Ian's tail and the room filled with demands for explanation.

"What do you mean? Cousin? What cousin? Where did this happen? Why didn't you just ignore her, or walk away? How could you guys let this happen? I knew I should have gone along."

"ENOUGH." I barked.

"She's my fucking family. She's not a problem, and no, Xander, you couldn't have 'stopped' it from happening if you'd been there. Don't be fucking ridiculous. And no, Mick, we don't need to move. And Ian? Ace? I can't believe you guys are talking about following her or 'paying her a visit'."

I shook my head and started angrily pawing through the refrigerator, looking for something carb-heavy and filled with sugar to deal with the high level of nonsense this had turned into.

"Hey, relax..." Ace started.

I whipped around fast, eyes blazing, a leftover donut in one hand, and a pie tin in the other.

"Relax? You are the one who is causing me this stress. You guys are the ones who need to relax. It's done. She saw me. She's just fucking happy I'm alive. Eddie told her I was dead. She really believed that."

"Really?" Mick looked incredulous. "Dead?"

I nodded vigorously as I dove into the lemon meringue pie and eyed the coffee pot.

Without a word, Ace was on it, probably grateful for a task.

"I'm just nervous about potential outcomes, Jade. It's my job, our job, to think of any and every eventuality. Berto loyalists hunting us down and converging on the house. Pierce or one of his rats following us and waiting for us to let down our guard. Friends, family, old associates... any of them can be a threat, even if it isn't their intention. Hell, they can be used against us. Did you think about that? This is nothing against your cousin. This is just us trying to determine what is the worst possible thing that can come from this."

I swallowed and nodded. "Okay. I get it, okay? You guys just came at me like I did something wrong. It really stressed me out."

Tears were blurring my vision and I focused on making short work of the pie. Ace set down my coffee and I could tell he wanted me to look up at him but I didn't want them to see that I was ready to blow. I mumbled a thanks and grabbed the donut.

Everyone was quiet. Mick squeezed my shoulder as he walked past and whispered something to Ian. Ian grunted an affirmation and Xander gave a quiet 'uh-huh'.

What is going on, now? I wondered.

I didn't have to wonder for long.

Minutes later Mick returned and set something down on the kitchen island I was seated at.

I looked down and nearly choked on my donut.

"My camera! My ring! How did you?"

Xander cleared his throat. "We ran some errands and decided to go back to the old safe house. A lot of stuff was cleaned out, but we found your stuff."

"Thank you so much. I'd written them off as lost."

I immediately put my grandmother's ring on my finger, remembering that I had taken it off before getting into the pool that day, that horrible day.

Then, I reached for my camera. It still had a little charge left on it and I scrolled through the photos. I'd had the same memory card in the camera for years because I didn't get many chances to go out and take pictures.

The guys could never know how much this meant to me. These things were far more valuable than this house, the view, my new clothes... anything. They were *my own things*.

There were pictures of Tish's wedding in Vegas. Pictures of the flowers out in front of our house. Pictures I'd taken walking around the city. Pictures I'd taken of Benny at varying stages since Eddie and I had gotten back together. I'd even gone to the cemetery and taken a photo of his mother's grave, in case he ever wanted to see it.

Finally, the photos I'd taken last, the ones from that day at the beach with Eddie and the baby. Tears slid down my face and I put the camera down and covered my face.

"What? What is it?" Ace hugged me from behind and I pulled away.

"Benny is not safe with Eddie. He's not safe and I'm not there to protect him."

I slid off the stool and pushed past Ian and put a hand up when Xander approached, letting him know I wasn't interested.

"I'm going to lie down. I don't feel good."

I closed the door behind me and hoped they would be considerate enough to just leave me alone. There was no way they could possibly understand how I felt. How I felt responsible for Benny, how much I missed him. Yeah, I shoved it down for a long time, but now that I was here, living in this beautiful mansion, with all the luxuries I could never have imagined, with all the food and clothing I could possibly want...

"He should have these things, too." I sobbed.

"Yes, he should."

I popped my head up and inhaled, ready to unleash a tirade on Ian for disturbing me, for not knocking, for sneaking up on me, which he had an enviable talent for.

"I'm serious, Ian. That baby deserves better. He deserves to be loved and safe. Not with that fucking monster. My parents? They aren't fit to care for a fucking goldfish. I'm surprised I survived."

I really was. My parents were two of the most despicable, irresponsible people ever.

"I hear you, Jade. I know this is killing you, not being able to be there for him. And I'm sorry for the way we all reacted to you seeing your cousin."

My eyes welled up, again. I brushed the tears away but Ian grabbed my hand and drew it toward him, pressing it to his lips. I swallowed the lump in my throat and dared to look into his eyes.

Ian's eyes were like a roiling storm. They were beautiful, mysterious. Ace's eyes reminded me of the beach, blue and sunny. And a little psychotic, because, you know, the ocean can kill you.

But Ian's eyes were a different story. They were deep, dangerous pools filled with things you shouldn't tangle with.

For a moment, I leaned toward him, so ready to taste his lips and fall into his depths.

But I stopped myself.

He exhaled and for a moment I thought he was disappointed, but as I studied his face I realized he was relieved.

"Jade, I'm here when you are ready for that, but I don't think now is a good time."

"Yeah, me either," I said dumbly, trying to decide whether it really was a bad time and realizing that all I'd be doing is distracting myself from the myriad of feelings I was being hit with.

"What?" He was looking at me as I scowled and chewed my lip.

I stood up and walked toward the window, staring down at the blue sea below.

"It's like I had just gotten to a point where I was feeling a little bit of peace. I was starting to feel like... myself, I guess. Whatever that means. I was feeling stronger and safer."

I turned to face him.

"Now it's like a different bandaid has been ripped off of me, exposing a wound I forgot I had. My family. My cousin. The baby. All of it. Now I feel vulnerable again and don't take this personally, but I feel alone in the world. I don't have a family anymore. They are dead to me, except Tish. But even though she's my cousin and she loves me and I love her, we aren't from the same world anymore. It'll never be like it was before."

Ian stood up and walked toward me.

"It can't be like it was before because it's not before, anymore. That is the past and at some point, it slips away and turns into the now. And the now isn't perfect but it's full of possibility to create something amazing."

He put his hands on my shoulders and gazed into my eyes.

"Jade, we're your family. And we get to create a new life. A life that's better than any before. Your cousin can be a part of that, we just need to take care of some things. You'll see. Life 2.0 is going to blow your mind."

His speech was rousing and I found myself feeling hopeful again. I leaned into him and he put his arms around me, holding me close. I felt safe and warm in his arms, and while I was content in that moment to just be held, I knew that soon I was going to want more.

And that scared the shit out of me.

Chapter Twenty-Seven

Mick

I DREAMT ABOUT JADE all night and woke up sweating and hard as a rock. Talking myself down wasn't working, either.

"To the shower I go."

I marched myself into the bathroom, naked and trying to push thoughts of her body out of my mind.

Jade was nowhere near ready for intimacy like that, and I was fine with it. Mornings spent jerking off in the shower were fine with me. I soaped up, grabbed hold, and pumped while I envisioned her soft skin, the curve of her waist, her thighs, my head between them, and her hard nipples as I pinched and pulled them.

I picked up speed as I thought about sitting her on top of me and watching her hair tumbling all over the place as she rode my cock, her perky tits bouncing up and down as her eyes rolled back in her head. I would grip those hips and pull her down hard, impaling her on my dick, making sure she felt every inch of my hardness inside her...

I was coming before I knew it, groaning in the shower as I envisioned filling her up and kissing her soft, full lips while I thrust myself inside her deeper and deeper.

The urge to collapse back onto the bed and get a couple more hours of sleep was strong, but I resisted. Instead, I pulled the drapes open, letting in the early morning light.

Today I would head out to grab our passports and identification. The first step toward our new life.

Except I was getting some pushback from Xander and Ian. Especially when I talked about heading to the Cayman Islands, at least for a while.

Yesterday, before the fiasco with Jade's cousin, Ian, Xander, and I had a heated debate about what we should do next. I thought back on the conversation, losing count of the red flags that I'd noted during the conversation.

It started off fine.

"Hey, Xander."

I'd wandered into the kitchen after my workout. The house had a complete gym, with weights, machines, bikes, treadmills, the whole shebang. Getting back to my workouts was comforting. I'd always burned off stress and worry by lifting and pushing myself. It felt good.

"Hey, Mick."

Xander sat at the island with a giant bowl of cereal and Ian was next to him, drinking an equally giant mug of coffee.

"Where's Ace?" I asked.

Ian jerked his thumb, gesturing toward the stairs.

"He's getting ready to take Jade down to the beach."

Xander frowned into his cereal bowl.

"What is it?"

"She's spending too much time out of the house. I don't like it. And what happened to two of us with her at all times?"

"I hear you, Xan, but someone needs to stay in the house, and we don't go out into the city alone. Ace can handle it. They are just going out onto the beach. You can probably monitor them right from the window."

"I don't understand why you don't want me to go with you, Mick," Xander complained.

I was noticing this about him more and more. Sure, Xander had always been given to bouts of depression and was often morose. But this wasn't his usual downtime. This was him being angsty. Complaining. Unsatisfied. I'd fully expected him to be consumed with Jade being back, and focusing all his attention on her. Instead, he was more consumed with Berto and Pierce. He was obsessed with what his uncle had left behind and what was going to happen to it. What was going to happen to his money, his houses, his businesses, and his will.

This interest in the business surprised me. He'd never been a flashy guy. Never been impressed with money. Never gave even one fuck about Berto's business.

Why now? What shifted?

"I told you. Me and Ian are on this. No big deal. We are heading over to the old safe house to see if there's any weapons left, any supplies. The security footage, anything."

"Yeah. Okay," he said, still staring into his bowl like it held the answers to the mysteries of the universe. Maybe it did.

Ian turned to Xander and gave him a long look.

"Bro, why don't you just talk to him?"

Uh-oh. Problems. We don't need problems.

Xander shrugged and put down his spoon.

"Yeah, sure."

I folded my arms across my chest and stood there waiting for the bullshit to begin. Drama was about to pour forth and I wasn't in the mood.

"I guess the first thing is I feel like we aren't doing enough to find Pierce."

Ah, this is where it's going. Fine.

"I hear you, but keep in mind that Pierce is probably laying real low. He murdered a bunch of women. Held them captive. Now those captives have escaped and now the police are actively looking for the kidnapper and murderer. You think he's going to be running around and showing himself at any of his old haunts?"

He seemed to consider that explanation, and for a minute, I thought I was going to get off easy.

No such luck.

"Yeah, but you forget this guy is a sick motherfucker who kills compulsively. It won't be too long before he does it again. He has to. He might have already."

I shook my head. "Doubt it."

Xander's nostrils flared at this, and he sprang up.

"I seriously don't think you understand the threat, here. He might go after the women he had captive. Because they got away. Because they know what he looks like, because he doesn't like unfinished business." Now he was pacing, pulling at the hairs sprouting from his chin. "And you know what? Neither do I."

"What's that supposed to mean?" I snapped.

Now it was Ian's turn.

"It means we have unfinished business here. I know you have your heart set on getting out of here, but it's starting to feel a lot like unnecessary running. And there are other things, too."

He looked at Xander, giving him an encouraging look, practically nudging him along.

"What, Xander? Spill it. We have shit to do today, you know that."

I was feeling progressively grumpier and thinking maybe I was getting too soft with these guys. There was a time not long ago when none of them would dare question me. Not even Ace, not Ian, and definitely not Xander.

What the fuck is going on with these kids?

"I'm just thinking, you know, about the Moreno organization. I mean, I know we were all set to get away from it, but that was when Berto was alive. And now, there are all these wannabes trying to edge in on our territory. Things we worked on. Things my dad built. I mean, doesn't it kind of bother you? And what if Pierce decides he wants to step up and take over? We can't let that happen, we can't let him get away—"

"I'm going to stop you right there, Xander. The whole reason we hatched a plan to retire in the first place was because you were done. You said it, you'd rather die than be a fucking gangster, killing people for a living..."

"Yeah. It's true. But I was just a stupid kid—"

This was insane. Insane.

"Are you telling me you *want* to be a criminal? You *want* to walk around with blood on your hands, always looking over your shoulder?"

I felt my face turning beet red.

"I already have blood on my hands, Mick. Don't you get it? Whatever innocence you were trying to protect is gone now. I killed half a dozen guys while we were working to get you and Ian free. That was me and Ace doing what we had to do for you. So yeah, that ship has sailed. And as far as looking over my shoulder? As long as Pierce is free to walk the streets I guess we'll be doing just that."

Okay, time to shut this shit down.

"Yeah? You want to take the helm? Take over the family business? You want to be the king of human trafficking and selling drugs to little kids? You want to go door to door sucking off of hardworking people and intimidating the local business people? You want to take away sons and daughters from their parents?"

Xander looked at me, wide-eyed. Ian looked away.

"You go right on ahead. But I want no fucking part of it."

Chapter Twenty-Eight

Ace

I HAD A STRONG feeling that things were about to go haywire and I didn't like that feeling at all.

Stretching out on the lounger on the third floor terrace, I marveled at the vivid hues of tonight's sunset. Fuck, I loved Southern California.

I'd spent a little time up in NorCal when Berto had some business, and by business, a couple of guys who owed him money that I needed to take care of.

San Francisco was awesome. I love cities and skylines and there was some really cool shit in that foggy, hilly, city by the bay.

But Los Angeles? There was no comparing it. The palm trees, the sunsets, the vibe. Yeah, some people called it a shithole, but to me, it was home.

And if you had the money, it was a nice home to have.

Jade brushed against my shoulder. The two of us had taken to watching sunsets together almost every night. It had been over a week since she ran into her cousin Tish. I felt like that had caused her to backslide a little. She was clearly hurting over her family.

I reached over and squeezed her hand, and turned to flash her my winning "everything is going to be alright" smile.

But I couldn't do anything but stare. She was fucking glorious, bathed in the sunset's glow, her eyes shining, her hair soft and flowing. Her smile was breathtaking and her body...

She was wearing those "yoga shorts" that defined her ass and showed off her shapely legs. And a bikini top. She was a vision and I felt my dick getting hard immediately.

I looked away and focused back on the sunset, trying not to get too worked up. We had all agreed that Jade and Jade alone would make a move when she was ready. She would be the one to initiate, and we would call it off in a heartbeat if it seemed for even a second like she was not in the right frame of mind, or in any way, shape, or form, not into it.

She reached over again, this time tracing her finger over my chest, now inching herself closer to me.

I was wearing nothing but swim shorts and at this point, there was no hiding my erection. I closed my eyes and swallowed roughly as her finger traced down my abdomen.

She drew her hand back and I turned to face her. A mischievous smile graced her pretty lips and I returned it.

"Look, Ace..."

I put my finger to her mouth to shush her.

"Hey, you don't have to explain."

"You shush. I *do* have to explain because I need you to know something."

"Oh?"

"Yeah. I need you to know that I want you. I think I'm ready to be with you."

I swallowed again and got even harder. I was ready to go, but I was freaking out because I didn't want to set her back. How was she sure she was ready? What if we did something and she regretted it? I couldn't bear the thought.

"See, I knew it," she said.

"Knew what?"

"I knew you would immediately overthink it."

That got a laugh out of me.

"Yeah, you got me."

She slowly rose off her chair and straddled the sun lounger I was reclining on, lowering herself until she was sitting on me. The feel of her weight on me, her skin against mine, and the little grind she instinctively did when she felt my hard dick against her about drove me insane with want.

But this was all about her. I took my hands off the wheel and vowed to myself that I would do everything in my power to make this good for her. To make her feel safe and loved.

She leaned down and kissed my lips, a slow, seductive kiss that sent chills running through my whole body. I reached for her, wrapping my arms around her but controlling myself. I wanted her to take the lead. Didn't want to make her regret one second of this.

After a good five minutes of making out like teenagers, she rose from me and extended her hand.

"I want you in my bed," she said with a smile.

Barely containing myself I followed her. She stripped off her clothes as we made our way to the giant bed, tossing pillows onto the floor and pulling back the coverlet, revealing decadent, silky sheets.

"Take off your clothes, Ace. I want to feel you, all of you."

I complied and she gazed at me in full appreciation, her eyes resting on my cock.

She licked her lips and I nearly exploded right there.

I crawled onto the bed and she pulled me on top of her and wrapped her arms around my neck and her legs around my waist.

"God you smell so good," she whispered in my ear, giving a playful nibble.

"Please touch me."

She let her arms fall to the sides and gazed at me with her gorgeous blue eyes, her hair fanned around her, spilling over the pillowcase.

"I've craved the feel of your skin, Jade."

She swallowed and grabbed for my hand, pulling it toward her, placing it on her breast, closing her eyes, and sighing deeply.

Her nipples were hard, begging to be licked and sucked, and I was so hard I could explode.

Deep breath, slow down.

Then she reached down and grabbed a hold of my cock, squeezing and moaning at the feel of how fucking hard I was.

"Fuck me, Ace. Now."

I mean, I can't exactly say no to a direct order, can I?

Chapter Twenty-Nine

Jade

His lips met mine, so warm and soft in contrast to the hardness of his body. Ace was lean and his smooth chest against mine felt so good.

There was still a part of me that feared I might freak out, that I might have second thoughts, but I knew if I did Ace would immediately stop and he would totally understand.

As if he read my mind again, he pulled away and smiled with his whole face, all the way up to the crinkle of his eyes.

"Hey, we can go as slow as you want. I can stop any time, and I am perfectly content to just hold you."

I laughed, my heart full of gratitude for this very nurturing yet devilishly sexy man in my bed.

"That's awesome, Ace. Now fuck me." I laughed and he leaned his head down, burying his face in my neck and giving me a playful bite.

I squirmed at the nip on my neck, squeezing my legs around him tighter as I pressed my body into him, desperate for friction and the feel of his skin.

"Oh my god, I want you inside me so bad." I gasped as his fingers finally drifted south and slipped into my wet pussy. I was so sensitive at this point, so ready and wanting. It felt like the slightest touch could bring me to climax.

He groaned as his fingers deftly worked, slipping over my swollen clit as he ran his tongue along the side of my neck. He scooted down to plant kisses down my chest before flicking his tongue over my nipple. His soft, teasing movements were just perfect, sending electricity through my body and making me even wetter.

His breath was more labored and his pupils were dilated as his body tensed. I knew he wanted me as bad as I wanted him, but he wouldn't rush, just kept teasing me, kissing me, caressing me.

Just as I was about to demand that he get to the business of fucking me before I changed my mind, he plunged his rock-hard cock inside me.

I cried out at the feel of him filling me, hiking my legs up and back further to give him more access to me. He had a giant dick, I think I forgot just how big he was until he pulled back and pushed back in.

I moaned, digging my nails into his back, arching my neck and squeezing my eyes shut, gasping as he drove into me again, his body trembling with urgency and also the strain of holding back. I knew he wanted to fuck me hard, harder than I could probably take right now, but his restraint made me even hotter for him.

"You feel so fucking good, Jade."

He slowed his pace and kissed me, a long, slow, passionate kiss that made me feel like he was savoring me. My body relaxed more and more as I surrendered to his love.

That's what it felt like. Making love. Not just hot and heavy fucking, but honest-to-goodness making *love.*

His slow strokes were bringing me closer to climax as he continued to ravish me with his kisses, trailing up and down my neck, back to my lips, with one arm wrapped around me and a fistful of my hair in his other hand.

We were truly joined, my body soft and accommodating, his hard and meant to bring me pleasure. Waves of warmth and electricity had me moaning and arching my back.

"Fuck." He gasped as he felt my body clench around him, practically convulsing with pleasure.

He increased his speed as I continued riding the waves of my orgasm, and within seconds he came, collapsing on top of me as he continued to push inside me, filling me with his hot cum.

Finally he kissed me again, then whispered in my ear.

"I love you, Jade."

"I love you, too." I nestled into the crook of his arm after he rolled onto his back and we just stayed like that for what felt like a long time, not talking, not doing anything but listening to the sounds of our own breath mingled with the crashing waves below the beach house.

After a while, he rolled onto his side and looked at me, tracing his fingers over my collarbone.

"Hey," he said. "How are you doing?"

I giggled a little and put my hand on his shoulder.

"You don't have to worry. I'm not traumatized or anything. I feel good. You felt good. I came so hard I saw stars, which is life goals, in case you didn't know."

He laughed and kissed me again, then wrapped his arms around me. The feel of his body and his embrace was pure bliss. *This is amazing. This is more than you could have ever hoped for.*

Chapter Thirty

Ian

There was a palpable tension in the house and it was getting to me. Xander was moody as fuck, holed up in his room poring over file after file in his uncle's computers, looking for answers to questions he never knew he had.

Mick was getting snappy, and Ace was desperately trying to mediate between the two of them.

"What's so funny?" Jade asked.

We were both in the kitchen enjoying the breakfast Ace had just made, and I couldn't help but marvel at the transformation he'd undergone since Jade had come into our lives. He was a new man. A man that would rather strap on an apron than a gun.

"Nothing."

"Oh, okay. I like to laugh at nothing, too. Just sit there cackling at jack shit for the hell of it."

She flared her nostrils and frowned at me but I just laughed some more.

"Ooh, you want to fuck around, huh?" she challenged.

I put up my hands in mock surrender.

"Now, Jade. I'm not trying to fuck around. I was just thinking about Ace. He makes a mean breakfast burrito."

"True." She narrowed her eyes. "But that's not funny."

"It is if you've known Ace as long as I have. I mean, he's always had a thing for cooking, but he also has always had a thing for torturing his victims before he caves their head in with a hammer."

Her eyes widened, and I realized my error immediately. Jade knew we'd killed, but she knew it in more of a "cops and robbers" kind of way. She didn't know that Ace was bloodthirsty as fuck, or at least he used to be.

She didn't really know how much I loved boosting shit. Pulling off big jobs, and that I didn't mind putting a bullet in someone to cover my tracks or to collect a debt, or for just about any reason.

She didn't realize that Mick was the softest one of us, but he'd done his fair share of horrible things, things she probably wouldn't understand. And she didn't realize that the only reason we'd decided to retire was because Mick was getting old and because we were worried about Xander.

And now Xander was coming into his own. No longer that timid kid. No longer that kid who couldn't hurt a fly.

Nope, he'd tasted blood, and he wanted more.

"Ian." She snapped her fingers. "You still with me?"

"Yeah."

"What were you thinking about just now?"

I looked down at her perfect face, staring into her eyes, so blue and despite all she'd been through in life, still somehow holding an innocence that defied all odds.

"Thinking about all the things you don't know about us. Thinking about how much Ace has changed. How much Xander has changed."

Her expression shifted at the mention of Xander.

"I'm worried about him."

"He'll be fine. Xander's been through a lot of shit and it haunts him. And this last few months? He felt like it was his fault that you got taken. He was mad with fear and guilt. For a little while, he didn't know if Mick had made it. Didn't know if you were dead or alive or what you were going through."

I paused, reading her expression. She'd never really asked questions about us, but she wasn't dumb and didn't exactly grow up sheltered.

"Him and Ace had to do a lot of stuff to get me and Mick free, and to try and find you. It changed him."

She looked down at her food and I could tell by the way her mouth was working that she was feeling like shit.

Strike two, dipshit. Why do you open your mouth sometimes?

"Mick and Ace just want to leave here, don't they?"

I nodded. "That's the idea. That was the original plan. We were going to get as much money together as we could and get our asses to paradise."

"And now?"

"Well, Mick and Ace still want to do that."

"This *is* paradise." She smiled for a second, then her eyes went dark. "We can't leave with Pierce still out there. We can't let him get away. Do you guys know anything? Any leads?"

We'd intentionally been avoiding talking about Pierce in front of Jade. There had been a couple of supposed sightings, but they hadn't panned out. Mick was sure he'd gone deep underground. Xander was sure he wouldn't stay down for long. There was too much money and power to grab for.

"I agree. He has to go down. He's only going to hurt more people. But we also can't endanger you—"

"I will be out of danger if he's dead, right? I mean, he can always come back for me."

I shook my head. "We won't let anything happen to you."

The look in her eyes said she didn't believe me. And that was soul-crushing.

After breakfast, she bounded upstairs, full of energy and announcing that she was "hitting the yoga mat" and then taking a shower. Two things I would love to sit and observe.

But it was time for business. Mick, Xander, Ace, and I were going to have ourselves a little meeting.

"Hey, yo." Ace bumped into me as we made our way to Mick's suite for our sit down.

"What's this all about?" Ace rubbed his chin nervously.

"We need to straighten some stuff out." Was all I said.

Xander and Mick were already waiting for us. Mick's room was the biggest bedroom in the house, with Jade's coming in second. It was more like an apartment within the house, with a separate living room, a bar, full-size refrigerator, sink, microwave, bathroom of course, and an extensive balcony with patio chairs and a foosball table.

The place was sexy as fuck, and I was a little jealous. Not that there was anything wrong with my room. It was big, it had an ensuite bathroom and gorgeous views. But this shit was next level.

I flopped down on the sofa while Mick sat in his leather chair. Xander plopped down next to me and Ace slid down onto the floor, resting his back against the loveseat.

Mick leaned his elbows on his knees and looked at me, then at Xander.

"Okay, here's the deal. I have passports, I have identification, and I can get us a private jet to take us to any island we want to go to. I say we head to the Cayman Islands, but if you have a better suggestion, I'm open."

Ace broke into a grin.

"I'll take the Cayman Islands, although I've always wanted to go to Jamaica. Maybe we can spend a couple of months in one place, then go somewhere else?"

Mick nodded. "I guess. I mean, I always saw us finding a spot and just staying put, but if you want to travel a bit, I don't see anything wrong with that."

I cleared my throat. "Are you guys forgetting something? Anything?"

Mick sighed and Ace pulled a face at me, kind of a "here we go" look.

"Ian, we've talked about this."

"No, you've talked about this. This is all you want to talk about. We made a promise, in case you forgot."

Mick nodded his head.

"Yeah, I made a promise that I was going to get you guys out of this life before it either killed you or ruined you. That's the promise I made. That's what I've been working on. Nothing has changed."

"Bullshit. Everything has changed. When they took Jade and put her in a cage, when we realized those cut up dead girls were Pierce's work, everything changed. When I slit Berto's throat and dumped him in the desert, things sure as shit changed. Why are you turning a blind eye to this? We swore we would find Pierce and make him pay. That's what I intend to do."

The three of them looked at me. Ace blinked at me like I'd grown a third arm out of my forehead. Xander was expressionless. Mick had the look of a man who thought he was off work for the weekend but realized he misread the schedule and still had another four hours to go.

He was weary. I got it, I did. But I was right, and he knew it.

I stayed silent, waiting for them to process what I had said, waiting for the argument or the acceptance.

Moments ticked by and I could see Xander biting his tongue, waiting for one of them to speak.

Finally, Ace did.

"I want Pierce dead, too. You know that. He's less than trash and he deserves a slow, painful death. Emphasis on slow and painful. I guess I just started thinking that our lives and the life of Jade is more important than him. Like, us running circles trying to find him and make him pay is just us wasting our energy. Energy we could spend building something good for once."

Xander flinched at that.

"But I hear you, Ian. We can't risk this fucker killing again, or coming after Jade. Eventually, we'll let our guard down, and eventually he'll come after us."

Now it was Mick's turn.

"You really think so? You think he's going to leave the country to find us and fuck with us? You think he's going to scour the globe in search of us? You think we are really that important to him?"

Finally, Xander spoke up.

"Yeah. I do. He's just like Berto. As far as he's concerned, we took something from him. Something that belonged to him. We got one over on him and he will not let it stand. Don't ask me how I know that, but I do."

Mick nodded and combed his fingers through his hair.

"Yeah, I could see that, especially if he knew we were in the area. The temptation to come after her would be huge. But again, I say he will not risk coming after us out of the country. He's going to get caught, no matter how slick he thinks he is. He'll fuck up."

I pointed at him. "Yes, he'll fuck up. And we'll be there for it. We'll be there to get him, to make him pay. To remove him from the earth like the stain he is."

Mick slumped in his chair a bit and looked off to the side, as though seeing the view out the window for the first time. I knew we were making sense to him. He knew that we couldn't just let him go. He was a fucking disease that needed to be cut out. We couldn't just let him fester and spread.

"So are you staying, Mick? Are you with us?" Xander asked.

Mick turned sharply to him. "Am I staying? Am I with you?"

Xander nodded. "Yeah, that's what I said."

I sucked in my breath a little and watched Ace's eyes widen. Xander was pushing Mick hard. And I hoped like hell he didn't start launching into his plan to revive the Moreno family, with him as head.

Because that was his plan. I knew it without him even saying anything. He wanted to step up into the role of head honcho. He wanted to be everything Mick had tried so hard to keep him safe from.

He had gone over to the dark side.

Chapter Thirty-One

Jade

I SANG IN THE shower, belting out my favorite Billie Eilish song while I massaged my scalp and swayed my hips, giving no fucks if anyone could hear my crappy voice.

I was feeling myself in a big way. Even with the tension in the house, even with the whole talk about Pierce and Xander and Ace being a fucking Norman Bates level psycho, I was good.

Hooking up with Ace could have gone one of two ways: It could have put me back into the darkness, or it could have brought me further into the light. Fortunately for me, it was door number two. Being with him felt so good, so right. He was gentle and patient and loving. He took such good care of me, and I couldn't wait to feel his touch again.

Now that I'd broken through that barrier, I found myself fantasizing about the other guys. Kissing Ian's pouty lips. Running my fingers through Xander's dark locks. Feeling Mick's powerful arms wrapped around me.

Time for a little self-love in the shower.

I reached down and found my pussy slick and engorged from want. It took less than a minute to get myself off, and far from satiating my hunger, it only stoked it.

Grabbing my fluffy towel off the counter, I caught a look at myself in the mirror. I smiled, pleased with the progress I'd made. Before being kidnapped on my twenty-first birthday, I'd been underweight and weak from stress and not eating enough healthy food. I lived on frozen burritos and plain peanut butter sandwiches on cheap white bread.

My short time at the first house with the guys helped. I was eating good. Lots of food. I'd put on weight.

Then the cage. They fed us enough to survive, and to be totally honest I probably ate better as Berto's captive than I did at home with my parents. But I was sick all the time, and the stress made it hard for me to eat. Sometimes I couldn't keep my food down and I would have to puke in the same bucket I pissed and shit in. If my keepers caught wind that I had thrown up, they would punish me by withholding food for a day or two.

I shuddered just thinking about it. My mind wandered to Missy and Darlene. I wondered what had happened to them. Wondered if Missy was still at Jesse's ranch, and whether Darlene had gone back to her former job as stripper, something I'd picked up eavesdropping on Nelson before his timely demise.

Whatever, who cares where those bitches are?

I was tan, strong and healthy. I wasn't just coming back to myself, I was blowing past the old me and not looking back.

My walk-in closet was filling out nicely. I had been shopping like nobody's business lately and I didn't feel bad about it at all.

"It's my turn, bitches."

I slipped on a gauzy sundress, applied lip gloss, and fluffed up my wavy hair, going for a sun-kissed, windblown look. Romantic, flirty, and carefree.

I'd never considered myself vain, but something inside me had shifted as I stopped focusing on everyone else and started focusing on me.

"This isn't vanity, this is self-appreciation," I declared, winking at myself in the mirror.

I grabbed my phone and remembered that Tish had programmed her number in it. My heart ached for her. I missed her so much. The guys didn't want me to text her or contact her anymore, but I really didn't see the harm. She wouldn't tell Eddie, and she didn't know anything about anything.

Taking a deep breath, I quickly fired off a text.

Hey Tish, it's me. Just wanted to say hi. This is my number, don't call it, but you can text me any time. My guy is super protective. He doesn't want anyone to know where I am for my own safety. Please don't tell that dickhead Eddie you saw me, or that you even know I am alive, okay? Just let's keep this between us. Love you, Tish.

On my way out of my bedroom door, I heard grumbling and sighing, and followed the sound to Mick's room.

He was sitting at his desk, arms folded across his chest, muttering words I couldn't make out, but he was clearly frustrated and irritated.

The guys were keeping some things from me, that was a fact. But I knew Mick wanted out of here. Wanted to get away from everything, to stop looking for Pierce and to put everything behind him.

It made sense. I understood. He wanted to be done, to move on with his life, to be happy.

And so did I. But first, we had to find Pierce. We had a duty to put that fucker down like a rabid dog.

I cleared my throat and stood there, smiling in his doorway like a complete dork.

He turned his head and for a split second his eyes darkened with desire as he took me in from head to toe. I felt my face get hot and for a second I lost the ability to speak, so I just waved like a dork until I could regain my verbal skills.

"Hey, whatcha doing?"

He shook his head. All business again.

"Just making a list of people we can go pay a visit to. People who might have some idea where Pierce might be. It's a short list, but it's a start."

I strolled into his spotless suite, decorated in shades of gray and crisp white. He was a simple guy. No fluff, just the minimum.

Something about him never failed to deliver full-body chills when he looked me up and down.

"Hey, Mick? I don't want to bug you or anything, but..."

He uncrossed his arms and looked at me, his eyes softening and brightening. He patted his lap and said,

"Sweetheart, you could never bug me. Not even if you tried. Come over here, let's talk."

I bit my lip and smiled, then climbed onto his lap, putting my arms around his neck.

"Do you have anything solid, or is it all a guessing game?"

"Xander knows a couple of guys Pierce spent a lot of time with that live in the area. These guys are heavy hitters with a lot of resources. One of them partnered with Berto in some kind of underground weapons business, the other ran part of his prostitution ring. These guys were inner circle all the way, and when Xander and Ace were trying to root out anyone who knew anything about anything, these two were nowhere to be found."

"Huh, so you think these guys would be more likely to help Pierce? Or would they see an opportunity and just make a grab for the Moreno throne?"

He smiled at me, looking right into my eyes, holding my gaze. I looked down at my manicured toes poking out of my sandals and shrugged, swallowing and willing my heart to stop thumping so hard.

"You're smart, Jade. I hate you worrying or thinking about any of this. What I want for you is zero stress, not a fucking care in the world. Go to the beach any time you want. Buy anything you want. Feel safe. Feel taken care of. Eat good, sleep good. Laugh and be happy. That's what I want for you."

I blushed, feeling a warmth in my chest at his words. My heart melted and I tightened my embrace.

"You *do* make me feel safe and cared for. And I've been doing so good, Mick. You know that?"

He nodded. "Yes, and I just want it to get better and better for you. That's why I wanted to leave. Why I want to take you away from all of this."

"I know. And I love you for that. And I know Ian and Xander do, too. But we have to take him down, Mick. We have to make him pay and make sure no one else goes through what I went through. You weren't there, Mick. You didn't see how he was, the things he did, how he laughed at our suffering. At my suffering. I don't even think he's human. I think he's pure evil. Evil like that can't exist."

His expression was drawn as I spoke, the emotion making my voice shake.

"Shhh. I know, Jade. That's why I agreed to this. And I promise, we will find him and put a stop to him."

I smiled, then leaned in and kissed him.

Chapter Thirty-Two

Jade

For a moment he stiffened, like he wasn't sure what to do. I stopped and pulled away, frowning and suddenly feeling like I shouldn't have kissed him.

"I -- I'm sorry."

He raised his eyebrows in shock at my apology and cupped my face in his hands, engulfing me. I couldn't believe a person could have hands that big, but then again...

"Oh, my god, Jade. Don't you dare be sorry. I just wasn't expecting you to kiss me like that. You kind of took me by surprise. In a good way," he added.

"You sure?"

I was officially questioning myself. I knew how Mick got when he was in work mode. All gruff and grumpy. Maybe I made a mistake coming in here.

He pulled my face close to his, kissing me softly and sending those full-bodied chills through my body.

"It's been so long since I've tasted those sweet lips of yours, Jade. It's like coming home."

That got a smile out of me, and the stirrings of desire became more insistent as I kissed him again, feeling his arms engulf me in a gentle embrace.

Gentle didn't last long, though. My kisses grew hungrier and I turned myself around so I was straddling him on his office chair, grinding my pussy against his hardness, wrapping my arms around his neck and trembling with anticipation because I knew he was ready for me but I wasn't sure I was ready for him.

Mick was a fucking giant compared to me, his biceps were easily the size of my waist and I felt like he could snap me in half if he wanted.

But he wasn't some clumsy oaf knocking shit over and lumbering around or anything. He was smooth and sure, always moving with purpose, never just barging his way through unless of course, he was taking someone down. Even that was graceful.

Mick made me feel safe always, but there was an element of danger to him. I felt it the first time I saw him and couldn't even look him in the eye.

"What do you want, Princess? Tell me."

He had hold of my hips and as he pressed me tightly against him, I moved them, giving an involuntary moan at the sensations the friction sparked inside me.

"I want you, Mick."

"What do you want me to do?"

He squeezed me, holding me against him as I squirmed against his rock-hard cock, begging to be let out, straining against his pants.

He skimmed one hand from my waist, up my torso, stopping briefly to cup my breast, then kept going, stopping to caress my neck, placing his thumb on my throat, gazing into my eyes intently as my heart pounded in my chest and my breath caught.

"Tell me what you want, Princess, so I can give it to you."

I whimpered as he squeezed a little. When he reached his other hand down, pulling up my skirt and slipping his finger under my panties, his pupils dilating when he felt how soaked I was.

"I want you to fuck me."

He growled, and with me straddling him, rose from the chair, just stood up like no big deal while I wrapped my legs around him, eager to see what he would do next.

I figured he would take me to the bed, but instead he just turned around and lowered me on the desk.

No words were exchanged as he pushed up the skirt of my dress, then pulled down the straps and top, revealing my bare chest.

He licked his lips and pulled off my underwear.

I reached for the button on his pants but couldn't reach. It didn't matter because he was already on it, pulling his shirt off with one hand while he unbuttoned his pants with the other.

He pulled down his pants and my eyes widened seeing the size of him. I hadn't forgotten, but still.

"You want me to fuck you, Princess? You want me to fill up your pussy till it can't take any more?"

"Yes," I gasped, my cheeks burning and my pussy aching for his cock.

He pulled me roughly toward him, pushed my legs back, and then trailed his hand down till it found me wet and slick.

"You're so fucking ready, but I want to play with you a little, baby."

I nodded, unable to speak as he teased my clit with one hand and pinched my nipple between his thumb and forefinger with the other.

The combination of the work he was doing on my clit and my nipples was driving me insane. I was practically frothing at the mouth I wanted him so bad. My release was close, but I didn't want to come yet, I wanted to wait.

"Please," I moaned. "I need you inside me."

"Hmm. You're lucky it's been a while and I need you as bad as you need me. Otherwise, I would tease you all day."

I whimpered and squirmed some more and he mercifully withdrew his fingers from me, taking a moment to suck the wetness from them as he looked me dead in the eye.

He took his cock in his hand and guided it to my opening. I was so wet but I still cried out when he entered me. He was slow and gentle going in, already knowing from before that it took a minute for my body to relax enough to accommodate his size.

"That's it, good girl. Take more of it."

He reached over and tapped my cheek. My eyes were squeezed shut and when I opened them he was smiling.

"Quit holding your breath."

I didn't realize I was, but I exhaled and took in a deep breath as he slid his cock deeper inside me.

"Yes," I whispered, feeling his size filling my body, dropping my legs back further to encourage him to go deeper.

"I love that you love my cock inside you. You want more?"

I nodded, once again unable to speak.

He started fucking me, slowly at first but quickly picking up speed as I cried out, calling his name, then covering my mouth because I was suddenly shy about the other guys hearing me scream and moan.

"I can do that for you."

He pulled my hand from my mouth, replacing it with his, covering it while he fucked me harder, my cries now muffled by his hand as he fucked me on his desk.

Mick could be gentle, I suppose. For a minute or two.

But there was nothing gentle about the way he was driving his cock into me. He went harder and harder, the sound of him slapping against my skin as he gripped me tighter and went at me with even more force, his cock driving deep into me.

I was seeing stars at this point and when he hitched my hips up and switched up his pace I felt like I could pass out. The angle was now just right and I was seconds from coming all over his dick.

"Fuuck," he moaned as he gripped me tighter, quickening his pace, his muscles rippling and his breath coming out in gasps. His eyes were dark with hunger and as he was fucking me it felt like he was consuming me, fucking his way into every part of me, engulfing me with his body, making me his.

An orgasm ripped through my body, taking me by surprise even though I knew I was on the verge.

He felt it, too, and took his hand off my mouth just as I cried out.

"That's it, Princess, scream for me."

He started thrusting harder as I went limp, satiated and gone full jelly mode.

Just when the stimulation was getting to be too much, he climaxed, spilling into me. He collapsed onto my chest, still careful not to crush me under his weight.

He wrapped his arms around my torso and lifted me off the desk, still inside my pussy.

"I'm going to lay you down right here, Princess." He withdrew from me but still held me in his arms, walking over to the bed and gently lowering me, keeping his eyes fixed on mine.

I relaxed into the blankets as he stood up and started to turn around.

"Where are you going?" I pouted.

He smiled and leaned down, kissing my lips and caressing my cheek.

"Just hold on." He disappeared for a moment, then returned. "I'm running you a bath."

He bent down and picked me up, walked into the bathroom, the whole way whispering in my ear. When we came to a stop in front of the bathtub, he stood me on my feet.

"I love you, Jade. I want you to know that I will always take care of you, protect you, and provide for you."

I nodded, feeling full and a little sore, content and sleepy, and loving that he was tending to my needs as I came down from my euphoric high.

He kissed my hand and helped as I stepped into the bath. "Hold on."

I nodded as I sunk into the marble tub, feeling the heat of the water embracing me as I closed my eyes and sighed.

He returned quickly with a glass of water and a plate of fruit.

"Damn, where did you pull that from?"

That got a chuckle out of him. "My fridge, Princess. I'm pretty well stocked up here, come by for snacks anytime."

"Wow." I gulped down some water and popped a juicy strawberry into my mouth while he climbed into the tub and slid down behind me.

I leaned back against his chest, positioned between his legs. He selected another strawberry and fed it to me while I relaxed against him.

"This is heavenly."

He placed his hand on my stomach, gliding over it, softly touching me, and kissed the top of my head.

"This is nothing less than what you deserve every single day, Princess."

We stayed like this for a while, and I allowed him to pamper, caress, murmur sweet words into my ear, and feed me.

It felt so fucking good.

"Mick?"

"Yes?"

"I don't want to leave here. I know you want to take us away from here, but I don't want to go. I don't want to run. I want to be able to feel safe anywhere."

He was silent but continued stroking my skin, nuzzling, and loving on me.

"And one other thing."

"Go ahead, Princess."

"I want Pierce to pay for what he did. Then, I want him dead."

Chapter Thirty-Three

Mick

Being with Jade was like putting on a pair of magic glasses that made everything crystal clear.

I was no longer plagued with indecision or doubt. She wanted Pierce dead, and she wanted to stay put. Those two things, which had seemed so complicated and filled me with dread and stress were now my ultimate mission. She loved it here. This was her dream house. This was where she felt strong and comfortable and inspired.

"What Jade wants, she gets."

That was a motto I could live my life by. Ace agreed. Even though I knew he shared my concern about the direction Xander and Ian were going in, he was clear on the same two things I was clear on: We kill Pierce, and we secure our position. We make it so Jade could feel safe on the beach, walking down the street, shopping at the mall, or getting a latte at her favorite coffee shop.

She was done running. That meant I was, too.

Deep down inside, in a place that I even hid from myself, I wanted a family and a home. A place to call my own. A safe place for the people I love.

I considered Ace, Ian, and Xander my family.

And now, Jade.

The last pink and purple glow of the sunset faded in the sky and the first stars started twinkling.

I grabbed a duffel bag and the keys to my truck.

Xander and Ian were going to stay with Jade. Ace was coming with me. Anyone who knew anything about Ace knew enough to want to avoid his bag of tricks, and the people we were looking for knew Ace.

Ace leaned against the doorjamb with his backpack slung over his shoulder and a familiar grin on his face.

He had been so ready to jump on board a plane and head out of the country, set up house in some beach village, and spend life drinking coconut juice and wearing flip-flops.

But here he was, ready to go. Berto used to call him the "Ace up his sleeve" but now he didn't belong to Berto.

Like me, he belonged to Jade.

Ace hopped in the truck and within minutes we were driving away from our exclusive beachfront community and on our way to Los Angeles, checking out the nooks and crannies most folks knew nothing about. There was a club, a couple of other locations to check, and a few other leads.

I had a strong feeling we were going to get our hands really dirty tonight.

"What's our first stop?"

"The club."

Okay, so there were plenty of clubs in Los Angeles, of course. There were famous clubs. There were very genre-specific clubs, hole-in-the-wall clubs, mainstream clubs, and gentlemen's clubs.

But then there were the clubs most people didn't know about. Clubs you couldn't find with a Google search.

"The club" didn't have a name other than that. It was Berto's haven and where he did a lot of his business. It was a place you weren't supposed to know about unless you were on the inside.

If you weren't on the inside and you found yourself here, you probably wouldn't be leaving alive.

And we weren't on the inside anymore.

It was early on a Monday evening. Chances were better than average there wouldn't be much of a crowd. Would Pierce be there? I doubted it.

But Stevie would be there, and he was tight with Pierce.

Stocky, red-faced, and chronically pissed was the best way to describe this guy. Oh, and dangerous. He was smart, too. Stevie handled a lot of the day-to-day stuff that Berto couldn't be bothered with. Collections, paperwork, accounting, paying bills and keeping abreast of what Berto's people were doing. He knew stuff about stuff. You wanted the latest gossip, numbers, news? You went to Stevie.

"You think he'll know? Where to find Pierce?"

I guided the truck into a parking lot about a block down. The lot was nearly full and people milled about, on their way to shop or coming off of work, or going to a nearby restaurant.

The Club was hiding in plain sight and I couldn't help but laugh, thinking about how many things went on there that people were blissfully unaware of.

"He knows. Or if he doesn't know exactly, he knows something."

I heard him exhale deeply. He was rubbing his palms on his jeans and had his head tilted back and his eyes closed. He was getting his head on right while I dug into my duffel back, grabbed two guns, a knife, and a stick of gum.

Put one gun in my waistband, another in my holster, and the knife under my pant leg.

Ace grabbed his "violence accessories" and we were on our way.

There was no talking as we walked down the sidewalk. We'd already covered everything we could think of before we left the house. Talking now would just be second-guessing and creating unnecessary anxiety.

Yeah, we were out of practice, but this shit is like riding a bike.

We turned down an alley, cutting through to the next block, came out of the alley, hung a right, opened a door, walked down a hall, opened the second door on the right, then went down the stairs.

"Secret knock time."

Ace winked and put his hand on his gun. I rapped twice, paused, rapped three times, paused, then rapped once.

We were strung tight with anticipation and while I had that pit of dread in my gut because I was actively doing something I'd promised myself I was done with, the old excitement was still there.

A big part of me loved this shit. Once upon a time, crime replaced drinking for me. I didn't need alcohol to leave my body and shut off my mind. I could just put a gun in my hand.

The door cracked open and a kid I didn't recognize opened it, looking first at me, then at Ace. He narrowed his eyes, then widened them as he recognized him. Everyone knew Ace, even if they'd never seen him before.

"Hiya," Ace said, beaming a bright smile at him. That was Ace. He was a ray of fucking sunshine.

He said nothing, but opened the door wider and stepped aside, letting us through. Then he disappeared into the darkness.

There was a soft thrum of music in the background and I felt my way to the curtain that led to the main room. The dark hallway was meant to disorient and put you at a disadvantage. I kept my hand on my gun and when I pulled aside the curtain and made my way inside, I couldn't help but smile.

This was going to be good.

Sitting right at the head table was Stevie himself. And with him was Rafe, the other guy we were hoping to talk to. My eyes scanned the room, and I saw some random dude, a couple of dancers and other entertainers, a bartender, and two bouncers guarding an exit. When I turned my back, I saw a guy bigger than me cradling his automatic weapon, guarding the door we'd just come in through.

We were here, for better or for worse.

Stevie didn't smile when he saw us, but Rafe did.

"Look at that, Stevie. The prodigal sons have returned. Maybe they want to rejoin the team?"

Stevie shook his head. "Nah. I don't think so."

He looked me up and down, and his eyes darted to Ace and rested back on me.

"You shouldn't be here, Mick. Neither of you should be here."

Ace cocked his head. "Nice to see you, too, Stevie."

He straightened himself in his chair. "I'm serious, kid. I took you boys for smarter than this. You have passports. Why are you still in town? You could be out of the country with your pretty little girl, but no, you're showing up here, in my club, to make trouble. Can't figure that out for the life of me, and I consider myself a pretty smart guy."

Ace looked at me, and I shook my head slightly. Stevie knew everything about everyone. He already knew we'd bought passports. Knew we had Jade back. He knew probably more. That's why we were here. He had to know that. He was just playing stupid.

"Now, Stevie," I said, making my way to the table.

The guys with guns moved in closer, but the girls didn't stop dancing, and the bartender didn't stop pouring drinks. The guys at the bar glanced over in curiosity but went back to their drinks. Everyone knew the drill. Mind your business.

"Don't 'now Stevie' me."

He looked genuinely alarmed, and it crossed my mind that he was afraid. Afraid not necessarily of me or even Ace, but of what our visit meant for him.

"Look, Stevie. You know why we are here. At least I think you do. If you don't, I'm happy to tell you," I said, keeping it good-natured.

Rafe patted the seat next to him and smiled. "Stevie boy, don't be so uptight. These guys are cool, you know that. Let's just have a drink and hear what they have to say?"

Stevie shot him a death look and shook his head. "No, we don't do business with these guys. They fucking killed Berto. They killed him and stole from him and they are traitors. Dead to us. If they are smart, they will turn around and get the fuck out of here before they bring us trouble."

"Too late," Ace said. "You are right, Stevie. We brought you trouble. You let us in here and now you are going to have to explain to Pierce how you let us in, talked to us, and let us go."

I smiled. Ace was great in these sorts of situations.

The poor guy's face fell for a minute, but he snapped back with a lopsided grin and an icy glint in his eye.

"You think you can come here and fuck with me like this? You're stupid and crazy. The both of you. And yeah, you're right, Ace. You don't just get to walk out of here, and Pierce is going to be real pleased to see you. Now that I think about it, this was just the stroke of luck I needed."

Rafe glanced at him, a wave of uncertainty sweeping across his face.

"Boss, you shouldn't be saying..."

"Cut it, Rafe. We can say whatever the fuck we want. These guys aren't leaving the club alive."

Rafe shrugged. "Might as well have a seat. Right after you give up your guns."

Ace grinned. "That's not going to happen."

Chapter Thirty-Four

Jade

I SAT ON THE couch drinking beers with Ian and Xander, trying my best to keep my mind from worrying about Mick and Ace. What they were doing was risky, but completely necessary. And scary.

"So they are going to do what? Talk to these guys? Ask them questions? Why would these guys tell them anything?"

Xander huffed a laugh and tipped back his beer. Something about him was getting to me. I missed the sweet, caring Xander. He'd changed. I still loved him, but he was distant. Ever since everything that happened in the desert. He was there for me. I knew he'd risked his life to save me and that he'd protect me no matter what.

But he was hardened. Closed off.

"They aren't going to just ask and hope they get answers. They aren't going to just walk away if they don't get cooperation. You know that, right? You understand that the mission might be to kill Pierce, but it's not just him that's going to die. Other guys are going to get killed. Most will deserve it. Some won't. Some might get caught in the crossfire. It's going to be messy, Jade."

I swallowed and nodded my head. I guess I knew that. Did I care? I checked in with myself to see how I felt about Ace and Mick going in, guns blazing, mowing down a bunch of guys in order to get to Pierce.

"Huh. I guess I don't give a shit." I shrugged. "That's bad, right?"

Xander looked over at me and smiled, then reached for my hand. I reached back, and he gave it a squeeze. "No, it's not bad. After what you've been through? None of them are innocent. And honestly, the more of his guys we take out, the better. Anyone who thinks Pierce is a 'cool guy' needs to go. Anyone who thinks they need to head up the Moreno family 3.0 needs to go. Basically, the more, the merrier."

Okay. That's a little extreme.

But I didn't really care how many of Berto and Pierce's guys they killed. He kind of had a point. By getting rid of anyone who was loyal to either of them, they were making sure we were safe and could stay put.

You're a fucking monster. Xander's not the only one who changed.

Bullshit, you are fine. You meditate and do yoga and read all those books.

Okay, that doesn't make you any less of a killer.

That was a punch to the gut. I'd successfully managed to "love and light" my way into stuffing that memory of blowing Lydia's head off, but now it was front and center, the look of raw, unadulterated fear on her face, the horror when she realized she was, in fact, about to die.

"What are you smiling about?" Ian asked me.

My eyes grew wide.

"I'm smiling? No, I'm not smiling."

Xander laughed and tossed a pillow at me. "You were smiling."

Great. Just fucking great.

"I don't know. I'm going to grab some more beers. Who wants one?"

Xander stood up and opened his arms out to me for a hug. “Hey, I’ll pass, I’m crashing. Gimme a hug.”

I smiled and melted into his arms. Yeah, he was different, but he was still Xander. I nuzzled my face into his sweatshirt and inhaled, then looked up at him and smiled. He leaned down and gave me a soft, quick peck on the lips. I fought the urge to pull his face back down for a deeper kiss, but decided against it. My gut told me that Xander was too preoccupied to be with me like that. Maybe I was wrong, but I had the feeling that until he knew Pierce was dead he was going to remain distant, distracted, and grumpy.

“Night Ian.” He waved at Ian and Ian raised his beer at him.

“Sleep good.”

That left Ian and me, and when I returned to the couch with two more brews, I snuggled in a little closer.

Ian held me in his arms, stroking my hair and occasionally planting a soft kiss on my temple. I felt content, mostly, but still worried about Ace and Mick. They’d been gone a good three hours.

“Hey, they won’t be home any time soon, if you are worrying about them.”

“How did you know?”

“Because I know you worry about us when we leave.”

“Yeah. I do. Especially with this. I just feel like Pierce is still a threat. I know Mick thinks he’s just lying low and trying not to get those murders pinned on him, but he’s crazy. And I feel like he’s going to blame everything that happened on me.”

Ian tensed at that, then leaned over and kissed me again.

“Pierce is a psycho, and yeah, he had it out for all of us. That’s why we will not stop till we find him and put an end to him. He will not hurt you again.”

I smiled and snuggled into him, inhaling his scent and feeling the warmth of his skin.

My phone started vibrating on the coffee table and I had a weird sinking feeling in my belly.

“Want me to grab it for you?”

I nodded. “Maybe it’s Ace, texting me. He knows I worry.”

He grabbed my phone and handed it to me without looking at it. I appreciated that about him. He was protective, but he respected my privacy.

I looked at my phone and saw that the text was from Tish. My gut went into immediate panic mode. My fingers shook for no apparent reason. She was probably just texting me back.

The message was simple: Call me.

I scrambled off of Ian and sat up on the couch, my heart pounding.

“I don’t know what’s wrong with me, Ian. Tish texted me—”

“She has your phone number?” Ian smacked his forehead and blew out an exasperated breath.

I nodded. “Yeah, look. It’s not a big deal. I just wanted to text with my cousin.”

“Okay, so what? She wants you to call her. Just text her back and see if everything is okay.”

“I have a bad feeling.”

He looked at me, and his eyes told me he took my bad feeling seriously.

“Call her. Put her on speaker.”

“Yeah, okay.”

I hit the call button, and it rang once, twice, three times. And then she picked up.

“Hello, Tish?”

“Ah, there you are, six.”

The blood drained from my face, and my vision fogged.

Ian’s eyes widened first, then darkened. He put his fingers up to his lips, then squeezed my shoulder, giving me a reassuring look and motioning for me to speak. He mouthed the words “Where’s Tish?” and again, motioned for me to ask the question.

I mustered up every ounce of fire I had in me, every part of me that Pierce hadn’t annihilated.

“Pierce, you dick. Where is my cousin?”

He laughed and I closed my eyes, my chest tightening and a sharp pain running through me. It was like my soul was cracking right there as I sat holding the phone out.

"You have me on speaker, six. Who is with you? Oh, I know. Ian. I know it's Ian because Mick and Ace are tied up at the club, and Xander, that traitor piece of shit, is on the phone right now. Talking to one of my guys. A guy who's loyal to me. And that leaves Ian. What a waste. Nothing but a pussy whipped pile of garbage. Over *you*. You fucking whore."

Ian shook his head and held his hand out for the phone. I gave it to him, at the same time asking again.

"Where is Tish, Pierce?"

He chuckled. "I'm texting you a photo of your beloved cousin now. Rule number one, six, don't have friends. Don't have family. Don't care about anyone."

I swallowed the lump in my throat as it tightened, restricting my airflow.

"Give me the phone." I mouthed. Ian shook his head.

When he clicked on the photo, his face went pale.

"Give it to me. Let me see." I hissed while Pierce laughed merrily in the background.

Ian shook his head. "No fucking way."

Then he sprang up as I charged him and tried to fight him for the phone.

Pierce continued.

"Oh, one more thing, six. You need to know that everything would have been fine had you just been a good little girl and gone back to Eddie. Isn't that right?"

My eyes widened and I felt a wave of nausea that quickly blossomed into a cold, numb horror.

"He agrees. You could have taken him back that night in the hotel room. You could have gone home to your family. But you chose betrayal, and that makes you a cheap whore. Everything you think you have? Everything you love? Depend on? It's all going away until you have nothing but the sidewalk. Then, I'm coming for you. And Eddie gets to be on the other end of it. As a reward for his cooperation."

I slumped down on the ground, the rage and fear in my body too much to hold. The urge to kill, to choke the life out of him, to shoot round after round into him until he was ground meat, to smash his head in... it was overwhelming, but at the same time, my heart was being ripped out. I didn't need to see the photo.

He'd killed her. Killed her in cold blood and Eddie fucking helped.

Chapter Thirty-Five

Ace

I HAD A GUN pressed against my temple while a hand reached under my jacket to pull my gun from my waistband.

"Did you really think you were going to just come in here and shake us down for information, then walk out? What the fuck happened? You get a head injury or something? Cause your brain ain't working right." Stevie clucked and shook his head.

"Look, Stevie. Pierce is a fucking psycho. We just want to know where we can find him."

Rafe put up his hand to silence me.

"Ace, I like you. Always liked you. But you are in the wrong here. Doesn't matter how you feel about Pierce. He was Berto's right-hand man. He was your superior. Berto was a father to you and you fucked him over. Now you have enemies, and Pierce is one of them. He's pulling people together, keeping things running. Doing what needs to be done, and that includes rounding up the trash."

"So you are taking orders from Pierce now?" I asked.

Stevie spoke up. "I don't take orders. I do what makes sense. Right now, dealing with Pierce and helping him out makes sense. Makes sense for my business. You, you don't make sense. If you guys were going to make a play for Berto's empire, you should have done it straight away. Maybe you could have gotten some guys on your side. But you hid yourselves away like cowards, leaving the family business to implode while you drained bank accounts, stole assets, and left the throne empty. Stupid as fuck. Now Pierce is sitting there and people don't mind."

"People don't mind? He's a fucking—"

Rafe cut me off. "What? He's not a nice guy? Go figure. Neither am I. Neither are you. Yeah, I've heard some things. Things I don't agree with. But that doesn't apply to me or my business. Doesn't affect my paycheck or my life."

Mick shook his head and glowered, but said nothing.

"Yeah, doesn't affect you now, but you gotta realize Pierce isn't loyal to anyone but himself. He doesn't care about you."

"Wah. I'm fucking crying. I don't need him to be my friend. I need him to protect my assets and help me make money. As long as he does that, we're good. What the fuck are you going to help me do?"

It was time for some quick thinking and talking, which just happened to be my specialty.

"You mind if I sit?" I asked, flashing the grin that's gotten me what I want since I was ten years old.

"Go right on ahead. Make yourselves comfortable. But don't pull any bullshit, because you aren't leaving here, and you will not win if you decide to fight back. You see my guys? Those are the ones you see. There are more where they came from."

"How long you known Pierce?" I asked.

He cocked his head. "What difference does that make?"

"It makes a lot of difference. He's been around maybe four years? And only risen up in the last two years? Why? Because he's fucking sick. Because he likes cutting up young girls. That's what the guy is bringing to the table. He got Berto involved in his sick little hobbies. That's why he had to go. Meanwhile, Berto was neglecting his businesses. You know that. You talked about it with me. He wasn't around, he was out in the desert playing with his toys."

Stevie's eyes shifted to Rafe, who said nothing but shifted in his seat. They knew I was speaking the truth. Pierce was a nobody with few friends. He had to be working overtime to get people on his side.

"Okay, but where have you been? Where's Xander? He took down Berto like a fucking backstabbing traitor. We can't let that stand."

I scratched my head as though trying to recall some information.

"Yeah, wonder where he learned that behavior from?"

The knife I had stashed was begging to be used. I didn't really think I was going to talk them into letting us go, but I could at least get them thinking and relaxed, then we'd fight our way out and start fucking shit up. These guys needed to live, though. They were power players with a lot of pull and resources. More and more I was starting to think Xander was maybe right. Maybe fuck Pierce and anyone else who thought they could run this organization.

"Hey, that was a long time ago."

Mick sat up straight.

"Yeah, a long time ago he took out his own brother and kidnapped and tortured his pregnant wife. But yeah, tell me again how he's the victim."

Rafe spread his fingers out on the table and looked at me. I could tell he agreed with me but his agreement wouldn't get us out of this place, nor would it deliver Pierce to us.

"Okay, I get it. But what Xander did makes no sense. He killed the head of the Moreno organization, with the help of Berto's own brother. That's a power play. Except that's not what happened. Jesse went back to his ranch, and Xander and you guys disappeared. If you'd have come straight to us with a plan, things might be different. But you didn't."

"I see. Well, we did some things. Xander did some things. We were just taking time, is all."

"Wasting time. Wasting time shacking up with some broad instead of taking care of business."

Stevie made a subtle gesture.

"I'm tiring of this conversation. It's time."

"Time for what?" Mick asked.

"Pierce asked me to have you guys packaged up and ready to go if you showed up here. Orders. He has a couple of questions for you first."

I laughed. "He has you guys asking us questions? What the fuck does that mean?"

"You know, questions. That's what you came here to do, right? Ask me questions about Pierce?"

I shrugged. "Yeah, I suppose."

"Okay, well, I am asking you a couple of questions. Answer them, and things will go easier for you."

I looked at Mick. He gave a slight nod.

"Ask the questions, then."

Stevie cleared his throat.

"First question, and I doubt you're gonna answer it, is Pierce wants to know where you are stashing Xander and that sweet little girl of yours?"

I rolled my eyes.

"Not gonna happen. What's the next question?"

Stevie sighed.

"Pierce wants to know what you guys did with his will."

"Pierce has a will? That's good. He should have a will." I smirked and cracked my knuckles.

"Cute," said Rafe. "Berto's will."

Mick leaned forward and declined a beer from the cocktail server. I accepted.

"Yeah, we wondered about a will. You know, he probably thought he was going to live forever. Doubt he made one."

"Two wrong answers. Berto made a will and you know it."

"Maybe I do. Maybe I don't. Not telling you shit. Not handing over anything. No wills, no addresses, no nothing. Just came here to find out where rat-faced Pierce was. That's all. You want to help us, or just wait for his psycho ass to kidnap one of your kids or something?"

Rafe and Stevie both turned several shades of red at that. I got them where it hurt. I happened to know that both of them had daughters.

"Shut your mouth, Ace."

Mick laughed. "Good luck, gentlemen. I still haven't figured out how to make that happen."

That actually got a slight smirk from both of them. Mick leaned back and unfolded his arms.

"Look. We go back a ways, you know I've been nothing if not loyal. I'm here to tell you that putting your money on Pierce won't give you the return you are looking for. He's not stable. He might be making pretty promises now, but down the road? I doubt he'll come through. He's not a professional. He's too preoccupied with his 'hobbies' to give this organization the attention it deserves."

I could see their wheels spinning. I knew full well they weren't just going to let us walk out of there, but they were distracted and their boys were relaxed.

Mick and I didn't need to exchange glances to know it was time.

"Stevie, Rafe, it's really been a pleasure. Remember what we said. Things can go good for you guys if you make the right choices."

"The fuck are you—"

He didn't get to finish his sentence because I had already jumped up, turned the table over, disarmed the bozo to my left while Ace had disarmed the bozo to his right. I fired off a few shots and knocked out a guy who sprung on me.

Others scattered and Ace had his knife out, slicing and dicing a path in front of him while I brought up the rear.

Our exit was relatively painless and easy. Maybe a little too easy.

Minutes later, we were in the truck and speeding down the highway, going in the opposite direction of the house.

"Anyone following us?" Mick asked me.

"I don't see anything obvious. But we have to assume they are."

“Text Ian.”

I reached for my phone and pressed the side button. There were several texts from both Xander and Ian waiting for me.

One caught my eye.

“Holy fuck.” I said, my eyes bugging out of my head.

“What? What is it?”

I looked at Mick, my guts lurching and my blood boiling.

“It’s Pierce. He fucking killed Jade’s cousin. He killed her. And Eddie was in on it.”

Chapter Thirty-Six

Jade

My world was crumbling. Ace and Mick were who fucking knows where. Maybe dead. Xander's guys, the guys he grew up with, the guys that could never quite stomach Berto, who loved Xander like he was their own nephew, that he was hoping would come to his side, turned out to be on team Pierce. Tish was dead, just to spite me.

Pierce left her husband and baby alive but beyond traumatized.

And fucking Eddie was a part of it. He led Pierce to her. He signed off on it. Profited from it.

"We gotta kill Eddie," Xander muttered.

Ian nodded. "Easy enough to do."

He was watching me warily as I drummed my fingers on the table, chewing my lip so hard I could taste blood. I wanted to grieve my cousin, but the flashbacks I was having had taken me to a place where I couldn't access those feelings. Not yet. Now, the only thing I could access was rage and my will to survive this.

"He'll expect us to come for Eddie," I said.

"Good," Xander muttered. "Let him think we are falling for his bullshit trap."

"Yeah, where did that thinking get us last time? We have to be smarter than him, and as much as it pains me to say this, he's a smart guy."

"Not smart enough," I said.

Ian's phone beeped and he pounced on it, looked at it, and heaved a deep sigh.

"It's Mick and Ace. They got caught up at the club. Sure enough, Stevie and Rafe are with Pierce."

"But Mick and Ace?" I leaned forward, grabbing hold of Ian's tee.

He closed his hand over mine. "They are okay. They'd be here now but they don't want to lead anyone here."

"Are we ready for a fight?" Xander stared at Ian, then at me.

"I showed Jade the safe room. We have weapons and supplies."

"There's too many windows here," I muttered.

"Hazards of luxurious beachfront living," Xander retorted.

I rolled my eyes. "But seriously. I mean, could Pierce have traced my phone?"

Xander shook his head. "Doubt it. It's a burner phone."

Ian looked at me, his brows furrowed as he considered the possibilities.

"Yeah, probably not, but it's possible. We have to assume that he could trace it. That his guys could be here any time."

"But how many guys?" Xander wanted to know.

"A dozen? More? Maybe just a handful. Enough."

My mind was reeling but there was one thought that hit me like a bolt of lightning and I was overcome with one urge and one urge only.

"We have to get the baby," I said.

Ian looked at me without a word, his expression impossible to read. Xander shook his head, his eyes soft but resolute.

"Jade, I understand, but honestly he's safer where he is than here."

I felt like I was going to jump out of my skin and start punching him in the face.

"Are you fucking kidding me? Eddie is bff's with Pierce. A killer. Eddie literally got my cousin killed. God knows what Pierce has that weak-minded shithead doing. But I tell you what he's not doing: He's not taking care of a baby."

Xander nodded in what was an infuriatingly dismissive manner.

"Yeah, but you said it yourself. He's not taking care of him. Your parents are. You may not think they are doing a good job, but you survived, right? So how about we worry on this later?"

I pulled away from both of them and headed for the stairs and the quiet of my room.

"Jade, I think you should stay near the safe room. It's better if you aren't up there by yourself."

"I'll be fine. Just like Benny."

"Jade..." Xander called. I ignored him. He meant well, but he was pissing me off.

About an hour later, Mick and Ace were back. They both came to check in with me and I was grateful for that.

"You're preoccupied, Jade. Talk to me? Are you afraid they are coming here? I swear, I won't let anything happen to you. None of us will."

Mick was so loving and reassuring, but there was no reassuring me. We would have to confront Pierce and whatever crew he had backing him up. That I could deal with.

What I couldn't deal with was Benny being in the hands of a killer.

I paced the length of my room for another hour, feeling broken, helpless, furious, and grief-stricken.

Then came a soft knock at the door. I had a feeling Xander would come at some point to talk to me, but it wasn't him. It was Ian.

"Hey," I said, my voice sounding miserable to my ears.

"Hey."

He approached me but didn't reach for me. He was giving me space, something he was good at. Ace and Mick had a tendency to invade my space sometimes, so did Xander, when he wasn't being ridiculously distant like he was now.

Ian had figured out the perfect balance of giving me space and being there for me when I needed him. I loved him for it.

"What's going on?" I asked.

He shook his head slightly. "Just strategizing."

"Yeah, that's good."

I was just getting ready to politely and lovingly ask him to make his way out of my room when he reached for my hand, grasped it in his, and looked me dead in the eye.

"Jade, sometimes the best thing you can do is forget about asking permission and just ask for forgiveness later."

I cocked my head, trying to suss out the meaning of his words.

"Look, it's crazy, but I am with you. I want to get him, too. They don't get it, but I do."

I put my hands out, reaching for him and pulling him toward me, searching his face to see if he meant what he was saying.

"Are you serious?"

He nodded.

"I bet Eddie isn't there. Bet he is staying in some hotel room or brothel getting his fill of booze and dope and chicks. Why would he be at your parents' house?"

I shook my head. "The only reason he would be there is if he thinks we are going there."

He pulled at his goatee. "Yeah, I thought of that. Or maybe they have a guy posted around there just in case. I say we take the chance. Worst case scenario is we have a fight on our hands. But are you prepared to deal with the fallout? Are you prepared to deal with the drama this is going to create?"

I nodded. "When can we go?"

He shrugged and put his finger to his lips.

"Get ready. I'll come get you when it's time."

Twenty minutes later we were sneaking out the back and sliding into a BMW I didn't even know we had. Probably Berto's.

"They already know we're gone," he said. "Don't answer your phone yet."

We sped down the winding road that led to the beachfront mansion and hung a right. He floored it for about four miles then eased us onto the freeway. Thirty minutes would put us at my parents' house. Southern California is like that. One minute you are cruising down Lifestyles of the Rich and Famous road and the next minute you are in one of "those neighborhoods" people worry about breaking down in. Stupid, really. Monsters live everywhere.

We cruised by twice and I didn't see any vehicles that were out of place.

Ian was armed, and so was I.

"You sure you are ready to do this? It could get ugly." He eyed me warily.

It occurred to me out of nowhere that 1. I hadn't seen my parents in months. 2. The baby hadn't seen me in months. 3. What if Eddie was there? 4. What if my mom or dad tried to stop me? Then what?

Too late now. We were in it to win it. I was taking Benny home and no one was going to stop me.

Kidnapping, Jade? Really?

"Yep. I'm ready."

We strolled right up to my parent's house. I still had the keys, they were in the purse that I'd been hauling around the day of the bank robbery. It came back to me just days ago and now I was using those keys to open the door and kidnap my ex-boyfriend's son.

"The living room lights are out, my parents spend most of their time in the bedroom," I whispered. "They don't hear well, and usually have the television blasting."

Ian nodded. "Any sign of Eddie?"

I shook my head. He would be in the kitchen sitting at the table. Always.

The door opened silently and I held my breath, stepping through the threshold and immediately tripping over my dad's shoes. He rarely left the house, but when he did, he immediately kicked off his shoes right as he came through the door.

"Fuck." I hissed.

"Would the baby be in your parent's room?"

I shook my head. "No, mine."

My nose wrinkled and I felt that twinge of shame and horror. The house smelled of mold, stale cigarettes, dirty, rotting dishes in the sink, and sour laundry.

There was the slight smell of souring baby milk, too.

I motioned for Ian to wait in the living room and I made my way to the hall.

Sure enough, my parents were in their room with the door closed, the glow from the television visible through the cracks, and the sound booming through the closed door.

I took a deep breath and approached my bedroom door. The light was off, the door cracked open about four inches.

I pushed it open and waited for my eyes to adjust to the dark. Then I remembered I had my phone in my back pocket. I pressed the side button and the soft glow of my home screen revealed a sleeping baby in the middle of my queen-size bed, surrounded by pillows and a few stuffed animals.

I shook my head and searched the room for a bag, diapers, something. I noted the baby monitor sitting on the dresser, and the green light indicating it was on.

Shit.

There was a small stack of diapers sitting on the dresser, and a tote next to it. I grabbed the tote, shoved the diapers and the wipes in the bag then made my way toward the bed.

Carefully, I slipped one hand under his neck and one hand under his bottom and lifted him off the bed. He immediately stiffened, stretching and grunting in that cute baby way, then started fussing and squirming in my arms.

I resisted the urge to soothe him or shush him and quietly pulled up the blanket he'd been on and covered him with it.

Then, I scurried out of the room while Benny started getting louder. I rushed past Ian, heading for the front door just as I heard my parents' bedroom door swing open.

"Come on." I hissed.

Ian eased the front door closed, but we got only ten steps down the sidewalk before the front door opened and my father stormed out of the house with my mother on his tail. He hunched down, putting his hands on his knees, wheezing from the effort of leaving his bed.

"Help!" My mom's shrill voice echoed down the street as I hustled away and tried to ignore the panic in my gut that told me there was no way we were getting away with this.

"Jade? Is that you?" She called after me. "It's you. I can tell by the way you are walking. Get back here! Bring him back here!"

Against my better judgment, I stopped and turned around as my dad came huffing and puffing toward me. Ian looked at me like I'd lost my mind.

"Let's go, what the fuck?"

I looked at my parents, their faces ghoulish from the shadows cast by the streetlamps.

"I'm taking him. His father is a fucking killer. He got Tish killed. You guys don't want this baby. You aren't taking care of him."

"The hell is wrong with you, girl? Give him to me. I'll call the cops!"

I laughed and shook my head. "No, you won't."

With that, I turned and started jogging with him down the street, Ian bringing up the rear. In less than a minute we were in the car and I was freaking out because we didn't have a car seat.

"Stay low in case the cops do come."

"I will."

I hunched in the back seat shushing Benny, who was worked up into a proper wail. We would need formula and supplies. This was crazy.

"We need to stop at a store, Ian. He needs formula. We don't have bottles."

"Are you serious?"

"Yeah, what did you think? You think he was going to eat pizza and drink beer?"

"Well, that would be convenient."

"Just stop at the nearest store that's open this late. Run in, I'll tell you what to get."

Once we were out of the immediate area, Ian pulled into a 24hr grocery store with the list I texted him.

He returned with all of it and more.

"There's some other stuff in the bag. A couple of toys, some kind of bottle organizer, some baby wash or whatever."

"Cool. Okay, let's go home. Drive carefully."

I looked at my phone and saw the long line of texts and missed calls from the guys. Ian's phone was likely the same.

We were in for a serious lecture.

"It's okay, baby. They're gonna love you."

Chapter Thirty-Seven

Ian

I STOOD THERE FEELING hungry and irritable as Xander, Ace, and Mick viciously railed me.

Not in a good way.

"What in the ever-loving fuck did you think you were doing?"

Mick was shouting at me while Xander paced, muttering and pulling at his hair. He was beside himself.

Ace wasn't quite as unhinged, but he was not happy.

"There's a fucking baby here," he repeated for the third time.

"Yes, Ace. Very good. You're figuring it out."

He shot me a fiery look.

"Bro, not the time. You're up shit creek. Might want to not talk shit."

I chuckled and put my hands out, fanning my fingers and trying to maintain a calm, collected demeanor, even though I was freaking the fuck out inside.

"Look, we did what needed to be done. That kid needed to be rescued. You guys weren't on board, so we did it ourselves. Now, we're back safe and sound, the kid is fine, Jade is fine. We're all fine."

"There's a baby here."

"Ace, we get it," Mick snapped.

Xander was morose as fuck and his pacing and hair-pulling were getting to me.

"Xander, buddy. Stop fucking pacing for one minute and listen to me. We can't freak out right now. We need to stay calm."

"Calm? You guys kidnapped a *baby*." Veins were bulging in his neck and his temples. He was officially losing it.

"Correction: We *rescued* a baby. We did the right thing. You should see the kid. He's pale, filthy, his clothes stink, and he has literal dark circles under his eyes. A *baby*."

"Yeah, we get it. This was a conversation we had, remember? And we told Jade that once this shit with Pierce was resolved, we would look into it."

Mick's face was beet red. Ace just looked tired but I think he was finally understanding that yes, there was a baby in the house.

"So what's Pierce going to do?" he asked.

Xander looked at him and waved dismissively. "He doesn't give a fuck about that baby."

"Yeah, but it was a bold move. I mean, we know he's enlisted Eddie, who knows what plans he has for him? And now we've kidnapped the kid."

"Don't know, but fuck them both," Xander muttered.

"Look, guys, I know you're mad, but what's done is done. We have him. Jade's going to take good care of him. We both are." I straightened up to let them know I meant business.

Ace slumped down onto the couch. "Okay, so now what? We got Jade and a baby to look after, Pierce is out there and he has it out for us. They're looking for his will, they want Jade, Eddie is going to want his kid back so he can keep getting checks. Am I missing anything?"

Xander shot me a scathing look and pointed at my chest.

"All I know is Ian and Jade just took everything and made it worse. Be ready. Pierce is coming full force. And now he's got even more ammo. You guys kidnapped a kid. You've put him on a righteous mission."

Now it was my turn to give Xander the "what the fuck are you talking about" stare.

"A righteous mission?"

"Yeah. Now not only is he avenging the death of Berto Moreno, his boss, and best buddy, he's helping to return an innocent little baby to his loving father. He'll make Eddie a fucking victim of his ruthless ex and a gang of heartless, disloyal, conniving traitors. He'll milk it for all it's worth just to get people on his side. Trust that."

I pulled the blade out of my pocket, flicked it open, and started cleaning under my nails.

"Look, we want Pierce dead, right? Well, that means we have to find him. So maybe he comes to us? You guys got a problem with that? You think we can't handle it? I say we should welcome him with open arms."

After what seemed like hours of lectures, projections, questions, and heated arguments, we broke and went our separate ways. We agreed that one of us needed to be awake to monitor the cameras at all times, so we set up shifts.

I went first. There was a wall of monitors in the safe room, but I also could bring up the feed on my computer.

I had dual monitors set up, each showing a feed of various outdoor and interior feeds. I could see the entire front yard, entrance, driveway, and the side of the house on one monitor, the terraces, back entrance, garage, and beach stairs on another monitor. Periodically I would switch to another feed, but this was my main view as I worked.

I was going analog with my work today, making lists of guys I thought we had a shot with. Making a list of women I knew for years that had no love for Pierce or Berto. There were plenty of them. None of them loved me much, either, but they loved Ace, Xander, and Mick. I wrote all their names down, surprised I even remembered them.

Everyone's first thought was to recruit the guys who knew how to fight and shoot.

Women were so often underestimated. Especially by pigs like Pierce and Berto, but even by "nice guys."

That's because they put them on a pedestal, completely disregarding women as a threat, as a weapon, as an ally. Maybe they would use them to gain information or get information, but they were rarely used to their full potential.

I suppose that's just because men underestimate the level of rage and pent-up violence so many women have. And they underestimate their capacity for ruthless self-interest.

Katy. Ellen. Candy. Moni. Sally. Layla. Veronica. Jane.

These were women that had beef with one or both of them.

Katy was just a kid when she was forced to work at one of Berto's houses. In fact, she was one of the girls Berto had brought to my birthday party one year. Later, she got wasted and told me that if she ever had the chance to kill Berto, she would take it for what he'd done to her mother. Berto was dead, but she was no fan of Pierce, either. From what Ace told me, her sister Charla had disappeared after Pierce forced her away from the house. I wonder if her body had been found.

Ellen and Candy, both in their early thirties. Pierce had severely beaten both on at least one occasion. Both were vicious, backstabbing, greedy women who had no problem spilling blood. Monique, well, she was really tired of the way Pierce was treating her and her girls.

The rest was more of the same. Women who were just trying to survive in an ugly world, and Berto and Pierce had done their best to make it even harder than it already was.

But how do I implement them? How can they help?

I heard soft footsteps and smiled. It was Jade, walking up and down the hall soothing the baby to sleep.

She crept into the room and seeing her holding the little guy close as she swayed back and forth made my heart happy. She was a natural, so nurturing, and sweet.

"I gave him a bath. Thanks for thinking to get the baby wash. He smells so good. All freshly changed and fed."

I nodded and smiled.

"He's going to need stuff."

She laughed lightly and rolled her eyes.

"Oh my god, I'm on it. Already put in an order for a crib, high chair, one of those bouncy things, a stroller, clothes, toys... you name it, it's going to be here tomorrow."

"Good deal."

"We did the right thing," she said, her voice resolute, but her eyes clouded with doubt.

"Yeah, we did. He deserves better than what they were giving him. And honestly, I think they'll all be relieved when it's said and done. Even Eddie. Perfect excuse for him to not have the responsibility."

She looked sad at that, and I reached out and stroked her cheek.

"I know it sucks that he got a raw deal, but you can make it better for him. We can make it better. He'll have a shot."

She nodded, her eyes welling up with tears. I knew she was still grieving her cousin, but the baby would help heal her.

"I better go lay down with him. He's pretty much out."

I kissed her forehead. "Night, Jade."

She left the room and I got back to my plotting and planning. We needed to trap Pierce, get him alone or nearly alone. We needed his inner circle to see he was just a piece of shit. Or we just needed to take him out and anyone who couldn't cope with reality.

The reality that Pierce wasn't in charge of the Moreno family. We were.

Chapter Thirty-Eight

Jade

It had been two days since we'd rescued the baby from my parents and his scumbag daddy. The odd thing is I felt guilty. Benny was confused, fussy, and looked like he'd been sick for weeks. I was determined to nurture him back to health and happiness.

"But did I have the right to do this?" I mumbled to myself as I watched him sleep.

The shiny gray truck had arrived just this morning, bringing all the things I could think that he would need: a crib, bedding, stroller, high chair, cases of formula and bottles, clothes, blankets, and toys.

I'd spent a pretty penny, but it was worth it. He was worth it.

"Kid looks good," Ace observed. He was still stressing about it but was coming around, joking and making faces to entertain him. In fact, Ace was the first one to get an actual laugh out of him.

"I see how it is, kid," Ian muttered grumpily as Ace beamed at his baby-entertaining prowess. "Was up half the night with you, then this joker comes in and you're an instant fan."

"What can I say? Kids love me." He chuckled while Ian rolled his eyes.

Mick and Xander weren't so easily won over. Mick had looked the baby over, concerned about his health, but not interested in him otherwise. Xander wouldn't stop fretting about our new "weakness" and considered the baby nothing more than a new "chink in our armor".

I felt so far away from Xander. It made me sad.

Ian put an arm around me and squeezed my shoulder. "Xander will come around. So will Mick. They are family men, but this is not an ideal situation. Xander is partially correct. It adds an extra dimension to the situation. Before we just had you to worry about, now there's a baby. It ups the stakes. And gives us more to lose, and more they can threaten."

I nodded. He was right, of course. But what he didn't realize was that this baby strengthened me. I would fight like a fierce mama bear to protect him.

"Remember, Jade. The first whiff of trouble of any kind, you take him and go to the safe room. You don't come out no matter what. When you do come out, you hightail it as far away as you can, and you don't look back if things go south."

"Things will not go that way," I said, tilting my chin up at him, giving him my mean mug face. "They are the ones going south. They are the ones who are going to run with their tails between their legs."

He sucked in his breath. "Yeah, that's the plan."

"Do you have a plan for real, or are you just saying that's the plan?"

He smiled, leaned in, and gave me a soft kiss. His lips felt warm on mine and my pulse quickened.

"Hope the kid sleeps good soon. I'm getting lonely and jealous."

"Oh, don't start that shit." I laughed and gave him a wink.

Hours later, I rocked Benny in my brand-new rocking chair, facing the sunset and the ocean below. I felt like I was living in a magazine, sitting there in my luxurious suite, furnished to perfection.

I dressed Benny in the softest organic cotton sleeper. I was wearing the kinds of clothes I'd often seen and envied when I was out and about on the streets of Los Angeles, seeing lithe, tan young women on their way to their spin glasses with their matchas and their hundred dollar leggings and Chanel bags.

Today I was wearing a super cute and flirty pink romper and I pulled my hair up in a high ponytail. I wore the diamond earrings Mick had presented me with, and my new smartwatch that Ian insisted was a good "investment in my health".

"Alright. Fed, burped, changed, rocked." I kissed his soft little forehead and gently laid him in his crib. For a few moments, I allowed myself to bask in the peace and domestic bliss.

Then, I came back to reality.

I flipped the monitor on and headed downstairs to the dining room, reluctant to leave him, but I wasn't about to be left out of the meeting.

Tonight was the night we were going to map out the plan to take Pierce out.

So far, there had been no further word from him or Eddie. At least not that I knew of. Mick had taken my phone. They forbid me to use social media, and I wouldn't care much except I really wanted to stay connected to the girls that I left behind at the ranch. I kept thinking of Rose, Sara, and Allison.

And Missy.

I stuffed down the grief from my losses and did my best not to give in to the belief that I would never have other women in my life I could trust, confide in, and have fun with.

Man, I really took those relationships for granted over the years.

Women I knew didn't trust other women. There was that underlying judgment, competition, and claims of "backstabbing" and "drama".

Of course, this was all a bunch of parroted bullshit put on us by insecure men, really. And the women that did backstab and play the "pick me" game were just women who didn't know their worth outside of whether or not a man wanted to sleep with them.

I understood that. It's how I spent years of my life with my disgusting, pathetic excuse for a man, feeling jealous of the other women that he cheated on me with, even though deep down inside I despised him. Even though if I was honest, I didn't really want him.

I just believed I needed him and wasn't enough without him.

I walked into a meeting in progress. Mick and Ian were muttering. Ace had a mouth full of chicken wings, and Xander was taking a bite of pizza.

"Wow, thanks for waiting for me," I snapped.

"Sorry, Jade. We really thought you'd just gone to bed. Wouldn't blame you. I know you were up with the baby a lot last night."

I sighed and rubbed my eyes. "I'm ready to get our shit figured out."

Ian cleared his throat. "Well, grab some grub, and let's get to it. We really haven't gotten to the meat of it yet. Been bullshitting, comparing notes, and shoveling food into our faces." He smiled and winked, and took a swig of his beer.

Ace jumped up. "Let me get you a beer and a plate."

I shook my head. "No beer for me, thanks. I want to be one-hundred percent present if Benny needs me."

Ian beamed at me, and Ace nodded. "Smart."

Xander looked disappointed.

"Aw, tell me you aren't turning into a stick in the mud because of that rugrat." He pouted.

My jaw dropped and Ian and Mick shot him "the look".

Ace presented me with a plate and squeezed my shoulder. "Here's a bottle of water. Let me know if you want some soda or something, and I'll grab it."

He turned to Xander. "Jade is being responsible. Responsible doesn't mean boring. And it's not her job to entertain us. We are a family here. We support each other."

"Yeah, well, if we're family how come they didn't tell us they were going to kidnap a kid and bring him home for us to look after? I don't recall signing off on that."

Part of me understood perfectly that he was right. It was a big, reckless, impulsive decision that made things complicated. And we did not give them any say. Xander had a right to be upset.

Yeah, that was part of me. The other part...

"Hey, I'll tell you what, Xander. How about I pack up my shit and get me and the rugrat out of your hair? Huh? Does that work for you? I mean, that way you don't have to worry about us. We'll just disappear, and you won't have to deal with the inconvenience anymore."

His eyes widened, and then he smacked his palm against his forehead.

"Jesus, Jade. Why would you even say that?" He looked alarmed and also irritated that I was calling him out.

"We don't have time for this nonsense." Mick shook his head and drummed his fingers on the table. "Xander, enough. Jade, come on. Those kinds of threats are childish. You aren't going anywhere. Now let's sit here like adults and figure this shit out. Ian has ideas, let's hear them."

Ian waited till we were all settled, then folded his hands on the table.

"We've been round and round trying to figure out who we could trust. But we've been looking in the wrong place.

We've been looking at men, men who really don't care what a monster Pierce is."

"Okay, so basically you're saying that there are no guys that would be willing to back you," I said, grabbing a third slice of pizza. "So what then? I mean, can't you just pay some people off? They like money, right?"

Mick snorted. "Pierce is promising them the world, promising stuff he won't be able to deliver. And all that's going to happen if we offer money is they'll take it, then fuck us over. No, you can't buy the kind of loyalty we need."

Ace tapped his chin, and Xander leaned in, eyeing Ian with interest. "Don't keep us in anticipation, bro. Tell us what you're thinking."

He pulled a folded-up piece of paper out of his pocket, carefully unfolded it, and smoothed it out.

"I compiled a list. A list of people who either have scores to settle with Pierce or with Berto. The individuals on this list are not sympathetic to his cause. Pierce can't bribe them with women, and they've all been bullshitted, lied to, screwed over, and ripped off enough times to not believe a fucking word he says. Not only that but he won't consider any of them a threat. He'll walk right into their house with his guard down and the safety on."

Ace looked at me, his brows raised, then at Xander and Mick.

"Go on, I think you have our attention, that's for sure."

Ian slid the paper across to Ace, and I watched him glance at it, cock his head, then shake it and slide the paper over to Xander.

"Okay, so I think I see what you are trying to do here, but I can't believe something would work. I mean, what are they going to do?"

Xander and Mick looked at the paper, and Mick rolled his eyes, pushed the paper away, then stopped, pulled at his chin, reached for the paper, and looked at it again, tilting his head back and forth as I reached for the paper, irritated that no one had given it to me to look at.

These guys didn't consider me a part of this at all. I was just someone to protect, a liability, really.

It was getting on my nerves.

"These are all girl names?" I frowned at the paper, reading each name, trying to comprehend.

"Even Jade thinks it's a bad idea," Mick grumbled.

Okay, now I'm getting really irritated.

"I just don't get it, is all. Didn't say it was a bad idea."

Ian shot me a smile and continued trying to sell his idea to the guys.

"I'm telling you. That list is everything. If we play it right, if we can get them on board, we will win. Easily."

Fuck this, they aren't interested in sharing their ideas with me. They don't care about my opinion, and at this point, my presence is just a hassle for them.

"I'm going to bed. Maybe let me know when you guys figure out your shit."

Maybe they're right. Maybe I'm tired. Or maybe I just miss my cousin. Or maybe I'm realizing that these guys aren't so interested in me anymore. Maybe I'm getting in the way, or getting on their nerves.

"Fuck it," I muttered as I pushed my chair in, glared at them, and turned to walk back upstairs.

Chapter Thirty-Nine

Xander

A sigh escaped me as Jade walked away and Ace pushed his chair back to go after her, but Mick intervened.

"Let her go," he said.

There was a knot in my belly, I hated that I'd been distant and shitty, but I was having an internal crisis unlike anything I'd ever known, and no one could help me.

Having the kid around wouldn't be a big deal except for the part where we were in mortal danger. It was bad enough knowing that Pierce could reasonably take her from us again. That she could be tortured, raped, and murdered. For real this time. Now add a baby in danger.

"Fuck," I muttered under my breath.

Mick lowered his voice and pulled Jade's phone from his pocket.

"I don't want her to see these messages. Don't want her to have to worry about this shit right now. Let her focus on the baby. It's better."

Ian shook his head.

"I disagree. She's a part of this and I think it's fucked up that you guys are treating her like a child. Her life is in danger and she deserves to know what we are planning. She wants to be a part of what we are doing."

Ace held up a finger and opened his mouth and I could just tell the four of us were about to bicker.

"Ian, while I wholeheartedly agree that we should treat Jade as an equal and keep her informed, I don't think she needs to be a 'part' of what we are doing. What we are doing is criminal shit. Thug shit. Go to jail shit. That's not her."

I chuckled and Ian cleared his throat. Before I could chime in with the obvious, Ian beat me to it.

"Hate to break it to you bro, but Jade just broke into a house and kidnapped a baby and she didn't bat an eye doing it. She pulled the trigger and took down one of Pierce's people and said that she'd happily do it again. I don't think you understand her."

"Don't understand her?" Ace sputtered, his eyes blazing with indignation.

I'd had about enough.

"Are we going to actually talk shop here, or are we just going to dick around and argue?"

That shut everyone up. Mick grunted an approval and pointed at the list Ian had compiled.

"I get where you're going - sort of. Please tell me you have a detailed plan and not just a list of women Pierce has pissed off."

Ian and I looked at each other. We'd been working on this for a little while and although I was doubtful about how this could work, by the time Ian had it all ironed out, he'd convinced me. We had a plan. A good plan.

"Let me see the texts he's been sending," I said.

Mick slid the phone over to me and I felt my blood boil as I read the filth Eddie was sending her.

... he'll cut off your tits, you stupid whore...

... you think you can raise a child? You're too ignorant. Too stupid...

... you won't ever have a kid of your own, that's why you had to steal mine...

... you're going to pay for what you have done...

... your own parents despise you, wish you'd never been born...

It went on and on. Dozens of threats, insults, sexually violent and explicit texts, demands to bring the baby back to her parents, and graphic details of what he and his "new friend Pierce" had in mind.

... meeting him was the best thing that could have ever happened to me, so I should thank you for that. I'm working now. I'm somebody. Got a nice, new car, a place, everything I need. Oh, and a real woman. A woman who can be a mother to Benny...

"Fuck's sake," I muttered, feeling sick to my stomach. It would be ridiculous and pathetic if we didn't already know who we were dealing with.

I slid the phone over to Ace.

"I don't need to see it. I can imagine. We just need Pierce dead. Is your plan going to get him dead?"

Ian grabbed for the phone and I watched his eyes as he read the texts one by one.

"Yeah," I said, "It's going to get him dead."

We'd ended the meeting and gone to bed, but long after that, I remained awake in my bed. There was no sleeping for me. I was exhausted but my mind wouldn't stop.

I was down with Ian's plan, but then what? What about the future? Mick told me not to think beyond what was next: Killing Pierce and eliminating any other threats to our family. Our objective was peace. And for us, peace meant killing anyone who stood in the way of us living our lives.

The baby was crying like he did every night right about this time. It didn't bother me, the soundproofing in the house was pretty good so wasn't loud or anything. I imagined Jade, with her silky, wavy locks piled on her head in her no-nonsense bun, as she called it. She was a glorious vision all tan and soft and everything beautiful and sweet and good. And she would walk him back and forth, cooing soft words of love and hope and soothing reassurance.

I'd seen her doing it and dammit if it wasn't its own kind of magic. Kind of made me fall harder for her, and I didn't even know the kid, really.

"And you've been a complete ass," I muttered to myself as I rolled out of bed, pulled on my pants, and went to her.

She needed to know right now, this instant that I was in love with her, that I supported her, and that I would do anything for her.

I reached her door just as his cries were subsiding and I froze. What do I do? Do I knock? Just barge in? What if I upset the baby? What if he starts crying again and it's all my fault?

"Shit."

I paced in front of her door for a couple of minutes, then raised my hand to knock on the door. A soft knock. But what if she's rocking him or holding him and she can't call for me to come in?

"You're going to fuck it all up." I clenched and unclenched my fists and was about to just go back to bed when the door cracked open.

"Xander?"

"Yeah, um, I just was coming to talk to you. Can't sleep."

She stepped back and swung the door open, gesturing me in but putting a finger to her lips.

"He just fell asleep," she whispered, padding over to the crib.

I looked around and marveled at both the baby setup and her suite in general. It was impressive and feminine and completely infused with Jade.

Not knowing what else to do, I followed her over to the crib, peering inside to see Benny, sound asleep and snoring loudly.

"Babies snore?" I asked, completely forgetting to whisper. Benny startled, looking like he was going to jump out of his skin, his arms flailing wildly. I nearly died right there, but he settled down right away, sighing deeply and not waking.

I clutched my chest as Jade shook her head slowly.

"This way."

She motioned me to follow her and I surveyed her room as we walked. There was a king-size bed piled with fluffy pillows and comforters, a sofa, desk, bookshelves already filled with books, baby equipment everywhere and there was a soothing lavender-vanilla scent that permeated the space which made me feel like I could fall asleep on the spot.

"Let's go sit outside, it's nice out."

We went out onto the terrace and she invited me to recline on one of the luxurious loungers that were set up with an unspoiled view of the ocean. It was dark, of course, but the nearly full moon gave just enough illumination to see the waves crashing on the shore below. The sound was soothing, as well, and I wondered if it helped the baby sleep better.

My room was on the other side of the house and I didn't have an ocean view.

"This is nice. I'm going to try not to be jealous that you have this amazing view," I said, half joking.

She reached for my hand. "You can come enjoy the view any time."

That got a smile out of me and my eyes instinctively raked over her body as she stretched out over the lounger, wearing nothing more than a camisole and silky pajama shorts that were barely there. Her nipples were hard and visible through the thin fabric and her dazzling and slightly mischievous smile lit up her face.

I sat up on the lounger and turned toward her, looking down at her perfectly beautiful face.

"Jade, I'm so sorry. I know I've been kind of a dick. I'm just going through some stuff right now, but I had no right to behave like I have. Please, you have to know I love you and I would do anything for you."

She crossed her arms over her chest and sighed.

"You *have* been a dick, that's true. And yeah, I get it. You are going through some shit. But you never talked to me. You refused to confide in me or share any of this with me. You shut me out, and you did it when I really needed you."

That last sentence was like a punch to the gut. I wasn't there for her when she needed me. When she was recovering from her nightmare and healing from her wounds I was busy worrying about my uncle's empire and how I was going to be the one to run it.

Even as I had the thought I was consumed with shame. No one but Ian really knew how I had gone from hating the criminal lifestyle and wanting out of it to being obsessed with taking over my family business. I didn't want to quit. I didn't want to get straight and be legitimate.

No, I wanted to take my uncle's place. I wanted to lead the Morenos and recreate the family to my liking.

And I wanted Jade by my side and my brothers, too.

"Let me make it up to you. I swear, Jade, we just need to get past this rough spot. We just need to deliver justice to that piece of shit and make sure no one rises up to oppose us. Then we can be happy."

She stuck her lower lip out slightly and looked up at me with puppy eyes.

"But I want to be happy now."

I squeezed her hand and raised it to my lips, caressing her soft skin, kissing it softly.

"What would make you happy, my angel?"

She swallowed and looked at me, her eyes grazing over my bare chest and then back up into my eyes.

"I could think of something." Her expression went from cute puppy dog to smoldering siren in two seconds flat and I felt heat rushing through my body as my dick started to get hard.

I looked around, feeling a definite sense of alarm.

"What about the kid?" I asked, feeling a little concerned and panicky.

"He's sleeping. He'll probably sleep till morning, and if he wakes up, I'll deal with it. That's what parents do. But it doesn't mean we can't have some fun, Xander."

Now I was rock hard. And my lips ached for her and my tongue wanted the taste of her.

"Where do you want to, you know..."

She laughed lightly and motioned me to come to her.

"Right here, silly. Right here in front of the whole ocean and all the stars in the sky."

Chapter Forty

Jade

I PULLED XANDER ON top of me and cupped his gorgeous face in my hands. He smiled, his eyes still uncertain.

"It's okay," I whispered.

His eyes lit up and he smiled before pressing his lips against mine. They were so warm and delicious. Xander's olive skin and full lips were beyond model sexy and his smooth skin and soft, shiny hair basically made him the most beautiful man I'd ever laid eyes on.

His soft touch was a contrast to Mick and Ian's rougher style. But I loved it and as he slipped off my shorts and I felt his hardness against me I sighed and surrendered to his love, to his worshiping of my body, so desperately needed and so welcomed.

"You feel so good, so soft and warm." He slid his hand under my camisole and let out a low moan at the feel of my breast under his hand. "It's been so long, Jade."

I nodded but said nothing. I didn't want to talk, I just wanted to feel him inside me.

"Here, get on top of me." He pushed himself off me and pulled me on top of him. I pulled off my top and planted my feet on the ground on either side of him, raising myself up so he could unbutton his pants and slide them off.

Now I was straddling him and we were both naked under the stars. I traced a fingertip from his collarbone down his chest and stomach, then leaned down to kiss his lips, sinking into him and reveling in the feel of his hands on my body, sighing as he gripped my hip with one hand, and squeezed my thigh with the other. He pulled me up and I leaned forward. With his hands, he was feeling every inch of my lower body, my thighs, my ass, my hips, and lower back. I was positioned so my breasts were at level with his face and I groaned as he took my nipple in his mouth, nibbling and sucking at one, then the other, tracing his tongue along my breasts, planting kisses all over my skin while his hands wandered and at last his fingers found me dripping wet.

"Yes," I whispered as he slipped his fingers against my clit, gently working, moaning at the feel of me.

"You're so fucking wet. So wet and warm and tight."

He continued working my clit while biting and sucking my nipples until I was quivering and grinding against his finger, loving the friction but craving the feel of more. Of his cock inside me, filling me up and thrusting into me.

"I want you inside me."

He pulled his face away from my nipple and reached out to caress my cheek, smiling in a sly and cheeky way.

"Make it happen then." He laughed lightly and pulled my face toward his while I slid down then grasped his cock in my hands, giving a couple of pumps before guiding it to my opening.

I teased myself with it for a minute, gliding it back and forth across my wetness, teasing my clit with it, then finally plunging it inside me as I lowered myself down on his hard shaft, groaning with pleasure.

"Fuck yes," he said, moaning and tilting his head back. When he gripped my hips, he bucked up against me and pulled me down. I instinctively grabbed for my breasts, pinching my nipples as I threw my head back and started riding him, bouncing on his cock while he effortlessly lifted me up and slammed me back down, grinding against me, plunging deeper and deeper, increasing in urgency until we were fucking hard and fast.

"I'm going to come," he gasped.

I was close myself and started grinding and playing with my clit as his thrusts became more urgent.

I gasped and moaned as I felt the wave of orgasm wash over me, my muscles contracting around his cock, my wetness increasing as he started to climax, gripping me hard as he plunged his cock into me one last time, emptying himself. I could feel his hot cum, filling me up.

"Fuck."

He finally slowed his thrusts and I fell forward, breathless and laughing, satiated, and content.

And more than a little grateful that the baby didn't wake up.

We stayed like that for a long time, me listening to the beat of his heart and the sound of the ocean waves, him caressing my back and kissing my forehead, murmuring words of love and affection until I finally drifted off to sleep.

Chapter Forty-One

Jade

THERE WAS TENSION HANGING in the house, and it was torture. I stayed in my room with Benny most of the time, longing to take him down to the beach, but knowing I couldn't. Too risky.

Sunlight flooded my room along with the sound of the ocean. I opened all the windows and the sliding doors to let the breeze carry the perfume of it into my space.

Soft music played while Benny kicked and rolled and gurgled at his toys on the soft play mat while I curled my hair and tried to calm my nerves.

Fixing my hair was meditation for me. It soothed me and today I needed soothing.

"This is frustrating, Benny. I feel so helpless. Like a sitting duck."

But what else was there to do?

"I'm going to think positive."

I took a deep breath in through my nose, counting to four. Then exhaled, repeating the mantra I'd been using.

Benny squealed his approval, and Ian poked his head through the door.

"Hey, you hungry? It's almost lunchtime."

He smiled at me and approached Benny. I watched as he scooped him up and held him like a pro.

"How's my big bruiser today?" He pressed his forehead against Benny's, making goofy faces and noises to go along with them.

"You're a dork, Ian." I laughed and squeezed his arm, standing on my tiptoes to give him a kiss on the cheek.

Another knock came at the door and Ace entered, looking absolutely gorgeous in his faded jeans and black tee. He had his hair slicked back in a vintage-looking pompadour and his tattoos and piercings and lopsided grin had me feeling like jelly.

He outstretched his arms and Benny gave a deep, gurgling laugh, opening his own arms wide as Ian handed him off.

"We're going to go make lunch. Give you a break, little mama."

Ace winked at me and leaned over, giving me a sweet little peck on the nose.

"Wait, what?" I was confused and flustered, but Ace was making his way out of the room with Benny, laughing and doing a little waltz.

"I'm giving you alone time. I read dads should take the baby so mom can have a break."

My jaw dropped, then I snapped it shut and grinned. "Okay, well you got about twenty minutes before he starts screaming," I called after him.

"Well, you better make that twenty minutes count," he called back.

I stood there and Ian came into view, shirtless, wearing his low-slung black pants that hugged his ass just right. He looked down at me, eyes twinkling with lust and mischief.

"Should I leave you alone so you can have some time to yourself?"

I bit my lip, thinking about how I walked the floor half the night, just thinking about how much I wanted to take a long shower undisturbed.

"Well, I was really wanting to take a shower without having to hurry or bring a bouncy seat into the bathroom."

He cocked his head.

"How about I wash your back?"

A flush crept up my cheeks as I unabashedly stared at his chiseled abs.

"Yeah. Let's do that."

I started toward the shower but Ian put up his hand to stop me.

"Just wait there, lemme get stuff ready."

I shrugged and took a seat.

He quickly scooped up some of the baby's clothes and toys, then went to my closet.

What the hell is he doing?

He emerged with some of my clothes, grinning as he laid them out on the bed.

"Just stay there, I've got this."

"Ookay..."

He disappeared into the bathroom and I heard the shower start running.

Seconds later, soft music was playing and he was approaching me, extending his hand.

I smiled and took it, and he led me into the bathroom.

"Stop."

"Stop what?" I said as I started to remove my shirt.

"Doing stuff." He chuckled as I froze where I stood.

He gently pulled my arms up so they were raised above my head and slowly pulled my shirt off. Then he took off my pants and underwear, helping me step out of them before leading me to the shower.

He had everything ready, my shampoo and conditioner, body scrub and gel, washcloth, everything.

I stepped in and he immediately went to work, positioning me so my hair could get wet, shampooing it, rinsing it off, and liberally applying conditioner.

He pulled me away from the water for a moment and repositioned me so it wasn't getting in my face or hair, but was still raining down on my body.

He knelt down, gazing up at me while the hot water rained on my chest and down my torso and legs.

When he kissed just below my belly button, I smoothed his hair and smiled down at him.

After a few moments, he grabbed my body oil, poured some out on his hand, and started massaging it into my thighs, working up and down as I tilted my head back.

"I feel like you are carrying some tension in your upper thighs, Jade." His eyes twinkled and I laughed out loud.

"Yeah, you gonna work that tension out?"

"Yes, Ma'am."

His strong hands did feel good massaging my legs and hips, and it felt especially good when his mouth traveled southward, planting soft kisses along my inner thighs while I enjoyed the feel of the warm water running down my body.

"Fuck, that feels good."

I gasped a little when his tongue found my clit, and immediately went to work.

His movements were efficient and effective, and I knew he wanted to get me off before things went any further. I appreciated it, because who knew how much time we really had. The fact that he was putting my relaxation and pleasure first made me feel loved.

I let my eyes close and my mind go blank as he slipped his fingers inside me while his tongue teased my clit, applying just the right amount of pressure to get me where I needed to go.

"I'm going to come. Holy shit, Ian."

Not going to lie, his skill with his tongue was impressive. I was so close to exploding in his mouth, just a few more seconds...

I gasped again as waves of pleasure moved through my body. My legs shook and my chest heaved. I moaned and with one hand on the back of his head pressed myself against him, milking the sensations for all I could get.

Once I had my fill of his mouth, he rose from his knees, lifting me up and leaning my back against the wall. I clung to him as he guided my body, moving it just right until I was lined up with his hard shaft. Then, as he pressed me against the tile, he lowered me down so he could easily move in and out of me.

The feel of the cool tile against my back and his hard cock inside me post orgasm was a mingling of sensations I didn't expect. The sound of the falling water and the feel of his wet skin... it was a whole sensory vibe and I wanted more of it.

"You feel so good," he whispered in my ear, his voice raspy and thick with hunger.

He started fucking me with steady, sure strokes, not going slow, but not rushing, either. I succumbed to him, relaxing into his body. My muscles relaxed, with my body warm and wet against his.

Soon he was gasping and driving into me harder as the water beat down on his skin. He trembled and tensed, throwing his head back as he came. I could feel the heat of him in my body and it was a delicious sensation. I was already fantasizing about the next time we would be together. How I would be the one to kneel down and take him in my mouth. How I would feel his hot cum hitting the back of my throat while I swallowed it down.

"Ugh, Ian. I already want you again," I said as he gently lowered me, my legs shaking and my head spinning.

"Soon, baby. Soon. I will never be able to get enough of you."

The sound of Benny's babbling brought a smile to my face as I bounced down the stairs, feeling deliciously warm and satiated. Ian followed me, smiling and humming to himself.

Ace was a vision, busily working in the kitchen while Benny smacked his hands on the tray of his high chair. Rock music was playing and it was a definite vibe in the kitchen.

"Where's Mick? Xander?" Ian gave Benny's curls a light tousle and took a seat.

"That's a good question. They left on some kind of mysterious errand this morning and said they would be back in the afternoon. Pisses me off, I don't feel like any of us should leave till... well till tonight, but they were on a definite mission. A secret mission." He turned and narrowed his eyes, looking half serious, half joking, like he so frequently did.

"Here, fill up your plate." He beamed as he watched me take a bite of pasta, then of the warm, buttery bread. I closed my eyes and moaned with pleasure. His cooking was so fucking good.

"I love you," I said. And I meant it.

When I opened my eyes I noticed Ian and Ace exchange an uneasy glance, and the feeling of contentment and safety came crashing down.

Tonight was the night they were going to kill Pierce and anyone else who was a threat to us.

If all went well, we could continue to live in this beautiful home together as a family.

But if it didn't...

Chapter Forty-Two

Ian

I COULD STILL SMELL Jade on me when we exited the truck and made our way to Moni's, an exclusive, invite-only brothel and club run by the Moreno family since the late 80s.

"You ready for this?"

I eyed Xander as I asked the question. Just a few months ago I wouldn't consider him strong enough for something like this. He was different now.

"Yeah, I'm beyond ready. Let's go."

We left Ace behind, along with Mick. It was Xander and me, and I knew Ace was stewing because he wanted a shot at Pierce, but he also wanted to protect Jade and Benny. So he agreed, and Mick did, too. I felt good knowing they were there. No way anyone was going to hurt them.

Never again.

"You think they'll be here already?" Xander asked.

"I don't know. I told them to get here at nine. They could show up early. Wouldn't be ideal, but no matter."

"What if the girls back out?"

"We deal with it when it comes. They won't all back out, so as long as we've got some of them on our side, it should be fine."

"What if one of them betrays us?"

I shook my head. "Let's hope not, but I trust Monique would sniff out a rat and deal with it."

"I fucking hope so."

We walked quickly and went to the back entrance. Sally let us in with a smile and a wink and led us to Monique's office.

Smelling of jasmine and opulence, her "office" featured a giant king-size bed covered in black satin, and candles were lit everywhere, filling the room with a hazy, golden glow.

She reclined in a leather chair, her feet propped up on a desk, and she was smoking a cigar.

"Moni. It's been too long." Xander stepped forward and she hugged him into her bosom like he was still a little boy. He flushed and grinned then waved his hand awkwardly at her. She smiled and poured herself a drink.

Her smile was coy and seductive, a smile she'd patented and registered as the deadly weapon it was. She was dark-haired with porcelain skin and had an ageless quality about her. I'd known her for years, and although I wouldn't consider her a friend, I'd always admired her spirit in the face of the constant darkness.

Also, she took care of her girls.

"So this is it," she said as she blew a series of smoke rings and snapped her fingers.

From the shadows, three young women emerged. They couldn't be more than teenagers, looking innocent enough until you really saw the look in their eyes. These girls were cagey. There was an underlying rage, just bubbling under the surface. They were intimidating.

Too many women underestimate the havoc they could wreak if they just allowed themselves to be dangerous.

"These young ladies are on our team. Look at them. Nubile, doe-eyed little sirens and each one of them could kick the living shit out of you."

I laughed and cocked my head, noting that all three girls were standing at attention.

"How long have you been waiting for this day?"

She looked at me, her eyes smoldering with a deep, seething hatred.

"A long time. It was inevitable, and I thank you for lighting the proverbial fire under my ass and making it happen."

The door opened and a woman I recognized as Katy walked to Moni, leaned down, and whispered something in her ear.

"Your friends are arriving. They should be here shortly. I recommend moving to the lounge."

I nodded and Xander looked at me, his mouth grim and eyes full of a mixture of doubt and determination.

We could easily fuck this whole thing up. The girls could fuck it up. Pierce's guys could outnumber us. Outsmart us. Who knew? All we knew was that it had to end here. Tonight.

"They're here."

There were at least two dozen women in the house. A handful of them was working the floor, serving drinks and doling out the charm. This included Moni's "secret weapons", the girls she'd been training.

Moni stayed in her office for now, with Katy and Sally waiting in the wings. Ellen, Candy, and Veronica were somewhere in the house. Waiting. There were some who had no inkling of what was happening, but most did. I glanced at one girl in her skin-tight dress. A white dress. She was a slight little thing and seeing the skin-tight, too-short dress made me think of the first time I'd seen Jade. She was so beautiful, so sad, vulnerable and angry. I would never in a million years forget that day.

Six men filed into the lounge. Pierce's men. I recognized half of them as Berto's guys. Joe was one of Berto's head guys. Always close to him. Rick was nobody special, but he'd been around for a while. He was the type of guy who just wanted to get promoted and didn't care what he had to do to get ahead.

Then there was Aaron. He was someone I'd hung out with, someone I'd sort of trusted. I mean, I don't trust anyone, but I trusted him more than a lot of Berto's goons.

Of course, I was also one of Berto's goons. And these guys knew that. They knew me and they knew Xander. They knew Xander killed Berto, and they knew why we were here.

"Just the two of you, huh?"

Pierce emerged from the shadows, and one of his guys took his coat and handed it to the redhead with the cute bob cut. White dress girl began offering drinks but Pierce waved her away.

"Let's have a seat, shall we?"

I nodded and sat next to Xander. One girl set down some glasses and Xander and I both accepted.

Seeing Pierce in the flesh was harder than I thought it would be. I wanted to slit his throat. I wanted to dump my booze on his head and toss a match at him and listen to his screams as he burned alive.

I glanced at Xander and could tell by his clenched jaw and look of absolute disgust, he felt the same way.

"I find it hard to believe that you two would show up here like this alone. I don't get it. Not at all."

Xander shrugged. "It needed to happen at some point, right?"

He nodded and stroked his chin. "I suppose so. Where are Mick and Ace?"

"Doesn't matter," I said.

Pierce leaned back in his chair and his eyes raked over one of the trio of terror, as I was calling them in my mind. She had long, wavy blonde hair, skin like glass, and huge blue eyes. She was tiny, and I realized that Pierce definitely had a type and she was it. Just like Jade. It made me sick and I could see in his eyes what he wanted to do to her.

The urge to put my hands around his neck was strong.

Moni entered slowly, smirking and approaching Pierce. She slid her hand across his arm and leaned down to plant a soft kiss on his cheek.

"So good to see you. It's an honor," she purred.

He gave a half-hearted smile in return and motioned for one of the girls to fill his glass.

My chest tightened, and I watched him sip as his crew stayed close.

"You checked them for weapons, right?" Pierce shot a hard look at Moni as she slinked toward the bar.

"Of course," she said. "Check them again if you'd like."

"I would like." Pierce snapped his fingers and two of his guys lumbered toward us, wearing too-tight shirts and gold chains, looking every bit like the thugs they were.

I stood up, rolling my eyes as they patted us down from head to toe. We were unarmed, as far as these guys were concerned.

But were we? I tried hard not to chuckle as the dull-looking dipshits Pierce had guarding him went back to their positions.

I didn't know for sure, but I would bet he had another half dozen guys outside.

"Water?" The redhead sidled up to Thug One, flashed a dazzling smile, and presented him with a glass of water.

He shrugged and took it, as did Thug Two.

Pierce nudged Aaron and Rick and whispered something to them.

"My boys would like a tour of the facilities," he said, his smile full of contempt and the honest belief that he was too good for this place. Too good for the women here. Too good to be sitting with the likes of us.

My heart sank a little as I watched the cute redhead lead Aaron and two of the other guys out of the room. But it was what it was. Everyone makes their choices in life. I'd put it out there just like Xander, Ace, and Mick. Plenty of Berto's guys had the option of coming over to our side. They chose Pierce.

They chose the losing side.

"Now, while my guys make a very thorough check to ensure that you were telling the truth about how many of you there are, let's talk shop."

Now it was my turn to smile. Shop. How silly did he think we were?

"Sure," Xander said, turning his glass and watching the lights dance in the cuts. "Let's talk shop."

Pierce cleared his throat and scowled at Xander.

"As you know, your uncle did not have any children of his own. At least none that I know of."

Xander shrugged. "That's also my understanding."

"So besides yourself, his dear and devoted nephew, the only other relatives he has are his brother, Jesse, and his children, of which there are many, from what I hear."

I nodded. "He's got a baseball team."

Pierce chuckled at that.

"Now, I know for a fact that Berto made a will. He talked about it. No details, no idea what or who appears in that will, but I know that I need it."

"Huh. Okay. What makes you think we have it?"

Again with the toothy sneer, followed by a deep sigh and a headshake.

"Don't play coy with me, Ian. I know Xander and Ace rooted through Berto's office at the warehouse, pillaged his house, and had a field day at our desert compound. You can't convince me that the will wasn't in one of those places."

"I haven't come across a will." I turned to look at Xander. "You?"

Xander shook his head. "Not me. Why is it so important to you, Pierce? You think he left you the farm?"

Pierce folded his hands in front of him on the table.

"Berto Moreno had a vast fortune in property, investments, businesses, precious metals, accounts, and personal assets."

He sat back and paused, then continued, keeping his gaze fixed on us.

"As the head of the Moreno Family, those assets are mine. Now, if he left some things to his brother, or to someone else, then that's fine. I'm willing to negotiate and be generous. However, I need that will so I can inventory what is now mine, and part out what I want to part out. So why don't we stop playing games? Give me the will, and I might let you two live."

I laughed at that, and I watched Pierce yawn and shake his head again.

"What's taking them so long?" He frowned and narrowed his eyes at us.

"You guys pulling some shit? Because I promise you won't get away with it."

I shook my head. "Wouldn't dream of it. What else did you want to discuss?"

Again, Pierce snapped his fingers, and one of his guards stepped out of the room. Now there were only two guys in the room with Pierce and I did my level best not to blow it right then and there.

Fortunately, I kept my cool and didn't jump on the opportunity, or else I would have missed this one.

The guard returned less than a minute later with none other than Eddie himself. He was wearing a suit now, too. It looked ridiculous on him but I guess A for effort.

"Eddie. Good to see you, man." I nodded my head at him and he glared, his eyes tinged with fear.

Xander burst out laughing. "This is Eddie? Are you fucking kidding me?"

"Hey, fuck you, man." Eddie's nostrils flared and his eyes went all wild, and it was hilarious. I didn't blame him for laughing, but this situation couldn't disintegrate.

Pierce scowled and motioned to his guy.

"Text Jamie and Teddy, let them know there is a possible situation."

I pasted a confused and hurt look on my face.

"Situation? What are you talking about?"

“Don’t fuck with me, Ian. I find it hard to believe that you are here alone. This place isn’t big. There’s no reason my guys shouldn’t be back by now.”

“Maybe they got distracted? This place is... full of distractions.”

I winked at the girl serving another round of drinks and she smiled.

“My guys are professionals and I didn’t authorize any bullshit.”

“Good help is hard to find.” Xander smiled.

Two more of Pierce’s guys arrived and went straight to the back. Eddie shifted from one foot to the other nervously.

“Tell him,” he whined at Pierce.

“Yes. Of course.” Pierce took another drink.

“You have something that belongs to my friend.”

“Oh?”

“Don’t fucking play dumb,” Eddie barked. “I want my son back.”

“Oh, the baby you were neglecting?”

“What the fuck do you know? You’re just a goddamn thief and a fucking killer. I’ve heard about you. What? You think you and that whore can do a better job of raising my son?”

He was beet red and breathless, furious and scared. It was actually kind of sad.

“Yes, I know we can.”

Pierce put his hand out to shut Eddie up and gave me a weary glance.

“You will give him back his son. We’ll arrange it. If you comply with my instructions, and by that, I mean returning Eddie’s son and handing over the will, I might decide to leave you guys alone. What do you think? Give back the baby, give up the will. We’ll call it good. We’ll leave you alone and you can go back to your original plan. Get out of here. Go somewhere far away from Los Angeles. How does that sound?”

I stroked my chin and casually glanced at my watch. Not including Eddie, there were two guys plus Pierce. If the girls had done their job, none of the guys who went on a "tour" or the guys who went after them would come back.

One of Pierce's guys started clearing his throat. Pierce first looked at him with an irritated expression that quickly turned to alarm.

"Get him some water!" He looked at me, then at Xander. "What the fuck is this? Is something going on here?"

The second guy followed, clawing at his throat and coughing. Soon, both of them were on their knees, puking and trying to breathe.

Eddie backed up but halted when he backed right into one of Moni's girls.

"What the fuck?" Eddie screeched.

Pierce clucked and shook his head and started reaching inside his jacket for his gun.

I pulled the gun that was strapped underneath the table and leveled it at him before he could get the chance.

"What the fuck is this, Ian?"

Xander laughed. "This is you getting royally screwed. You really shouldn't be so casual about pissing people off, Pierce. You never know when that shit is going to bite you in the ass."

Moni strolled from behind the bar, followed by three of her armed girls. Katy emerged from the shadows, and Sally and Veronica joined them. Each of the women stood in a semicircle, staring down Pierce.

Meanwhile, Xander and I just sat back and watched as Eddie and Pierce were both disarmed and tied up.

The guys that Pierce brought to protect him were on the floor, dead from whatever it was the girls put in their drinks. I'd left specific instructions that Pierce's drink would not get spiked.

"Well, well, well," Moni drawled, tracing her finger along Pierce's forehead. "You certainly are in a pickle, aren't you, lover boy?"

"You're going to die a slow, painful death, you bitch." He seethed, his face red and sweat dripping down his temple.

Moni's smile was sweet, but her eyes were steely.

"I think not, Pierce. You see, it's your turn to die, and no one is coming to save you because you don't have any real friends. There's not one woman here that would piss on you if you were on fire. We all know what you did with those girls you took. You are a fucking pussy, Pierce. You hurt women and you think you're smart and tough, but you fucking underestimated us. Did it never occur to you that you could only hurt us for so long before we retaliated? You checked these guys for weapons, but it didn't occur to you we might be armed? You just let you and your guys drink what we served you, not even thinking for one minute that you were among enemies?"

"You bitches think you are so brave, but you would never have done this without help from men." He jerked his chin at me and Xander, but I put my hands up and shook my head.

"You're wrong, there. This plan has been brewing since long before we approached them. They were ready. We just moved things along a little."

"Fuck you. Fuck all of you," he spat.

"What now?" Xander asked.

I took a delicious minute to savor the growing fear in Pierce's eyes. His guys weren't coming to save him. Anyone outside had already been flushed out and dealt with. Bodies were cooling down upstairs. The guys on the ground weren't getting up. Eddie was tied up and now gagged for good measure. Pierce was opening and closing his mouth like a fish, trying to decide what fountain of bullshit he could spew that had the best chance of getting him out of the mess he was in.

"I'm going to make this short and sweet." I stood up, keeping my gun trained on Pierce's forehead just in case.

"Ian..."

"Nope, you don't get to talk or interrupt."

He sighed and fidgeted against his restraints.

"Eddie, you are definitely coming with us."

Eddie's eyes widened, then narrowed before he started struggling against the ropes and screaming through his gag. Nobody gave a shit because everyone knew what a worthless loser Eddie was.

With that out of the way, I focused on Pierce. This situation was more complicated.

"So, you're going to die, Pierce. That isn't a question. The question is, do we off you here?"

Some of the girls started whispering and gesturing, and I could tell by the vibe I might have a problem.

"Ian? A word, please?" Moni drifted toward me and put a hand around my forearm, pulling me into the shadows.

"What's up, Moni?" I whispered.

"I'm going to be honest here. The girls want blood. That's the whole reason we did all this. We have a mess to clean up now and we need our payoff."

I pressed my lips together and nodded. Of course they did, and it was understandable. But killing Pierce without Ace would not fly. In fact, we all needed to be there. Jade needed the option of justice and closure. This guy had kept her captive in a cage. Raped and tortured her. Killed her friend. Killed her cousin. We couldn't take away her opportunity to say something to him. To hurt him. Only if she wanted to. Maybe she wouldn't want to see him. But the option needed to be there.

"I hear you. But I have to bring him home with me. Don't worry, I promise you this guy is dead and will never bother you again, but justice needs to be served slowly, and Jade needs closure."

She pursed her lips, looked at the girls waiting for the word, and nodded slowly.

"Fine. He can die with you, but he's not leaving here without some pain. We will still take our blood."

"Agreed. Just don't fucking kill him."

Moni smiled. "We won't. But we'll make him wish he was dead. What about the loser?"

"It's a huge bonus we got him. Mick and Xander seem to have something in the works. I honestly don't know, but I know we're bringing him with us."

"Sounds good. Now, why don't you two give Pierce and my girls some privacy."

I nodded and shot her a warning look. If I came back in the room and he was dead, there would be hell to pay.

Chapter Forty-Three

Jade

I PACED THE LENGTH of my room more times than I could count, and every hour I would check in with Mick and Ace.

"Anything? A text?"

Over and over I'd burst into Mick's room while he kept his eyes on the exterior cameras. Ace was in the living room, sticking by the phone and trying to act casual.

"No, nothing."

Benny was sound asleep in the safe room, at Mick's insistence. He didn't want to have to waste time gathering him and all his stuff up in case Pierce's guys showed up. So I'd been in there with him since the guys left, hoping like hell there would be no uninvited guests, no guns or dirty cops this time around.

And no Pierce.

Because if Pierce and his men showed up that meant two things: One, Xander and Ian were dead. And two, I would soon wish I was dead.

Two more hours went by. Then three. Then four.

"It's almost morning," I wailed. "There's something wrong."

Ace was pale and quiet, and that told me he knew it, too.

"We won't panic, but we need to think about next steps if they don't return by the agreed upon time."

My head felt like it was going to explode. I'd had three cups of coffee and two slices of cold pizza.

"Fuck."

Tears welled up in my eyes and I struggled to relax while giving Benny his morning feeding. He could tell there was something wrong, so he was extra fussy.

Finally, he dozed off. He would wake up again in a couple of hours.

"Fuck," I said again as I cried silent tears of dread, fear, and helplessness.

"They can't be dead."

Trauma resurfaced as I waited, sure that Pierce's guys were going to show up like they did last time. Positive that Xander and Ian were unsuccessful and either dead or captive. Absolutely knowing that this time, there would be no escape for me.

Just as I laid Benny down Ace burst into the room.

"I got a fucking text. They are on their way."

An hour later we stood together, anxiously awaiting Xander and Ian. I was a fucking mess. Because they didn't just have Pierce, they had Eddie, too.

The truck backed in and I held my breath as I watched.

Mick and Ace pulled a struggling Eddie out of the truck first, and I felt like I was going to pass out.

I kidnapped his kid. Doesn't matter that it was justified and that I hated Eddie and he helped murder Tish. I still felt a horrible sinking feeling as he glared at me, foaming through his gag and kicking and jerking around.

"We've got the perfect little home for you, Eddie. Don't worry, you're going to be just fine."

Now it was time for the main attraction. The sound of his grunts filled me with a darkness I couldn't explain. Watching him struggle as Mick and Xander pulled him out of the truck was exhilarating. I couldn't wait to see him suffer. I was angry and excited and not afraid.

It was so weird, the contrast. Seeing Eddie gave me the most sickening sensation of shrinking and dreading. Like I was that thirteen-year-old girl just trying to find safety, only to be traumatized all over again. And again. Eddie reduced me.

But not Pierce. Despite my instinctive fear of him, I did not shrink in his presence. My hunger for revenge and desire for his suffering trumped my fear.

"Damn, you guys already tee off on him? I thought we'd agreed..." Ace shook his head as he examined our catch.

"We didn't do this. The girls did. That's what took us so long."

"The girls? They did this?" I raised my brows and got a little closer, aware of Pierce's eyes on me. I could see the raw hatred in his eyes and somehow it made me happy.

"Wow, I wondered if I'd ever see your ugly face again, and here we are." I tapped my foot as Mick and Ace held him while Xander and Ian watched from the sidelines.

"I thought you guys were just going to kill him," I said.

"Yeah, that was our original plan but we decided that a quick death was better than he deserved. And we didn't know if you had anything you wanted to say to him. Or do."

Xander added in that last part and my heart fluttered as I considered his statement.

"How long will we keep him?"

"As long as we want."

"You guys are stupid. My men will come looking for me," he said, lifting his chin defiantly.

I tentatively approached him, then landed a square kick right in his jaw.

"Nice," Ace praised.

Pierce winced at the impact, but it wasn't something that was going to break him or anything.

I was just getting started.

Ian smiled and motioned for me to come closer to him.

"And while he's here as our special guest, we wanted to make sure he was comfortable, of course."

I took a few steps forward and saw that Ian was next to something that was covered with a tarp.

"What's that?"

He whipped the tarp off with a flourish, revealing a cage.

My heart jumped nearly out of my chest and gooseflesh sprouted all over my arms.

The cage looked to be about the same size as the cage I inhabited during my stay at Berto's desert compound.

Mick moved toward the cage as Ace, Ian, and Xander guided Pierce inside. He struggled and swore, his eyes wild with rage and fear. My chest tightened and the blood rushed in my ears, providing me with a visceral reaction to the sight of him, my torturer, captor, and the murderer of my friends and family, being stuffed into a cage.

"You're all gonna die, you hear me? No mercy for any of you. Especially you, pretty. You are going to wish you'd died in the desert by the time I am finished with you."

Logically, I knew this was absurd, but there was a part of me that was triggered, that was certain the rug would be pulled from under me and he would somehow escape, somehow he would find a way out and come for me like he'd promised.

Ace kicked at the cage and motioned to Xander.

"Grab the hose."

Xander nodded and I watched in awe as he returned with a brand-new hose, clearly purchased for the occasion, screwed it into the spigot, and turned it on Pierce, full blast. He hit him with the water for about forty-five seconds and turned it off.

Pierce sputtered and whined, but said nothing.

"Lesson one: Don't talk to Jade. Don't threaten her or address her unless she is asking you a question. Do you understand?"

Pierce glowered but nodded miserably. Too easy, I thought. He was certainly trying to figure out how to get out of his predicament.

Several times I thought about approaching the cage and either kicking it, spraying him down, screaming at him, or heckling him. But I wasn't ready. I think I was still in shock. Still in a state of disbelief that we'd finally bested the monster.

It felt too good to be true.

Mick and Xander came back with celebration pizza, sodas, beer, candy bars, and a bottle of pricey whiskey.

"Pizza time, Benny. That means mushy baby food for you." Ace laughed.

He swooped him up and I got misty-eyed at how naturally and willingly he'd stepped up for Benny, taking part in his care. He loved to take him into the kitchen and talk about all the food and gadgets in the kitchen, then put him in the high chair so he could watch everything.

"You know, Jade. I was thinking we should just start making his baby food. It's healthier, and it's not that hard. I watched a whole YouTube video on it."

He was doling out pizza slices while I grabbed Benny's food out of the fridge. Ian cracked open a beer for me, and Mick went to double-check everything was secure in the garage.

"Neither of them are going anywhere, Jade. Don't worry." Xander said.

I shrugged and shoved the pizza in my face while air-planing a spoonful of green bean mush toward Benny's mouth.

"That stuff looks vile. Why don't you just give him some apples or peaches?" Ian wrinkled his nose at the store-bought concoction and I smiled, offering him a sniff.

"Keep that shit away from me. I think you're abusing him." He joked.

I rolled my eyes. "He has to be accustomed to eating vegetables, to eating bitter flavors. If I get him hooked on bananas and peaches and shit, he'll have a sweet tooth and reject the vegetables."

"She's making sense," Xander said as he grabbed another slice of pizza.

My logic did not move Ian. "I think she's mean."

I punched him playfully in the arm and Benny burst out laughing, a deep belly laugh and so I punched him again and Benny lost it, shaking with gleeful laughter like it was the funniest thing he'd ever seen.

"The boy already has a taste for violence." Ace beamed at him and I facepalmed, half horrified and half proud.

After all, he would grow up with violent criminals, right? We had his father locked in a cage in the garage, right? Every one of us had killed. Who was I kidding to think this kid was going to have a normal childhood?

Later, after Benny was sound asleep in his warm bed and Xander and Ian regaled us with stories of how the women from the brothel had coordinated an attack involving poison and a great deal of throat-slitting, I found myself wanting to go pay Pierce a visit.

I'd just scooped up a nice bowl of ice cream when I realized I had to go in there. I wouldn't be able to sleep if I didn't.

"Hey, I'm going to go fuck with Pierce."

I made this announcement then took myself and my bowl of ice cream and marched myself out to the garage.

Eddie was still gagged because he wouldn't shut the fuck up for even one minute, but Pierce was quiet. He had his knees drawn up to his chest and was glaring off into space when I walked in, Ace and Xander behind me.

Pierce's head popped up and his eyes met mine as I squatted down on the concrete floor in front of the cage. I took care to leave a few feet in case he got any crazy ideas like spitting on me or worse. I'd seen more than a few girls get bold and pull a move like that.

One girl had flung her piss through the cage and right at Missy's face. It would have been hilarious if we didn't all know what it meant.

Now I was on the other side of the cage and Pierce was inside, confined, restricted. The top of his head was just about touching the roof of the cage and he couldn't even stretch his legs out in front of him. I was smaller than him so for me, I'd had a little wiggle room. Not Pierce.

"I'm going to get out of this cage," he said, carefully. I was sure he would have added several expletives to his statement but didn't dare with Ace and Xander standing right behind me.

"Yeah, you think so?"

He leaned forward. "Yeah, I think so."

"You think someone is going to rescue you?" I took a bite of my ice cream, closing my eyes in ecstasy as he swallowed and pretended not to look at it. He'd been there all day and into the evening with no food and very little water.

"Someone rescued you, didn't they?" he responded.

I nodded and pointed my spoon at him. "But then again, someone gave a shit about me enough to come for me. No one cares about you, Pierce. No one gives a fuck if you live or die."

He curled his lip at me but said nothing.

"You know it's true. You didn't really have friends. You bought friends, and those kinds of friends aren't going to stick their neck out for you."

I spooned some more ice cream into my mouth.

"We'll see who shows up here, six."

Against my will, I flinched when he called me that. Cursing myself silently, I hated that he'd noticed.

"Hand me the hose," I said. My bowl was empty and it was getting late, but I had some shit to say to this fucker.

"You comfy in there? Cozy?"

Xander handed me the hose and I sprayed him right on the forehead. He shielded his face with his hands and I sprayed him some more.

"Fuck you, it's cold."

"Oh, I know, Pierce. Nothing like a nice hose down at night right before bed. Nothing like shivering for hours until every inch of your body is tense and hurting from shaking so hard. Nothing like your clothes soaked and freezing and sticking to your body while you desperately fight for just a little sleep on the hard, cold, concrete floor. Yeah, it really sucks."

He shook his head, as though he couldn't believe I was so petty as to bring up the past.

"You didn't have to do this. You got away. You escaped with your life and a good amount of money. You could have left and had a good life somewhere."

I curled my lip and rapped my knuckles on the cage.

"But then we wouldn't have this time together, Pierce."

Ace chuckled behind me and Xander bent down, picking up my bowl and giving me a wink.

"You want us to take him out? Have a little fun?"

I shook my head.

"No, I'm tired." He helped me to my feet and I stretched luxuriously before kicking his cage.

I avoided Eddie at all costs but had to ask what their plans were with him. I suppose he needed to die, too, for what he'd done to Tish. He may not have pulled the trigger but he was still responsible.

"We have plans for him, don't worry, Jade. All will be revealed tomorrow."

I nodded sleepily and leaned into Ace as we made our way out of the garage.

"I need to snuggle. Who's going to snuggle me?"

Ace laughed and pulled me in closer to him. "I'm in."

Xander came up behind me and caressed the back of my neck.

"I'm calling dibs on the other side of the bed."

"Just till Benny wakes up."

Ian greeted us in the kitchen.

"Why don't you go lie down in Ace's room for a bit? I can keep an ear out for Benny. That way you don't have to worry about Ace's fat mouth waking him up."

"Are you sure?" I asked, feeling dubious.

"Dude, I know how to make a bottle. If I can't settle him down I'll come get you."

"Okay, promise me you won't let him cry for too long. Come get me right away if he gets all frantic."

Ian rolled his eyes at me and nodded. "No problemo, Princess. I got this."

"Where's Mick?"

Xander jerked his thumb toward his room. "Already sawing logs. Old-ass."

I giggled at that, knowing full well he was only crashed out because he'd worn himself out the last few days worrying, preparing, and not sleeping.

"Goodnight, Ian." I stood on my tippy-toes and kissed his pouty lips. He smiled down at me and as I followed Ace to his room and slid between his silky sheets, with Xander climbing in behind me, I felt so content, so safe, and so loved.

And it scared the shit out of me.

Chapter Forty-Four

Mick

I DIDN'T SLEEP FOR shit, even though I was exhausted. From my room I could hear snippets of conversations here and there, I could hear Benny cry a couple times, and I knew they had gone out to the cage to mess with Pierce.

We needed to kill him fast. I didn't feel comfortable keeping him around too long. It would be too easy to be lulled into a false sense of security. Ace and Xander thought for sure there would be no one to come for Pierce, no one to try and rescue him in the hopes of a fat promotion and reward.

And, while Moni and her girls did a bang-up job of taking out Pierce's men, there could be repercussions if it was discovered that they had aided us in our scheme.

This thought disturbed me way too much to just leave it alone, so I dialed up Moni. She was a good person. The school of hard knocks and all, she was rough around the edges. But she had a heart and tried her best to help in whatever small ways she could, I didn't want to see her or her girls get hurt over what they'd done.

The phone was on the third ring before a sleepy voice picked up.

"Who's this?"

I couldn't help but laugh at the slight snarl in Moni's normally smooth, unaffected voice.

"It's Mick."

"Oh, good morning," she purred. "To what do I owe this honor?"

"Just wanted to check in with you, make sure you girls are okay."

She sighed. "Yes, us 'girls' are just fine, thank you. We can handle ourselves."

"Good to hear, Moni. I just want to reiterate that there could be backlash. Be ready for visitors."

"Oh, we're ready. But what about you guys? I mean, what's your plan?"

"Plan? As far as what?"

"Well, I'm assuming you guys are taking over, right? Before some other dipshit gets any ideas. You have a small window here. If you guys don't step up and claim this territory, someone else will. And I really don't want that. None of us do."

The conversation ended, and I felt better. Seemed like she had things under control... for now.

But she was right. Someone would come. Rarely were women just left alone to make their money and live in peace. Soon enough, some ambitious prick would sniff out opportunity and profit, content to take a large piece of the pie for very little effort.

And while the next guy might not be as awful as Pierce or Berto, they would still do what they always do: take advantage, take liberties, and leave a trail of trauma and tears.

Unless we stepped up and made things different.

"But that's not what I want to fucking do."

More and more, I was seeing my dream of getting the fuck out of the lifestyle disappearing in the rearview.

I took a quick shower, dressed, and jogged downstairs, smiling just a little at the sight of my family busy cooking breakfast, sipping their coffee, joking around, and gathering together around Jade and the baby.

Speaking of the baby...

"Hey Jade?" She was walking back and forth, putting away dishes and munching on strawberries, singing to the baby, and looking fine as hell in her linen shorts and pink crop top with her hair in a high ponytail.

She stopped and flashed a shy grin, cocking her head at me and waiting to see what I had to say.

I paused for a moment because she had no idea what was coming. No clue. Xander and I had pulled off a little secret mission, and I was about to drop that bomb right now.

"What's that?" Ace pointed at the papers in my hand.

"That's what I want to talk to you guys about. Especially you, Jade."

Xander sidled over and gave me a knowing look.

"Oh? What's up?"

I motioned her over to me and she approached. I placed the papers on the counter and slid them toward her.

"I know you have worries about the future with Benny. Yesterday, Xander and I paid a visit to a judge and he had these papers drawn up for us. Your name is in that box and once Eddie signs those papers, you will be Benny's permanent guardian."

Her mouth dropped open while she shuffled through the stack of legal documents, her hands shaking as she did.

"These are really legal?"

"Yep. They need your signature and Eddie's. The judge is taking care of the rest. Xander called in a favor, which was easy to do because the Moreno name still has a lot of pull."

Ian and Ace perked up at that. The conversation about this needed to happen soon.

"Yeah, it's nice to be able to call in favors," Ian said. "But Eddie has to agree to sign them."

I nodded. "Yeah, that was the caveat. Judge won't move forward without that, but he cleared out all the bureaucracy. The CPS stuff, the red tape, all of it."

"Cool," said Ace. "So that's what you guys were up to yesterday?"

"Yeah."

Jade looked at me, tears welling in her eyes. She threw herself at me and I lifted her off the ground as she wrapped her arms around my neck.

"I can't believe you guys did that. Oh, my god. So it will be official. We'll be able to do stuff like take him to the pediatrician and enroll him in school."

Ian laughed. "Let's not get ahead of ourselves. Kid has a while before he hits the books."

She sniffled and let go of me, then turned to Xander and mauled him with her patented Jade bear hug.

"You guys are amazing. I'm so glad you did this. I'm so glad you are all here and okay."

She sniffled some more and Ace reached out and wiped the happy tears from her face.

"Now we gotta go talk to Eddie."

"Are we going to let him go? What's the plan?" Her eyes widened as she started calculating the reality of it all.

"Good question. What's our next move? We have to figure some shit out, right?"

An hour later we were gearing up to play bad cop, good cop. I pulled Eddie out of his cage and Ace and I marched him straight into the bathroom to get him cleaned up, fed, and ready to sign papers.

"Alright, Eddie. Now I know we are the last people you want to deal with, but we have an offer for you. A really generous offer."

He eyed me and Ace warily and shook his head.

"Nah, there is no offer. I'm not betraying Pierce. He's my friend. His guys are coming any time and I am not fucking up what I had going. Besides, you fuckers stole my kid."

Ace leaned toward him and smiled. "Your kid is fine. He looks ten times better than he did when we first got him."

"What the fuck does that mean? He was fine. He was fed and happy. I don't know what kind of bullshit lies Jade has fed you about me, but she's a lying—"

I put my finger up in warning. "Now, Eddie, I'm going to stop you right there before you get yourself in trouble."

He swallowed and huffed out a sigh of resignation and frustration. I almost felt bad for him. Almost.

"No one is coming for Pierce, I promise you that. And if by some miracle they show up, I'll blow his fucking head off before they come anywhere near him. He is not leaving that cage alive, I promise you that."

Eddie's face paled. I realized then that he'd truly believed Pierce was really getting out of there. That he would somehow get free and Eddie would walk out of here with his kid and a long career being one of Pierce's lackeys.

"Like I said. I'm prepared to make you a generous offer. Ian thinks I shouldn't do it. Neither does Xander. They're real pissed about what you did to Jade and her cousin, Tish."

Now he was really pale.

Xander entered the room and gave Eddie a baleful once-over.

"See, we could just kill you. No big deal. Just like we killed Berto Moreno. Just like we had all the guys Pierce brought with him killed. We don't give a shit about you. Far as I'm concerned, you are a cancer and we should cut you out. Pierce is going to die. We are going to kill him, that's a fact. Killing you is no big deal."

"Please. Please don't kill me. I swear I won't rat you guys out. I won't do anything."

I waved Xander off and spoke to Eddie, lowering my voice to a kind, conspiratorial tone.

"I know you won't, Eddie. Like I said, I'm prepared to make you an offer."

He wiped at his nose and Ace handed him a paper towel, giving his shoulder a friendly squeeze.

"Jade is prepared to take responsibility for little Benny."

Eddie stiffened, and I motioned for him to let me finish.

"I know that maybe you have other ideas for how Benny should be raised, but let's just be honest here. Jade's parents are old and sick. They can't give Benny the attention he needs."

Eddie shook his head, then paused, then opened his mouth to argue.

"I met a girl. She's real nice and young, and she already says she'll take care of him. I don't need Jade to raise my son."

I nodded and stroked my chin and pretended like I was thinking shit over.

"Yeah? What happens when you tire of her? What happens when you want to take your girl out somewhere fun for the weekend? You want a girl or you want a nanny?"

He laughed. "I can have both, you know that."

"Hmm. I suppose. But how are you going to keep them? The money Pierce gave you? That's about done. That car he bought you? It's sitting in a garage somewhere right now. You don't have it anymore. That pad you were staying in? Not yours anymore. You aren't getting any more paychecks. Not from the state, not from Pierce. We run the Moreno family now."

Eddie was furious at this last statement. His knuckles were turning white and his eyes flashed.

"How the hell do you have rights to claim the Moreno family?"

Xander slid right in on that one. "Name is Xander Moreno. Did you not know who the fuck I am?"

"Nice. You killed your own family." Eddie turned up his nose as though such behavior disgusted him.

Xander turned a little red himself and got right up in Eddie's face.

"I was just returning a favor. That fucker killed my father and was responsible for the death of my mother. So yeah, I killed him. And Pierce? Pierce killed Jade's cousin. She was a mother with a baby and he killed her. Killed dozens of young women. Daughters, mothers, sisters. He was going to kill Jade, and the fact that you don't care only makes me want to kill you more. Give me one good reason, Mick. Give me one good reason I shouldn't cut this piece of shit right now."

I smiled as Eddie tried to walk back everything he'd just said. I waited for him to finish.

"Would you like to hear the deal I am offering you?"

He nodded, pale, sweating, and miserable.

I leaned forward, and Ace materialized with the paperwork.

"Sign off on this paper. Relinquish your parental rights and give the baby to Jade. You sign that paper and I'll give you half a million dollars."

His eyes widened. "You can't be serious."

I nodded slowly.

"I'm dead serious. Five hundred grand and you just walk away. I'll even give you back your fancy new car. You can go back to your new girlfriend and take her somewhere nice. You have no responsibilities to anyone. Don't have to worry about raising a kid. I hear it's expensive. You can come and go without worrying about babysitters or jealous girlfriends or keeping formula and food in the house. No more buying diapers. No more worrying about him getting sick or crying or shitting his pants. Jade will take good care of him, raise him up like he's her own."

He narrowed his eyes and pretended to scoff at the idea, but he was already crumbling.

"You can have more kids, Eddie. And now you'll have money for them. Knock up your new girl. Marry her and make an honest woman of her. Or don't. Hire a nanny. Or just go be free with a fat stack of cash and zero responsibilities. Be honest, Eddie. Do you really love that kid? Do you really want to be responsible for him for the next seventeen years and change?"

At that, he stopped cold. He knew full well he didn't love the kid. He had that low-class mentality that trash like him gets when they have a son. Like they actually achieved something special by blowing their wad and getting someone pregnant and producing a boy child. Big fucking deal, but for guys like Eddie with nothing else to offer the world, it *was* a big deal.

"One million dollars, Eddie. Or I let Xander take you back out into the garage. Ian's out there now, waiting. Hoping you make the wrong decision."

Eddie swallowed.

"I want to see him."

That threw me for a loop. I guess I should have figured he would ask that, but somehow I didn't think he would.

I was wrong.

Xander shook his head, but Ace shrugged. "I mean, let him see the kid."

"Won't it fuck him up? Confuse him?" Xander wondered.

"It will be fine. You get to see him. You don't touch him or hold him. Period. But yeah, you can see him."

Ace went up the stairs while I studied Eddie some more. He was a fucking loser, but again, part of me felt bad for him. I'd been a loser in a past life, an abusive drunk. I would never see my daughter again, and I hated myself for that.

One day, he might have a wake-up call, but it would be too late. He would have regrets over the way he had treated Jade and neglected his son.

Or maybe he wouldn't.

Ace returned with Benny. The baby was dressed in the cutest little overalls and he'd put on weight. He was a total roly-poly with rosy cheeks and a mop of curls. He was grinning broadly and babbling cheerfully, completely content and safe.

Eddie saw him and I saw the understanding on his face. For all his fuckery, he could clearly recognize that his son was doing amazingly.

Benny looked straight at him and continued grinning. I had wondered what we would do if he reached for him or cried for him, but I think we all knew that wouldn't happen.

Eddie pressed his lips together and nodded, reaching for the paperwork. Xander handed him a pen and he started signing.

Chapter Forty-Five

Jade

I'D SPENT TWENTY MINUTES straight crying a river of happy tears. Once the rest of the paperwork was finalized, Benny would be my son. All because Xander had connections, and the guys had a shit ton of money. Money and a name bought me custody of Eddie's baby.

They had promised Eddie a half a million dollars. Were they really going to give it to him? Or did they lie? Would they kill him, instead?

My chest tightened. I didn't like the idea of the guys fooling anyone, not even Eddie. Why be shady like that?

So you can get what you want, that's why. He's the one who allowed Tish to be murdered in cold blood. He deserves to die, not rewarded for being a selfish loser.

My own thoughts shocked me. I guess it didn't matter how much I meditated or how many affirmations I said or self-help books I read. The truth was I didn't care anymore. The idea of "offing" someone carried no shock value.

It could easily be me, Mick, Ace, Xander, or Ian.

So why not Eddie?

I blew out a breath because it finally hit me. I was changed. The old Jade no longer existed, and this new Jade was wiser, darker, and more than just a little...

Jaded.

"We're going to let him go. But first, we gotta take care of Pierce. We can't have him running off to whatever is left of Pierce's guys."

"That won't happen. We appealed to his better nature and bribed him with money and freedom. Both of which we will take away from him if he steps a foot out of line."

Mick grunted in agreement. "Yeah, and I truly believe a part of him is relieved that he no longer has the responsibility."

I nodded. That felt true. Eddie loathed responsibility. He cared for Benny as much as he was capable, but that was it. He didn't really want to take care of him.

"But it's time we did Pierce. So if there's anything else you need to get closure from him, now's the time."

Ace cracked his knuckles and was giddy with excitement.

The sound of footsteps descending the stairs at an urgent rate caught our collective attention.

"Guys, we got company."

The blood drained from my face and I froze for a second but willed my feet to move so I could go get the baby and make it into the safe room before anyone could burst through the doors.

"Fuck. Move, Jade. Get into that room. We'll get the baby." Mick snarled, guiding me into the theater while Ian thundered up the stairs.

Oh my god. We were wrong. Pierce has people and they are coming for him. They'll let him out of that cage and I'm fucked. It's over.

My lungs refused to work properly, and for a split second, I thought I would pass out.

"Wait. It's... Jesse."

We all stopped and Xander relaxed his shoulders a bit. "It's Uncle Jesse. He's got some people with him."

I chose to observe rather than participate, so I grabbed Benny and headed to the safe room anyway. I flipped on the monitors so I could see and hear what was going on. There were three other men with Jesse, and a woman.

Not just any woman.

"Fucking Missy."

Fury coursed through my veins as I watched Mick clap Jesse on the shoulder and the lot of them strolled into the house, with Missy bouncing right along behind them. Into *my* house.

"Fuck her."

Thanks to the microphones, I could hear everything that was transpiring and Jesse was laughing, joking, and being his usual jovial self.

"Xander, heard you boys bagged Pierce. That's admirable, good job."

Ian spoke up. "Yep, killed him graveyard dead. Tossed him over a very steep cliff. Shame what happened to him."

Jesse laughed and I relaxed a little. I guess if they thought he was dead they'd have no motivation to go searching the house for him.

"What's next for you guys?" Jesse asked.

There was a few seconds of awkward silence then Mick, ever the straight shooter, dropped the bomb.

"We're not sure yet, and we could ask you the same question. You came here for a reason. You heard about Pierce, I'm guessing. So what's next for you?"

"Well, there are some things I wanted to talk to you about. It's true."

Xander and Mick looked at each other and shrugged.

"Let's hear it."

Missy walked through my kitchen and opened the fridge. "You guys got anything to drink? I could use a snack, too. Long drive." She giggled and started pawing through the refrigerator.

The anger inside me swelled to epic proportions and I started thinking some pretty dark thoughts.

When she cracked open one of my beers and sat her ass on one of my stools, leaning her elbow on the island like she owned the place, it was almost too much.

"Deep breaths, Jade. One, two, three, four..."

Visions of Missy torturing Saysha swam through my brain and had me nearly hyperventilating.

Meanwhile, Jesse was regaling everyone with tales of a showdown in Barstow and a harrowing job in Vegas. There was laughter and more beers cracked open.

I watched Missy eyeballing the house, looking around, poking her nose where it didn't belong.

The rage and trauma were so loud in my ears, I stopped hearing what was being said in the kitchen among the guys. When I finally tuned in, the topic had taken an interesting turn.

"So there really was a will?" Is what I heard when I got Benny settled and could focus on what they were up to.

A will. That's what Pierce had been freaking out about.

"Yeah, we found it tucked away at that compound when you guys rescued your girl."

I watched Missy as Jesse spoke and she laughed and rolled her eyes.

"Watch it, Missy, we rescued you, too. That place was a fucking horror show and you know it."

"Easy, Jesse. That's in the past, now," Missy's man warned. He was a big guy. Big as Mick.

I wanted to kick the living shit out of her.

While Benny was rubbing his eyes and nodding his head, I had a front-row seat to all the tea.

Jesse was finally getting to the point of why he had crawled out of the desert. I remembered the day he told us how much he hated Los Angeles. How he loved the desert and would never in a million years wanted to come back here.

But maybe things had changed.

"According to Berto's will, everything goes to Ace. All of it. The property, accounts, everything."

Holy shit. I did not see that coming.

"So Berto left everything to Ace, and you want him to reject it or something? Is that what I'm hearing?" Ian crossed his arms and glared at Jesse because that's exactly what he was saying.

Xander was quiet. I wonder if it hurt his feelings that his uncle left his fortune to Ace and not him? I'd heard the way Berto talked about Ace. He revered him because I think he believed he was like him.

Ace was a killer - although I'd personally not seen that side of him. Not really. He was so sweet and nurturing. I struggled to believe that he truly enjoyed harming anyone.

But he did. I'd heard enough to know it was true. And if he got his fondest wish, he'd be killing Pierce.

And I'd be watching.

"What if I don't want to decline this inheritance, Jesse? After all, he left it to me."

Ace just asked the wrong question, of course.

"Well, Ace. You know I like you, I do. But Berto was my brother. I'm his next of kin, not you. Not even Xander. By the law, it's me."

"Unless there's a will that says otherwise, right?"

"I can fight you in court, boys. And that could get expensive. And it could get dangerous."

Mick crossed his arms, and the entire room shifted. Now things were getting tense, and I wondered what Jesse's strategy was going to be.

Fuck. If Ace is dead, then the inheritance goes to the next of kin, right?

Shit, shit, shit.

"Look, I just want what's fair. Berto killed my brother. He exiled me to the desert, using me when it suited him. I helped build this family, too. And it's just another fuck you from him leaving me out of the will."

Ian pulled at his goatee and regarded Jesse, trying to size him up and determine if he was a threat.

"So you're butthurt. I get it. But what else do you want? I mean, what do you really want? Just the money? The homes? The investments? Or is there something more?"

Jesse shook his head. "I came here in good faith to ask you to do the right thing, Ace. Do the right thing and bow out of the will. Xander is family and I'm okay with making some concessions if there's something he really wants, but..."

Xander cut him off.

"But really, what do you want? Because last time we talked, you said you weren't interested in taking over Berto's territory or operations, and now—"

"I said that. And I meant it. I'm not interested in moving to Los Angeles, and I'm not interested in taking over Berto's territory or leading the family operation."

"Okay, so what are you interested in?"

"I've been over this will back to front. My brother's assets are... considerable. Homes, offshore accounts, property, stocks, bonds, precious metals, businesses, you name it."

"Yeah, my uncle had a lot of shit. We helped him build it, too," Xander said.

Jesse laughed. "Don't flatter yourselves. While you were certainly at Berto's side while he built his empire, he's the one who ran the business, built it, expanded it, worked the deals, authorized the expansions, and took a majority of the risks, including taking on rivals and winning new territories and assets. You know this, Xander."

He paused, looking each of them in the eye before continuing.

"I know you have a ton of his cash and some of his possessions. You've raided everything you could get your hands on as far as his low-hanging fruit. That's fine. Keep it. Run the family as you see fit. Take over. But know that the businesses he owns will remain in my name, and the profits will come to me. You can take your cut for running them, you can build the operation out, you can keep your ties, your hustles, run your jobs, and whatever else you got going, but the clubs, the fronts, the mom and pop businesses he'd invested in, that's all mine. What do you say?"

"Oh, hell no," I whispered. This was bullshit. And I really, really didn't like that Missy was still standing in my kitchen. Fuck all that.

Mick looked at Ace, then at Ian. Finally, he turned to Xander.

"Look, we already agreed that we were done with the organization. We accomplished what we set out to do. We dealt with Pierce, we did what we had to do to get Jade. Now, we just want peace, right, Xander?"

There was an uncomfortable silence and Mick set his jaw and glared at Xander, waiting for him to say that he was willing to walk away not just from everything that Berto had left to his friend, but also to the family business that his father began and that his uncles had built.

I knew Xander had no desire to leave the business, to abandon the lifestyle. He was in deep now. Maybe a few months ago, he wanted out, but no more.

Ian didn't want out, either.

Jesse stepped into the rescue.

"Look, Mick. I hear you. You don't want to pull jobs anymore. You are tired of the lifestyle. I was too. That's why I didn't mind getting out of Los Angeles. That's why I never fought hard to stay here or to take what my brother had stolen. But I think you'll find that life gets boring real fast when you are living on the straight and narrow."

Mick shrugged. "I got no issues with being bored."

"Yeah, but these boys will. You can't pretend that these boys are going to be satisfied with Joe jobs and a peaceful life."

"Is that true, Xander? Ace? Ian? Because we've talked about this. Planned our exit a million times. You telling me you want to give up the life we've been planning to keep this fucking bullshit going?"

Jesse held up his hand.

"Just know if you guys don't do it, there are plenty of guys that are happy to take over. And you might not like what that ends up looking like."

Just when I thought I was over Missy being in my house because now they were wrapping shit up and getting ready to leave, she did it.

She opened her mouth.

"So where's Jade? She too scared to come out here and face me?"

The smile on her face was broad and self-satisfied.

A feral growl escaped my lips, and I didn't hesitate. Benny was fast asleep. I had been reluctant to come down there because I hate an awkward entrance but this bitch was running her mouth.

I left the safe room, closed the door behind me, and made a beeline for the stairs.

I skipped steps and hit the ground running. In seconds I was striding through the kitchen entryway and heading right for that red-headed bitch.

"What the fuck did you say?"

I didn't wait for an answer because I didn't give a fuck what she had to say for herself.

A quick pull back and I shot out my fist, making contact with her face and sending her sprawling onto the tile floor.

Her face registered shock, pain, and fury and I stood over her, daring her to get up and try me some more.

Of course, she did.

"Hey, what the fuck..." Her man started for me, but Jesse stuck an arm out and Mick and Ian stepped closer.

"Let them be," Mick said.

"But she just..." he whined.

"Jay, you just let them work it out." Jesse gave him a warning glance as Missy scrambled to her feet and we squared off against each other.

"You fucking whore. Who do you think you are?" she hissed.

"This is my house, bitch, so I'll ask you the same question."

She laughed. "Maybe it is, maybe it isn't."

I stepped toward her and struck, but she easily evaded and came back with a strike of her own.

I partially blocked and caught a hit on the chin, but immediately went back in and made contact. Then again, and again.

She stumbled backward but regained her balance.

"You fucking killed Saysha."

"Nope, not me. That was all Pierce and Berto. She was mouthy, and that's not my fault."

I punched her in the nose and blood splattered all over my face, hands, and the refrigerator.

"Fuck you. You singled her out. Singled us out. If not for all the times you snitched and bitched about her, tattling off to Berto and Pierce, provoking her, and doing everything you could to get under her skin..."

"It's your fault, shorty. Your fault she's dead. Pierce fucking hated you and wanted you to suffer. And you knew that. You're the one who made it clear that she was your friend, she was your favorite. Otherwise, he would have had no reason to use her against you. That's all he did. He picked the girl that you cared about most. So it's your own damn fault you betrayed her, not mine."

Her words stung me because they rang true. If I wouldn't have made it clear how much I cared about her, Pierce wouldn't have had any reason to single her out. To pull her out of her cage and take her out into the desert as a weapon against me. A way to hurt and break me.

It didn't matter. Missy was still a part of the game. Of the hunt. Of the torture and death.

I roared and flung myself at her full force, putting us both on the ground. I quickly straddled her and punched her repeatedly until my fist and her face were dripping with blood.

Finally, Mick pulled me off her and tried to settle me down as I fought, kicking and screaming obscenities.

Eventually, I stopped and glared at her bloody, swollen face.

"You deserve way worse than this. I never want to see you in my house again. I'll kill you next time."

She was a sniveling wreck at this point, and her man carried her out, narrowing his eyes at us as he passed by.

"Welp, I guess they got it figured out." Jesse seemed unfazed by what had transpired. In fact, his expression as he made his way out was more amused and impressed than anything.

"Look, Jesse, leave the will. We'll go over it and be in touch. Does that work for you?"

He looked at Ace, then Xander. Finally, at Mick and Ian.

"I can wait, but I would seriously reconsider your idea about leaving the family business, Xander. You're a good kid. Not like Berto, or even your old man. Not like me, either. And you've got a group of guys to help you out and keep you grounded. You could really build something special. Hell, you could even start making it legitimate, if you wanted to." He smiled and hooted at the idea. "Not that I recommend that, but you theoretically could."

Jesse looked at me and smiled.

"You're a firecracker, that's for sure. You could probably run the damn organization single-handedly if need be. I'm willing to bet you got some smarts in that brain."

I rolled my eyes. He sounded surprised that I might have "smarts in my brain".

Finally, he clapped Mick on the back. "I'll show myself out. Looking forward to your call."

Chapter Forty-Six

Ace

THERE WAS A PLEASANT tension in my body, an anticipation that I'd not had the pleasure of experiencing in a long time, it seemed. This was not the same as the feeling you get when you stumble into a situation that requires you to kill. For example, you get rushed and you have to defend yourself, or you are in the middle of a job and you have to take out a guard or something.

No, this is different. A planned kill is where I thrive. This is why Berto loved me and why he left me all his shit.

I needed to put that in the back of my mind, though. Xander was kind of butthurt and now we had some major decisions to make, but for now, there was me and Pierce.

And Jade, who decided to come along for the ride.

She eyed the tarp on the floor and I thought she was going to duck out on me.

"Wow, full Dexter mode. Crazy."

I laughed and had to admit to myself I was nervous about her seeing me like this.

Then again, I'd just watched her fly into a murderous rage and tee off on that redheaded bitch in a way that made me simultaneously aroused and disturbed. My girl had some venom in her, some killer instincts.

And now I was going to show her what I had hidden behind the curtain.

The truth of it was I was terrified. Terrified she would think I was a real monster, just as bad as Pierce.

Pierce sat hunched in his cage and watched my girl flush and smile at the sight of him scrunched up, unable to stretch or move. His gaunt face had a sickly pallor to it.

"Part of me wants to let him live, Ace," she whispered, brushing her body against mine.

I looked at her, ready to talk her off the "let him live" ledge.

Pierce perked up, thinking he might have a chance.

"You don't have to kill me. Look, I'm not a threat to you guys. You've won. You can let me go and I swear, I will never—"

"Because I want to see him live out the rest of his miserable life in this cage, Ace. I want to feed him table scraps through the bars and watch his body weaken from not being able to move or stretch. Watch it atrophy."

She approached the cage, squatting down so she was at eye level with Pierce.

"That's the word for it. I looked it up," she said.

"That's how I felt when I was let out of the cage so you guys could fuck with me and my legs were so weak. From not being able to walk or stand."

"Cry me a river," he spat.

I chuckled at his feeble attempts to be a tough guy, and I gave Jade a squeeze.

"Don't worry baby, this trash will never hurt anyone again, and you will never, ever have to worry about anything. I will let no one hurt you."

Pierce let loose a hooting, hollering, braying laughter that made my hair stand on end and filled me with a white-hot rage that begged for violence. It was at this point I felt the urge.

"You're the one who's going to be crying a river, dick." Jade pointed at him as I opened the cage and hauled him out. "A river of blood." She slapped her knee and giggled and I couldn't help but grin. But would she still be cracking jokes when I started cracking his skull?

I put him on his knees and chained him in place so he couldn't stand and his arms were out wide on either side of him.

"Jade, sweetie?" I paced back and forth now, my blood rushing through my veins and the adrenaline simmering and ready to boil over.

"What?" she asked, eyeing me.

"You can stay for a little while, okay? But I'm going to need you to leave when I say. Don't want you having nightmares."

"I can handle it, Ace. I've seen some pretty awful shit."

Pierce chuckled again, and I punched him in the mouth. He spit out a tooth and some blood and kept laughing.

"Cut off his fucking nipple," she said, completely out of the blue.

His eyes widened.

"Isn't that what you do?" she asked, her voice all sugary and innocent.

"To the girls? I know you do. That's how they found at least two of your victims, and that's what I heard them talking about in the cages. So I think it's super important that you understand how that feels."

"You're crazy, bitch."

She smiled. "Maybe I am, maybe I am."

"A nipple, huh? Just one?" I was starting to actually believe that Jade might have more than just a little sadistic streak in her. Good girl.

I muzzled him so he couldn't bite me and to muffle his sounds.

His body jerked as I cut the thin slice of flesh from him, fresh, red blood dripping down his torso and onto the tarp.

I watched Jade's reaction carefully and noted that Mick and Ian had come to watch, too.

Pierce choked and I realized he was vomiting. I took the muzzle off and he started screaming, so I punched him again and wiped his face with a towel, replacing the muzzle.

"No more puking, dipshit. You'll choke."

I clapped him on the back and looked at Jade.

"The real work is going to start soon. If you want to get anything in before that, this is your chance."

She took a deep breath and walked around him, cupping her chin, frowning as she gave it deep consideration.

"Yeah, I need to get a few things off my chest."

She grabbed the hose and turned it on him full blast in the face. I chained him in place so he couldn't do much besides shake his head back and forth. He was sputtering and trying his damndest to cringe away from the water.

She stopped the flow of water while he coughed and sucked in gulps of air.

After a few seconds, she blasted him again.

"Isn't this some kind of water torture?" She laughed as she sprayed him a little longer, then stopped.

He was sobbing now, helpless and scared. He knew it was only going to get worse.

"Maybe we cut off his dick?" Jade suggested.

I tilted my head back and forth.

"I mean, it's not a bad idea..."

He howled at that, sobbing and begging.

"But I really don't want to touch his dick."

Jade nodded, completely understanding.

Then she kicked him in the solar plexus, knocking the wind out of him.

He struggled to breathe.

"If we were out in the boonies, I would let you go, Pierce," she said.

"I would give you a head start."

He couldn't speak because he was still choking.

"Take off the other nipple."

Her eyes were lit up with excitement. She smelled blood. I realized in that moment that with the proper set of circumstances, anyone could become a killer.

He whimpered and twitched as I cut off his other nipple.

She blasted him with the hose again. And again.

"Okay, I'm getting bored," she said.

"Well, princess, you could stay while I finish up, or you could go."

She considered it, then sighed.

"I think I'm going to go."

I nodded, feeling a wash of relief.

She walked out of the garage with Mick, Ian, and Xander on her heels. They'd already washed their hands of Pierce. He was already in the rearview mirror.

"Just me and you, Pierce."

"Fuck you," he gasped.

I laughed and grabbed my toolbox.

"Now here's the question, friend. How do I do it? I love a good, satisfying whack to the skull, but that's quick. But goddamn Pierce, you have pissed me off to no end."

"Ah, you love me, Ace. We're alike."

Now that stopped me in my tracks.

"No, Pierce. I know you think we are, because yeah, I'm sick. Sure. Do I like to kill? Yeah. But not like you."

He laughed.

"Of course. You aren't a monster like me."

"How many kids you killed, Pierce? How many little girls did you torture? Women that were just minding their own business?"

"Those bitches were nothing. They won't be missed."

"Those women had mothers. Some of them had kids. So yeah, they will be missed."

He cocked his head. "I suppose for a while, but eventually they'll fade away like we all do. People aren't shit, Ace. You're just soft for the females and that's your mistake. They don't count, buddy. They don't matter."

"You don't matter, Pierce."

His laughter was maniacal at this point.

"Oh, but I mattered. I mattered to every one of those girls in cages. I was their god. I decided who lived and died. Who ate. Who got raped, beaten, hunted. I called the shots, so I very much mattered. I mattered to your little bitch Jade, and I still do. I bet she has nightmares about me. I bet that sometimes she hears a certain word or sound, or smells something, and it triggers her and she sees my face and hears my voice. And she always will."

I resisted the urge to respond to his words.

"Remember I told you, Pierce? I told you I would kill you. I keep my promises."

"Yeah, you can kill me, but I'll still matter to those bitches who lived."

He laughed some more, and I grabbed the hammer.

"Goodnight, loser."

The first crack didn't kill him, but it dislodged his eyeball from its socket.

He drooled blood and made a gurgling, rasping noise, trying to form words but unable to do so.

The second crack was lights out.

"Piece of shit. No one is going to miss you. You *don't* matter."

Chapter Forty-Seven

Xander

We sat around the table, Mick, Ace, Ian, Jade, and Benny. He was a regular part of the family now. It was getting where it felt like he'd always been there, babbling away and smiling. He had dimples, and he was almost always happy. The kid was definitely growing on me.

Jade looked beautiful, so poised and calm, but what I knew about her now was that she was a force to be reckoned with in her own right. There was no naivete in her smile, no innocence, no wide-eyed wonder. Just Jade, a woman who had shown so much resilience and strength. A woman who loved fiercely but also had a darkness in her, just as we all did.

I thought back to when I first saw her at the coffee shop and thought she was an angel, just all beauty and goodness and light.

As much as I loved her light, knowing her shadow made me love her even more. Our eyes met from across the table and she winked and smiled. Her hair was smooth and wavy, falling over one eye like she was a movie star. She wore black jeans and a tight black shirt that showed her curves. She was wearing more makeup than usual, especially around the eyes.

Ace squeezed the back of my neck and planted a kiss on the top of my head.

"Feels weird to be here, right?"

"Yeah."

"Been a long time," Ian said as he looked around, then at me. He smiled and we all looked at Mick.

"You cool with all this, Mick?"

Mick had been quiet about everything. I knew there was a part of him that was disappointed that we'd decided to stay, to come back to Berto's old house and meet with Jesse's crew, and whoever else showed up.

"As cool as I'm going to be. I mean, someone's gotta run the show, right?"

Ian nodded.

Ace picked up his phone and looked at it and whispered something to one of Jesse's guys.

"Frankie B. is here. Derek, will you meet him at the gate and show him in? He has a couple guys with him."

I nodded and nudged Mick. "Frankie was always cool, yeah?"

"Yeah, he was okay. Trusted him more than most. I know he had wanted to steer clear of the fallout after Berto died. I'm kind of pissed he didn't step up until now, but we can hear what he has to say about it."

Derek left and Jesse joined us at the table with his wife, Laurie. Moni was coming, too.

There were some stragglers we were waiting on and then we would get the meeting underway.

"Uncle. Glad you're here before everyone else shows up. We can talk."

Jade pulled some documents out of a small leather briefcase and set them on the table.

"We've discussed your proposal, and your requests at length, and we feel confident that you'll be pleased with what we've worked out."

Jesse nodded, and Jade slid the papers over.

I observed him. Jade had definitely made her wishes clear, and Mick and Ian had some input, too.

Ace, funnily enough, didn't give a shit, even though everything was technically supposed to be his.

Jesse smiled.

"The house in Hawaii? Really?"

Jade tapped her nails on the table. "Really."

He raised his brows, and the corner of his mouth pulled back in a feigned, painful smirk.

"If it's what the lady wants."

Laurie scowled and Jesse nudged her, showing her some of the paperwork he had already rifled through. Her jaw dropped and he chuckled.

"What about this? I don't get it?"

Ace leaned forward and Jesse handed over the document.

"Ah, yeah. Moni takes over as owner of the establishment she's been running for well over a decade. She's earned it. That's one we aren't willing to negotiate on. There are several other clubs and houses that you are free to take possession of. We will happily help you run them, and you'll take the larger cut of the profit for very little work on your part. It's a win for you. But Moni gets to own her club."

Jesse nodded, looked at Laurie, and she nodded, too.

"The rest is basically what you proposed if you look at it. The offshore accounts and investments are intact and all yours. The businesses on that list are yours. We keep the house in Hawaii, Moni keeps her club. We keep this house as Moreno headquarters, which means it's your house, too, since you are a Moreno. We cooperate and have each other's backs. We keep the assets we've already taken possession of, you keep everything else."

Jesse pursed his lips and drummed his fingers on the table. There was a heavy silence while we waited for him to give the yay or nay on the proposal. He was getting almost everything he wanted.

Almost.

"I'm not going to lie, I'm a little disappointed that we aren't coming away with that sweet spot on the island, but with the assets that we'll be coming into we can probably buy three houses, so I'm going to let that go. Moni gets her business. You're right, she deserves it. We'll work with you, send you some of our guys while you build your organization back out."

I nodded. "Thank you, Uncle. Means a lot to me."

"You boys are going to do a fine job. Don't forget about me out in the desert. I'm thinking of expanding my territory out there, come see me when you can."

"Sounds good, Jesse."

"Derek and Sam and a few other boys will stay here. I'm heading home tonight. I fucking hate Los Angeles."

"Oh, one more thing." He started pulling something from inside his denim jacket and we all tensed. Ace reflexively put an arm out toward Jade and I saw Jesse roll his eyes.

"You kids are going to have to learn to trust your old uncle."

He pulled some papers out and handed them to me.

"You know I helped you get into that beach house as a rental because I know a guy, right? Real estate guy I've done a lot of business with."

Mick nodded and Ian looked on curiously.

"Turns out the owner of the property met with some misfortune and is looking for a quick sale. I agreed to purchase the property, and I'm gifting it to you."

Great. Now we looked like assholes for taking the Hawaii house.

"You need a nice house or two for your growing family."

"Well, I mean we only got the one kid." Ace grinned and fluffed Bennie's curls.

Jesse eyed Jade, then Laurie. She laughed and nodded.

"I bet you a house in Hawaii Miss Jade is about to be a mama. You mark my words. I know these things. I knew Laurie was prego before she did."

"It's true."

We all turned and looked at Jade and found her blushing furiously while shrugging her shoulders.

Then she smiled and raised her hand. "I have a request that's not on the paper."

"Oh? What? You want to know if there are any other island houses lying around you might want?" Jesse sounded annoyed but his eyes were laughing.

"No, this is about my friends. The girls from Berto's compound. The ones that have been staying out at your ranch."

He shifted in his seat and looked at Laurie.

"Yeah, I got a couple of them working for me."

She tapped her finger on the table.

"Look it's up to them, but if they want to come out here, I'd like to put them up and find them jobs. Like, jobs that don't involve taking off their clothes. Unless that's what they want. But I'm just putting it out there. They've suffered enough, and I would love to give them a chance at a better life."

Jesse cleared his throat and shrugged. "Way I see it, they have a better life than what they had when we found them, but it's up to them. You want to give them work and get them put up here, they're free to go. I don't own them."

She smiled and I patted her hand.

"Okay. It's settled. Agreement reached?"

Jesse nodded and so did Ace and Mick. Ian looked the way I felt: relieved.

"Let's get some drinks going in here to celebrate."

Hours later the table was full with Jesse, his guys, Moni and two of her inner circle, Sam, Frankie, and a few others who showed up and pledged their loyalty to me, the new head of the Moreno family organization.

Sitting at the same table as my uncle had so many times, and my father. I was also sitting in the home where my mother had taken her own life. The home where I'd been bullied, ridiculed, and put down.

For years I hid behind the lie that I wanted nothing to do with this family, but in truth - it was all I wanted.

I was now the head of the Moreno family. Me, a scared kid who wanted nothing more than to run away from it all, to never fire a gun or pull another job. Now I was in charge. These guys worked for me. Looked to me for leadership.

Well, maybe not Mick. He was his own man.

"You know, Mick. You are family, but you don't have to pull jobs. You don't have to do anything."

He smiled and slung an arm around Jade.

"I know. But I have to keep an eye on everyone. Make sure everyone is doing the right thing and behaving themselves.

He winked at the table at large.

"God help you if you aren't. You'll answer to me."

Jade grinned and leaned on his shoulder.

Everyone looked at me, questions in their eyes.

I rapped my knuckles on the table.

"Meeting adjourned. Let's go home."

Chapter Forty-Eight

Jade

I WALKED OUT ONTO the sun-drenched terrace wearing a pale blue sundress, my hair blowing in the Hawaiian breeze.

Today was my birthday, and this was my party.

My guests cheered and clapped as I blushed and giggled nervously. My cake was three-tiered and covered in roses. Ace had hired a fancy catering company to provide the food. He was busily supervising the operation while I greeted my guests, a mix of Jesse's crew, my friends, and of course, many of our "associates" who were flown out to celebrate with me.

It hadn't been difficult for me to adjust to the life of organized crime. In fact, it was quite easy. These days, I was steering clear of things, but they kept me informed and a part of decisions.

Jesse's wife smiled and rubbed her belly, and I laughed and rubbed mine back. We were due within weeks of each other. Jesse was busy wrangling their toddler daughter and my best friend Rose was beaming at Benny as she held hands with her new boyfriend.

We all laughed and cheered when Benny reached out and grabbed a fistful of cake and shoved it in his mouth.

Ian came up behind me and put his arms around me, then rubbed my belly and whispered in my ear, "How's my baby?"

I laughed and replied, "She's good."

"How do you know it's a she?"

I looked down and placed my hand over his. "I know."

Moni came up and wrapped her arms around both of us and I giggled at being in the middle of the sandwich with my baby bump.

"You are glowing, girl." She smiled and planted a kiss on my cheek. "When are we opening presents? It's my favorite part."

"Mine too," I laughed.

Hawaii was everything I'd imagined it would be. The turquoise ocean dazzled me and I couldn't get enough of the warmth and beauty of it.

"Presents!" Yelled Micah, one of Jesse's higher ups that I actually liked and got along with. He was with Allison, and that made me happy.

Allison had moved back to Los Angeles and was doing admin work for our organization. I'd moved her into a high-rise apartment on Wilshire Blvd and we met for coffee and lunch regularly. She was also one of the few people I would let babysit Benny. Sara was also in Los Angeles, attending college and waiting tables, dating one of our guys but steering clear of any "business".

"Here, this is for you." Xander grinned and dropped a small bag on my lap.

I opened the bag and found a small box. In the box was a key.

"What's this?" I asked.

"Go look in the garage."

I shook my head in confusion and made my way to the garage, opened the door, and gasped, covering my mouth.

"Jesse really felt like you needed a motorcycle, but given your current condition, we got you a Range Rover instead. Hope you love it."

I squealed and clicked the key fob, unlocking it. I climbed behind the wheel and adjusted the mirror.

"Oh, my god."

Mick, Ace, Ian, and Xander stood in a row, arms crossed and beaming from ear to ear.

I climbed out. "I want to go for a drive. Oh my god. Thank you so much."

Ace slipped an arm around me. "You can't go yet. You've got guests and more gifts to open. I know you were tired of not having your own ride."

I kissed him and then turned to Mick, then Ian and Xander, hugging each of them and kissing them before hurrying back up the stairs.

The gifts kept coming. Diamond earrings. Expensive perfume, a gold chain from Tiffany's, a Chanel bag. New shoes, gift cards to boutiques and eateries, spa treatments, and more. It was dizzying.

But most important was the friends. Okay, so some of them were more like work friends, but I found myself getting more and more attached to the people that were part of the organization, the family.

After a very exhausted Benny finally passed out, I went out onto the lanai and watched the waves as the sun dipped down on the horizon. The sky was brilliant with color and I closed my eyes to feel the warmth of it on my skin while focusing on the sound of the waves below.

For now, we were safe and happy. The family business was running like a well-oiled machine. I was treated like a queen, loved and protected. I had a beautiful little family with Benny and the baby growing inside me.

I wanted for nothing and I felt safe and loved every second of the day.

There were times, of course, when doubt crept in. When I saw Pierce's face sneering at me as he told me I was a victim and always would be. When I wondered when the other shoe would drop. Who would come for me? The ghosts of Pierce and Berto, even Lydia haunted my dreams still.

But then I would open my eyes and see the beauty around me, the love and protection.

"I fought for this. I fought and survived, and so did my men. We earned this with blood and tears and it is ours."

I'd proven to myself that I could defend myself and my family, over and over again. No one would ever take from me what was mine.

I wandered downstairs, feeling beautiful, sexy, and powerful as my belly grew.

My guys were waiting for me.

"Hey beautiful," Ace called as I descended the stairs and made my way into the living room.

"I just made popcorn."

"How's junior?" Mick asked as he moved closer to me and kissed my temple.

"She's kicking like crazy."

We decided not to find out the baby's sex, but I knew she was a girl.

"Good. Now let's watch this movie."

Ace slid down to the floor, his back against the couch, motioning for my foot. He loved to rub my feet while we watched television. It felt heavenly.

"Xander, grab another bowl of popcorn."

Mick wrapped an arm around me and pulled me closer, and Ian stretched out on the other side of me, resting his head against my belly.

"I can't believe it's almost time."

"Yeah, me either."

Mick laughed, and I snuggled in, ready to zone out on a movie and bask in the love of my men. I was the happiest I'd ever been, and I knew things were only getting better. We'd been in Hawaii for a couple of weeks and tomorrow was our last day on the island.

"I want to have my birthday in Hawaii every year."

Xander stopped rubbing my feet and looked up at me.

"You know, it's almost my birthday, in case anyone is wondering."

I laughed and patted his head. "And what do you want, almost birthday boy?"

"Can we get a puppy?"

Ace huffed and glared at him with his brilliant blue eyes.

"No. Absolutely not. We get anything, we're getting a cat. Period. You don't understand, I've been waiting my whole life for a cat."

Mick frowned and shook his head. "Sorry, I'm team dog."

"So Xander and Mick are team dog, Ian? What about you?"

"Cat."

They all turned and looked at me.

"Jade? You know it's up to you, anyway."

I sighed and rubbed my belly. Hell, we were about to have two kids. But with a mom and four dads...

"Easy-peasy. We get both. A puppy and a kitten, and they grow up together with the babies."

Mick groaned and Ace laughed.

"It's settled," said Xander.

"Yeah."

Later that night, I thought back to my last birthday, and how I woke up in a place where I wasn't loved, valued, or cared for. I thought about that horrible white dress and the way Pierce looked at me when I was tied up in the van.

Then I flipped through my phone, looking at the pictures I'd taken of this birthday. The floral arrangements, my goofy guys hamming it up, Benny's chubby face, and my friends.

And I was happy. I was happy and I would never, ever let anyone take that away from me.

Also By

Lana Black

Jaded
Jaded 2: The Hunt

KEEP IN TOUCH!

I would love to keep in touch with you! If you want up-to-date info on new releases, cover reveals, events, and fun bonus stuff, you can subscribe to my newsletter by clicking HERE.

You can stalk me on TikTok by clicking HERE.